V

THE GOLDEN MEAN

THE
GOLDEN
MEAN

Annabel Lyon

ALFRED A. KNOPF   NEW YORK   2010

THIS IS A BORZOI BOOK
PUBLISHED BY ALFRED A. KNOPF

Knopf, Borzoi Books, and the colophon are registered trademarks
of Random House, Inc.

Originally published in Canada by Random House Canada, a
division of Random House of Canada Limited, Toronto, in 2009.

Grateful acknowledgment is made to the Trustees of the Loeb
Classical Library for permission to reprint an excerpt from
Diogenes Laertius: Lives of Eminent Philosophers, Volume II, Books 6–10
(Loeb Classical Library Volume 185), translated by
R. D. Hicks (Cambridge, Mass.: Harvard University Press),
copyright © 1925 by the President and Fellows of Harvard
College. Loeb Classical Library® is a registered trademark of the
President and Fellows of Harvard College. Reprinted by
permission of Harvard University Press on behalf of the Trustees
of the Loeb Classical Library.

Library of Congress Cataloging-in-Publication Data
Lyon, Annabel, [date]
The golden mean : a novel of Aristotle and Alexander the Great /
by Annabel Lyon.—1st U.S. ed.
p. cm.
ISBN 978-0-307-59399-3 (alk. paper)
1. Aristotle—Fiction.   2. Philosophers—Greece—Fiction.
3. Alexander, the Great, 356–323 B.C.—Fiction.   4. Greece—
History—Macedonian Expansion, 359–323 B.C.—Fiction.
5. Athens (Greece)—Fiction.   I. Title.
PR9199.3.L98G65 2010
813'.6—dc22   2010017548

Manufactured in the United States of America
First United States Edition

For my parents,
my children,
and Bryant

Cast

(IN ORDER OF APPEARANCE)

Aristotle, *a philosopher*
Callisthenes, *Aristotle's nephew and apprentice*
Pythias, *Aristotle's wife*
Hermias, *governor of Atarneus, Aristotle's former patron*
Philip, *king of Macedon*
Phila, Audata, Philinna, Nikesipolis, *wives of Philip*
Olympias, *wife of Philip, queen of Macedon*
Leonidas, *one of Alexander's tutors*
Carolus, *a theatre director*
Demosthenes, *an Athenian orator, enemy of Philip*
Arrhidaeus, *son of Philip and Philinna, elder half-brother of Alexander*
Philes, *Arrhidaeus's nurse*
Alexandros, *king of Molossos, Olympias's brother*
Antipater, *a general, regent in Philip's absence*
Alexander, *son of Philip and Olympias*
Arimnestus and Arimneste, *twins, Aristotle's younger brother and sister*
Proxenus, *husband of Arimneste, Aristotle's guardian after his parents' deaths*
Amyntas, *Philip's father, king of Macedon*
Illaeus, *a student of Plato, Aristotle's tutor*
Perdicaas, *Philip's elder brother, king of Macedon after Amyntas's death*
Euphraeus, *a student of Plato, Perdicaas's tutor*
Hephaestion, *Alexander's closest companion*

Ptolemy, *another of Alexander's companions*

Lysimachus, *one of Alexander's tutors*

Pausanias, *a Macedonian officer, later one of Philip's bodyguard*

Tycho, *a slave of Aristotle*

Artabazus, *a Persian refugee in the Macedonian court*

Athea, *a slave of Aristotle*

Meda, *sixth wife of Philip*

Little Pythias, *Aristotle and Pythias's daughter*

Xenocrates, *a philosopher, Speusippus's successor as director of the Academy*

Eudoxus, *a philosopher, director of the Academy in Plato's absence*

Callippus, *a philosopher, companion of Eudoxus*

Nicanor, *son of Arimneste and Proxenus*

Plato, *a philosopher, director of the Academy*

Speusippus, *Plato's nephew, director of the Academy after his uncle's death*

Herpyllis, *Pythias's maid, Aristotle's companion after Pythias's death*

Cleopatra, *seventh wife of Philip*

Attalus, *father of Cleopatra*

Eurydice, *daughter of Philip and Cleopatra*

Pixodarus, *governor of Caria, Arrhidaeus's potential father-in-law*

Thessalus, *an actor*

Nicomachus, *Aristotle and Herpyllis's son*

IT MUST BE BORNE in mind that my design is not to write histories, but lives. And the most glorious exploits do not always furnish us with the clearest discoveries of virtue or vice in men; sometimes a matter of less moment, an expression or a jest, informs us better of their characters and inclinations, than the most famous sieges, the greatest armaments, or the bloodiest battles whatsoever.

—Plutarch, *Alexander*
translated by John Dryden

THE GOLDEN MEAN

ONE

T HE RAIN FALLS IN black cords, lashing my animals, my men, and my wife, Pythias, who last night lay with her legs spread while I took notes on the mouth of her sex, who weeps silent tears of exhaustion now, on this tenth day of our journey. On the ship she seemed comfortable enough, but this last overland stage is beyond all her experience and it shows. Her mare stumbles; she's let the reins go loose again, allowing the animal to sleepwalk. She rides awkwardly, weighed down by her sodden finery. Earlier I suggested she remain on one of the carts but she resisted, such a rare occurrence that I smiled, and she, embarrassed, looked away. Callisthenes, my nephew, offered to walk the last distance, and with some difficulty we helped her onto his big bay. She clutched at the reins the first time the animal shifted beneath her.

"Are you steady?" I asked, as around us the caravan began to move.

"Of course."

Touching. Men are good with horses where I come from, where we're returning now, and she knows it. I spent yesterday on the carts myself so I could write, though now I ride bareback, in the manner of my countrymen, a ball-busting proposition for someone who's been sedentary as long as I have.

You can't stay on a cart while a woman rides, though; and it occurs to me now that this was her intention.

I hardly noticed her at first, a pretty, vacant-eyed girl on the fringes of Hermias's menagerie. Five years ago now. Atarneus was a long way from Athens, across the big sea, snug to the flank of the Persian Empire. Daughter, niece, ward, concubine—the truth slipped like silk.

"You like her," Hermias said. "I see the way you look at her." Fat, sly, rumoured a money-changer in his youth, later a butcher and a mercenary; a eunuch, now, supposedly, and a rich man. A politician, too, holding a stubborn satrapy against the barbarians: Hermias of Atarneus. "Bring me my thinkers!" he used to shout. "Great men surround themselves with thinkers! I wish to be surrounded!" And he would laugh and slap at himself while the girl Pythias watched without seeming to blink quite often enough. She became a gift, one of many, for I was a favourite. On our wedding night she arrayed herself in veils, assumed a pose on the bed, and whisked away the sheets before I could see if she had bled. I was thirty-seven then, she fifteen, and gods forgive me but I went at her like a stag in rut. Stag, hog.

"Eh? Eh?" Hermias said the next morning, and laughed.

Night after night after night. I tried to make it up to her with kindness. I treated her with great courtliness, gave her money, addressed her softly, spoke to her of my work. She wasn't stupid; thoughts flickered in her eyes like fish in deep pools. Three years we spent in Atarneus, until the Persians breathed too close, too hot. Two years in the pretty town of Mytilene, on the island of Lesvos, where they cobbled the floor of the port so enemy ships couldn't anchor. Now this journey. Through it all she has an untouchable dignity, even when she lies with her knees apart while I gently probe for my work on generation. Fish, too, I'm studying, field animals, and birds when I can get them. There's a seed like a pomegranate seed in the centre of the folds, and the hole frilled like an oyster. Sometimes moisture, sometimes dryness. I've noted it all.

"Uncle."

I follow my nephew's finger and see the city on the marshy plain below us, bigger than I remember, more sprawling. The rain is thinning, spitting and spatting now, under a suddenly lucid gold-grey sky.

"Pella," I announce, to rouse my dripping, dead-eyed wife. "The capital of Macedon. Temple there, market there, palace. You can just make it out. Bigger than you thought?"

She says nothing.

"You'll have to get used to the dialect. It's fast, but not so different really. A little rougher."

"I'll manage," she says, not loudly.

I sidle my horse up to hers, lean over to take her reins to keep her near me while I talk. It's good for her to have to listen, to think. Callisthenes walks beside us.

"The first king was from Argos. A Greek, though the people aren't. Enormous wealth here: timber, wheat, corn, horses, cattle, sheep, goats, copper, iron, silver, gold. Virtually all they have to import is olives. Too cold for olives this far north, mostly; too mountainous. And did you know that most of the Athenian navy is built from Macedonian timber?"

"Did we bring olives?" Pythias asks.

"I assume you know your wars, my love?"

She picks at the reins, plucks at them like lyre strings, but I don't let go. "I know them," she says finally.

Utterly ignorant, of course. If I had to weave all day, I'd at least weave myself a battle scene or two. I remind her of the Athenian conquest of Persia under the great general Pericles, Athens at her seafaring mightiest, in my great-grandfather's time. Then the decades of conflict in the Peloponnese, Athens bled and finally brought low by Sparta, with some extra Persian muscle, in my father's youth; and Sparta itself defeated by Thebes, by then the ascendant power, in my own childhood. "I will set you a task. You'll embroider Thermopylae for me. We'll hang it over the bed."

Still not looking at me.

"Thermopylae," I say. "Gods, woman. The pass. The pass where the Spartans held off the Persians for three days, a force ten times their own. Greatest stand in the history of warfare."

"Lots of pink and red," Callisthenes suggests.

She looks straight at me for a moment. I read, *Don't patronize me.* And, *Continue.*

Now, I tell her, young Macedon is in the ascendant, under five-wived Philip. A marriage to cement every settlement and seal every victory: Phila from Elimea, in the North; Audata the Illyrian princess; Olympias of Epirus, first among wives, the only one called queen; Philinna from Thessaly; and Nikesipolis of Pherae, a beauty who died in childbirth. Philip invaded Thrace, too, after Thessaly, but hasn't yet taken a Thracian wife. I rifle the library in my skull for an interesting factling. "They like to tattoo their women, the Thracians."

"Mmm." Callisthenes closes his eyes like he's just bitten into something tasty.

We're descending the hillside now, our horses scuffling in the rocky scree as we make our way down to the muddy plain.

Pythias is shifting in the saddle, straightening her clothes, smoothing her eyebrows, touching a fingertip to each corner of her mouth, preparing for the city.

"Love." I put my hand on hers to still her grooming and claim back her attention. My nephew I ignore. A Thracian woman would eat him alive, tender morsel that he is, and spit out the little bones. "You should know a little more. They don't keep slaves like we do, even in the palace. Everyone works. And they don't have priests. The king performs that function for his people. He begins every day with sacrifices, and if anyone needs to speak to a god, it's done through him." Sacrilege: she doesn't like this. I read her body. "Pella will not be like Hermias's court. Women are not a part of public life here."

"What does that mean?"

I shrug. "Men and women don't attend entertainments together, or even eat together. Women of your rank aren't seen. They don't go out."

"It's too cold to go out," Pythias says. "What does it matter, anyway? This time next week we'll be in Athens."

"That's right." I've explained to her that this detour is just a favour to Hermias. I'm needed in Pella for just a day or two, a week at most. Clean up, dry out, rest the animals, deliver Hermias's mail, move on. "There isn't much you'd want to do in public anyway." The arts are imported sparingly. Pig-hunting is big; drinking is big. "You've never tasted beer, have you? You'll have to try some before we leave."

She ignores me.

"Beer!" Callisthenes says. "I'll drink yours, Auntie."

"Remember yourself," I tell the young man, who has a

tendency to giggle when he gets excited. "We are diplomats now."

The caravan steps up its pace, and my wife's back straightens. We're on.

Despite the rain and ankle-sucking mud, we pick up a retinue as we pass through the city's outskirts, men and women who come out of their houses to stare, and children who run after us, pulling at the skins covering the bulging carts, trying to dislodge some souvenir. They're particularly drawn to the cart that carries the cages—a few bedraggled birds and small animals—which they dart at, only to retreat, screaming in pleasure and shaking their hands as though they've been nipped. They're tall children, for the most part, and well formed. My men kick idly at a clutch of little beggars to fend them off, while my nephew genially turns out his pockets to them to prove his poverty. Pythias, veiled, draws the most stares.

At the palace, my nephew speaks to the guard and we are admitted. As the gates close behind us and we begin to dismount, I notice a boy—thirteen, maybe—wandering amongst the carts. Rain-plastered hair, ruddy skin, eyes big as a calf's.

"Get away from there," I call when the boy tries to help with one of the cages, a chameleon as it happens, and more gently, when the boy turns to look at me in amazement: "He'll bite you."

The boy smiles. "Me?"

The chameleon, on closer inspection, is shit-smelling and lethargic, and dangerously pale; I hope it will survive until I can prepare a proper dissection.

"See its ribs?" I say to the boy. "They aren't like ours. They extend all the way down and meet at the belly, like a fish's. The legs flex opposite to a man's. Can you see his toes? He has five, like you, but with talons like a bird of prey. When he's healthy he changes colours."

"I want to see that," the boy says.

Together we study the monster, the never-closing eye and the tail coiled like a strap.

"Sometimes he goes dark, almost like a crocodile," I say. "Or spotted, like a leopard. You won't see it today, I'm afraid. He's about dead."

The boy's eyes rove across the carts.

"Birds," he says.

I nod.

"Are they dying, too?"

I nod.

"And what's in here?"

The boy points at a cart of large amphora with wood and stones wedged around them to keep them upright.

"Get me a stick."

Again that look of amazement.

"There." I point at the ground some feet away, then turn away deliberately to prise the lid off one of the jars. When I turn back, the boy is holding out the stick. I take it and reach into the jar with it, prodding gently once or twice.

"Smells," the boy says, and indeed the smell of sea water, creamy and rank, is mingling with the smell of horse dung in the courtyard.

I pull out the stick. Clinging to its end is a small crab.

"That's just a crab."

"Can you swim?" I ask.

When the boy doesn't reply, I describe the lagoon where I used to go diving, the flashing sunlight and then the plunge. This crab, I explain, came from there. I recall going out past the reef with the fishermen and helping with their nets so I could study the catch. There, too, I swam, where the water was deeper and colder and the currents ran like striations in rock, and more than once I had to be rescued, hauled hacking into a boat. Back on shore the fishermen would build fires, make their offerings, and cook what they couldn't sell. Once I went out with them to hunt dolphin. In their log canoes they would encircle a pod and slap the water with their oars, making a great noise. The animals would beach themselves as they tried to flee. I leapt from the canoe as it reached shore and splashed through the shallows to claim one of them for myself. The fishermen were bemused by my fascination with the viscera, which was inedible and therefore waste to them. They marvelled at my drawings of dissections, pointing in wonder at birds and mice and snakes and beetles, cheering when they recognized a fish. But as orange dims to blue in a few sunset moments, so in most people wonder dims as quickly to horror. A pretty metaphor for a hard lesson I learned long ago. The larger drawings—cow, sheep, goat, deer, dog, cat, child—I left at home.

I can imagine the frosty incomprehension of my colleagues back in Athens. Science is the work of the mind, they will say, and here I am wasting my time swimming and grubbing.

"We cannot ascertain causes until we have facts," I say. "That above all must be understood. We must observe the world, you see? From the facts we move to the principles, not the other way round."

"Tell me some more facts," the boy says.

"Octopuses lay as many eggs as poisonous spiders. There is no blood in the brain, and elsewhere in the body blood can only be contained in blood vessels. Bear cubs are born without articulation and their limbs must be licked into shape by their mothers. Some insects are generated by the dew, and some worms generate spontaneously in manure. There is a passage in your head from your ear to the roof of your mouth. Also, your windpipe enters your mouth quite close to the opening of the back of the nostrils. That's why when you drink too fast, the drink comes out your nose."

I wink, and the boy smiles faintly for the first time.

"I think you know more about some things than my tutor." The boy pauses, as though awaiting my response to this significant remark.

"Possibly," I say.

"My tutor, Leonidas."

I shrug as though the name means nothing to me. I wait for him to speak again, to help or make a nuisance of himself, but he darts back into the palace, just a boy running out of the rain.

Now here comes our guide, a grand-gutted flunky who leads us to a suite of rooms in the palace. He runs with sweat, even in this rain, and smiles with satisfaction when I offer him a chair and water. I think he is moulded from pure fat. He says he knows me, remembers me from my childhood. Maybe. When he drinks, his mouth leaves little crumbs on the inner lip of the cup, though we aren't eating.

"Oh, yes, I remember you," he says. "The doctor's boy. Very serious, very serious. Has he changed?" He winks at Pythias, who doesn't react. "And that's your son?"

He means Callisthenes. My cousin's son, I explain, whom I call nephew for simplicity; he travels with me as my apprentice.

Pythias and her maids withdraw to an inner room; my slaves

I've sent to the stables. We're too many people for the rooms we've been allotted, and they'll be warm there. Out of sight, too. Slavery is known here but not common, and I don't want to appear ostentatious. We overlook a small courtyard with a blabbing fountain and some potted trees, almond and fig. My nephew has retreated there to the shelter of a colonnade, and is arguing some choice point or other with himself, his fine brows wrinkled and darkened like walnut meats by the knottiness of his thoughts. I hope he's working on the reality of numbers, a problem I'm lately interested in.

"You're back for the good times," the flunky says. "War, waah!" He beats his fat fists on his chest and laughs. "Come to help us rule the world?"

"It'll happen," I say. "It's our time."

The fat man laughs again, claps his hands. "Very good, doctor's son," he says. "You're a quick study. Say, 'I spit on Athens.'"

I spit, just to make him laugh again, to set off all that wobbling.

When he's gone, I look back to the courtyard.

"Go to him," Pythias says, passing behind me with her maids, lighting lamps against the coming darkness.

In other windows I can see lights, little prickings, and hear the voices of men and women returning to their rooms for the evening, public duties done. Palace life is the same everywhere. I was happy enough to get away from it for a time, though I know Hermias was disappointed when we left him. Powerful men never like you to leave.

"I'm fine here," Pythias says. "We'll see to the unpacking. Go."

"He hasn't been able to get away from us for ten days. He probably wants a break."

A soldier arrives to tell me the king will see me in the morning. Then a page comes with plates of food: fresh and dried fruit, small fish, and wine.

"Eat," Pythias is saying. Some time has passed; I'm not sure how much. I'm in a chair, wrapped in a blanket, and she is setting a black plate and cup by my foot. "You know it helps you to eat."

I'm weeping: something about Callisthenes, and nightfall, and the distressing disarray of our lives just now. She pats my face with the sleeve of her dress, a green one I like. She's found time to change into something dry. Wet things are draped and swagged everywhere; I'm in the only chair that hasn't been tented.

"He's so young," she says. "He wants a look at the city, that's all. He'll come back."

"I know."

"Eat, then."

I let her put a bite of fish in my mouth. Oil, salt tang. I realize I'm hungry.

"You see?" she says.

There's no name for this sickness, no diagnosis, no treatment mentioned in my father's medical books. You could stand next to me and never guess my symptoms. Metaphor: I am afflicted by colours—grey, hot red, maw-black, gold. I can't always see how to go on, how best to live with an affliction I can't explain and can't cure.

I let her put me to bed. I lie in the sheets she has warmed with stones from the hearth, listening to the surf-sounds of her undressing. "You took care of me today," I say. My eyes are closed, but I can hear her shrug. "Making me ride. You didn't want them laughing at me."

Redness flares behind my closed eyelids; she's brought a candle to the bedside.

"Not tonight," I say.

Before we were married, I gave her many fine gifts: sheep, jewellery, perfume, pottery, excellent clothes. I taught her to read and write because I was besotted and wanted to give her something no lover had ever thought of before.

The next morning I see the note she's left for me, the mouse-scratching I thought I heard as I slipped into sleep: *warm, dry.*

My nephew is still sprawled on his couch when I pass through his room on my way to my audience. He's drunk and has been fucked: face rosy and sweet, sleep deep, smell of flowers unpleasantly sweet. We'll all want baths, later. Another grey day, with a bite in the air and rain pending. You wouldn't know it was spring. My mood feels delicate but bearable; I'm walking along the cliff edge, but for the moment staying upright. I may go down to the city myself, later, to scrounge a memory, something drawn up from deep in the mind's hole.

The palace seems to have rearranged itself during my long absence, like a snake might rearrange its coils. I recognize each door and hall but not the order of them, and looking for the throne room I walk into the indoor theatre instead. "Bitch," someone is yelling. "Bitch!"

It takes me a moment to realize he's yelling at me.

"Get out!"

My eyes adjust to the smoky dimness. I make out a few figures on the stage, and one very angry man climbing toward me over the rows of stone seats. A plume of white hair over a good face, a great face. Killing eyes. "Get out!"

I ask him what play they're preparing.

"I'm working." A vein throbs by his eye. He's right up to me now, his breath in my face. He's wrecked, he's a killer.

I apologize. "I got lost. The throne room——?"

"I'll take him."

I look down at the boy who's suddenly appeared at my side. The boy from the gates, the one I pretended not to recognize.

The director turns away and stalks back down to his position. "Places," he barks.

"They're doing the *Bacchae*," the boy says. "We all love the *Bacchae*."

Back in the hall he raises a hand and a soldier appears. The boy goes back into the theatre before I can thank him. The soldier leads me across another courtyard and through an ante-room with an elaborate mosaic floor, a lion hunt rendered in subtly shaded pebbles. It's been a long time since I was here. The lion's red yawn is pink now; the azure of a hunter's terrified gaze has faded to bird's-egg blue. I wonder where all the colour went, if it brushed off on the soles of a thousand shoes and got wiped across the kingdom. A guard holds a curtain aside for me.

"You refined piece of shit," the king says. "You've spent too long in the East. Look at yourself, man."

We embrace. As boys we played together, when Philip's father was king and my father was the king's physician. I was taller but Philip was tougher: so it remains. I'm conscious of the fine, light clothing I've changed into for this meeting, of the fashionable short clip of my hair, of my fingers gently splayed with rings. Philip's beard is rough; his fingernails are dirty; he wears home-spun. He looks like what he is: a soldier, bored by this great marble throne room.

"Your eye."

Philip barks once, a single unit of laughter, and allows me to study the pale rivulet of a scar through the left eyebrow, the permanently closed lid. We are our fathers now.

"An arrow," Philip says. "A bee sting for my troubles."

Around us courtiers laugh. Barbarians, supposedly, but I see only men of my own height and build. Small Philip is an anomaly. He wears a short beard now, but is as full-lipped as I remember him, broad-browed, with a drinker's flush across the nose and cheeks. An amiable asshole, sprung straight from boyhood to middle age.

I left off my accounting to Pythias with Philip's invasion of Thrace. From there he went on to Chalcidice, my own homeland, a three-fingered fist of land thrust into the Aegean. An early casualty was the village of my birth. Our caravan passed by that way, three days ago now; a significant detour, but I needed to see it. Little Stageira, strung across the saddle of two hills facing the sea. The western wall was rubble, the guard towers too. My father's house, mine now, badly burned; the garden uprooted, though the trees seemed all right. The fishing boats along the shore, burned. Paving stones had been prised up from the streets, and the population, men and women I'd known since childhood, dispersed. The destruction was five years old. News of it had first reached me just before I left Athens and the Academy for Hermias's court, but I couldn't face it until now. Weeds crept their green lace over doorsteps, birds nested in empty rooms, and there was no corpse smell. Sounds: sea and gulls, sea and gulls.

"An easy journey?" Philip asks.

Macedonians pride themselves on speaking freely to their king. I remind myself we were children together, and take a breath. Not an easy journey, no, I tell him. Not easy to see my father's estate raped. Not easy to imagine the cast of my childhood banished. Not easy to have my earliest childhood memories splotched with his army's piss. "Poor policy," I tell him. "To destroy your own land and terrorize your own people?"

He's not smiling, but not angry either. "I had to," he says. "The Chalcidician League had Athens behind it, or would have if I'd waited much longer. Wealthy, strong fortifications, a good jumping-off spot if you felt like attacking Pella. I had to close that door. You're going to tell me we're at peace with Athens now. We're on the Amphictyonic Council together, best friends. I'd like nothing better, believe me. I'd like to think they're not building a coalition against me as we speak. I'd like to think they could just learn their fucking place. Reasonably, one reasonable man to another, are they going to rule the world again? Did they ever, truly? Are they hiding another Pericles someplace? Could they take Persia again? Reasonably?"

Ah, one of my favourite words. "Reasonably, no."

"Speaking of Persia, I think you have something for me."

Hermias's proposal. I hand it to Philip, who hands it to an aide, who puts it away.

"Persia," Philip says. "I could take Persia, with a little peace and quiet at my back."

This surprises me; not the ambition, but the confidence. "You've got a navy?" The Macedon of my childhood had twenty warships to Athens's three hundred and fifty.

"Athens has my navy."

"Ah."

"You can't be sweeter than I've been," Philip says. "Sweeter or more accommodating or more understanding. I let them off easy every time, freeing prisoners, returning territory. Demosthenes should make a speech or two about that."

Demosthenes, the Athenian orator who gives poisonous, roaring speeches against Philip in the Athenian assembly. I saw him once in the marketplace when I was a student. He was buying wine, chatting.

"What do you think of him?" Philip asks.

"Bilious, choleric," I diagnose. "I prescribe less wine, more milk and cheese. Avoid stressful situations. Avoid hot weather. Chew each bite of food thoroughly. Retire from public life. Cool cloths to the forehead."

Philip doesn't laugh. He cocks his head to the side, looking at me, deciding something. It's unnerving.

"The army's moving?" I say. "I saw the preparations as we arrived. Thessaly again, is it?"

"Thessaly again, then Thrace again." Abruptly: "You brought your family?"

"My wife and nephew."

"Healthy?"

I thank him for his interest and return the question, ritually. Philip begins to speak of his sons. The one a champion, godling, genius, star. The other—

"Yes, yes," Philip says. "You'll have a look at the older one for me."

I nod.

"Look at yourself," Philip repeats, genuinely perplexed this time. "You're dressed like a woman."

"I've been away."

"I make it twenty years."

"Twenty-five. I left when I was seventeen."

"Piece of shit," he says again. "Where do you go from here?"

"Athens, to teach. I know, I know. But the Academy still rules a few small worlds: ethics, metaphysics, astronomy. In my job, you have to go where the best minds are if you want to leave your mark."

He rises, and his courtiers around him. "We'll hunt together before I leave."

"It would be an honour."

"And you'll have a look at my son," he says again. "Let's see if you have some art."

A NURSE ADMITS ME to the elder son's room. He's tall but his affliction makes his age difficult to guess. He walks loosely, palsied like an old man, and his eyes move vaguely from object to object in the room. While the nurse and I talk, his fingers drift up to his mouth and pluck repeatedly at his lower lip. Sitting or standing, awkwardly turning this way and that as he is instructed, he seems affable enough but is clearly an idiot. His room is decorated for a child much younger, with balls and toys and carved animals strewn on the floor. The smell is thick, an animal musk.

"Arrhidaeus," he slurs proudly, when I ask him his name. I have to ask twice, repeating myself after the nurse tells me the boy is hard of hearing.

Despite the mask of foolishness, I can see the king his father in him, in the breadth of his shoulders and the frank laughter when something pleases him, when I take deep breaths or open my mouth as wide as I can to show the boy what I want him to do. The nurse says he's sixteen, and had been an utterly healthy child, handsome and beloved, until the age of five. He fell ill, the nurse says, and the whole house mourned, thinking he could not possibly survive the fever, the headaches, the strange stiffness in the neck, the vomiting, and finally the seizures and the ominous lethargy. But perhaps what had happened was worse.

"Not worse." I study the boy's nose and ears, the extension of his limbs, and test the soft muscles against my own. "Not worse."

Though privately I thrill to the various beauty and order of the world, and this boy gives me a pang of horror.

"Take this." I hand Arrhidaeus a wax tablet. "Can you draw me a triangle?"

But he doesn't know how to hold the stylus. When I show him, he crows with delight and begins to scratch wavering lines. When I draw a triangle, he laughs. Inevitably I think of my own masters at school, with their modish theories about the workings of the mind. *There have been always true thoughts in him . . . which only need to be awakened into knowledge by putting questions to him . . .*

"He is unused," I say. "The mind, the body. I will give you exercises. You are his companion?"

The nurse nods.

"Take him to the gymnasium with you. Teach him to run and catch a ball. Have the masseur work on his muscles, especially the legs. You read?"

The nurse nods again.

"Teach him his letters. Aloud, first, and later have him draw them with his finger in the sand. That will be easier for him than the stylus, at least to start with. Kindly, mind you."

"Alpha, beta, gamma," the boy says, beaming.

"Good!" I ruffle his hair. "That's very good, Arrhidaeus."

"For a while my father taught both children," the nurse says.

"I was their companion. The younger one is very bright. Arrhidaeus parrots him. It doesn't mean anything."

"Delta," I say, ignoring the nurse.

"Delta," Arrhidaeus says.

"I want to see him every morning until I leave. I will give you instructions as we go along."

The nurse holds out his hand to Arrhidaeus, who takes it. They rise to leave. Suddenly Arrhidaeus's face lights up and he begins to clap his hands, while the nurse bows. I turn. In the doorway stands a woman my own age in a simple grey dress. Her red hair is dressed elaborately in long loops and curls, hours' worth, fixed with gems and amber. Her skin is dry and freckled. Her eyes are clear brown.

"Did he tell you?" she asks me. "Did my husband tell you how I poisoned this poor child?"

The nurse has gone stone-still. The woman and Arrhidaeus have their arms around each other's waists, and she fondly kisses the crown of his head.

"Olympias poisoned Arrhidaeus," she singsongs. "That's what they all say. Jealous of her husband's eldest son. Determined to secure the throne for her own child. Isn't that what they say?" Arrhidaeus laughs, clearly understanding nothing. "Isn't it?" she asks the nurse.

The young man's mouth opens and closes, like a fish's.

"You may leave us," she says. "Yes, puppet," she adds, when Arrhidaeus insists on giving her a hug. He runs after his nurse.

"Forgive me," I say when they're gone. "I didn't recognize you."

"But I knew you. Philip told me all about you. Can you help the child?"

I repeat what I told the nurse, about developing the boy's existing faculties as opposed to seeking a cure.

"Your father was a doctor, yes? But you, I think, are not."

"I have many interests," I say. "Too many, I'm told. My knowledge is not as deep as his was, but I have a knack for seeing things whole. That child could be more than he is."

"That child belongs to Dionysus." She touches her heart. "There is more to him than reason. I have a fierce affection for him, despite what you may hear. Anything you do for him, I will take as a personal favour."

Her voice rings false, the low vibrancy of it, the formality of her sentences, the practised whiff of sex. More than reason? She sets off a simmer of irritation in me, hot and dark and not entirely unpleasant.

"Anything I can do for you, I will," I hear myself say.

After she leaves, I return to my rooms. Pythias is instructing her maids in the laundry.

"Only gently, this time," she's saying. Her voice is weak and tight and high; petulant. They bow and go out with the baskets between them. "Callisthenes found a servant to show them down to the river. They'll beat my linens with rocks again, wait and see, and say they mistook them for the bedding. They'd never have dared back home."

"You'll have new linens once we're settled. Just another day or two here. Look at you, trying not to smile. You can't wait."

"I can wait a little longer," she says, trying to bat my hands away.

Pretty, I called her; once, maybe. Now her hair hangs thin and lank, and her brows, ten days without tweezing, have begun to sprout rogue hairs like insect legs. The lips—thinner on top, fuller beneath, with two bites of chap from the cold and damp—I want to kiss, but that's for pity. I pull her to me to feel the green hardness of her, the bony hips and breasts like small apples. I ask her if she'd like a bath, and her eyes close for a long moment. I am both a gross idiot and the answer to her most fervent prayer.

When we come back from the baths (which, to my deep satisfaction, made her gasp: the pipes for hot and cold, hot hung with warming towels; the spout in the shape of a lion's mouth; the marble tub; the stones and sponges; the combs and oils and files and mirrors and scents; I will bring her here every day we remain), Callisthenes is up and eating the remains of last night's meal. Pythias withdraws to the innermost room, to her maids and her sewing. The boy looks abashed but pleased with himself also. Laughing Callisthenes, with his curls and freckles. He has a sweet nature and a nimble mind and makes connections others can't, darting from ethics to metaphysics to geometry to politics to poetics like a bee darts from flower to flower, spreading pollen. I taught him that. He can be lazy, too, though, like a sun-struck bee. I worry about him from both sides of the pendulum: that he'll leave me, that he'll never leave me.

"Had a good time?" I say. "Out again tonight?" Jealousy pinches my sentences, but I can't stop myself. The pendulum swings hard left today.

"Come with me," he says. I tell him I have to work—the reality of numbers, I remind him—and he groans. "Come with me," he says. "You can be my guide."

"I can be your guide here," I say.

"I thought I caught a glimpse of the number three last night, by the flower stall in the market," he says. "It was hiding behind a sprig of orange blossom."

"Known for shyness, the number three," I say.

"Is Pella much bigger than you remember?"

"I wouldn't remember a thing," I say truthfully. "The city has probably tripled in size. I got lost this morning trying to find the baths just here in the palace."

"Wouldn't you like to find your father's old house?"

"I think it's part of the garrison now. Shall I show you the baths now that I know the way? We can work after that. You still have a headache, anyway."

"Headache," Callisthenes confirms. "Bad wine. Bad everything, really. Or not bad, but—vulgar. Have you seen the houses? They're huge. And gaudy. Like these mosaics everywhere. The way they talk, the way they eat, the music, the dancing, the women. It's like there's all this money everywhere and they don't know what to do with it."

"I don't remember it that way," I say. "I remember the cold, and the snow. I'll bet you've never seen snow. I remember the toughness of the people. The best lamb, mountain lamb."

"I saw something last night," Callisthenes says. "I saw a man kill another man over a drink. He held him by the shoulder and punched him in the gut over and over until the man bled out of his ears and his mouth and his eyes, weeping blood, and then he died. Everyone laughed. They just laughed and laughed. Men, boys. What kind of a people is that?"

"You tell me," I say.

"Animals," Callisthenes says. He's looking me in the eye, not smiling. A rare passion from such a mild creature.

"And what separates man from the animals?"

"Reason. Work. The life of the mind."

"Out again tonight?" I ask.

THE NEXT MORNING I return to Arrhidaeus in his room. His face is tear-stained and snot-crusted; his nurse gazes out a window and pretends not to hear me enter. The boy himself smiles, sweet and frail, when he sees me. I wish him good morning and he says, *"Uh."*

"Any progress?" I ask the nurse.

"In one day?"

I help myself to a cloak hanging on the back of a chair, which I drape over the boy's shoulders. "Where are your shoes?"

The nurse is watching now. He's a prissy little shit, and sees his moment.

"He can't walk far," he says. "He doesn't have winter shoes, just sandals. He never goes outdoors, really."

"Then we'll have to borrow yours," I tell him.

Eyebrows up: "And what will I wear?"

"You can wear Arrhidaeus's sandals since you won't be coming."

"I'm obliged to accompany him everywhere."

I can't tell if he's angry with me or frightened of being caught away from his charge. He glances at Arrhidaeus and reaches automatically to wipe the hair from the boy's face. Arrhidaeus flinches from his touch. So, they've had that kind of morning.

"Give me your fucking shoes," I say.

Arrhidaeus wants to take my hand as we walk. "No, Arrhidaeus," I tell him. "Children hold hands. Men walk by themselves, you see?"

He cries a little, but stops when he sees where I'm leading him. He gibbers something I can't make out.

"That's right," I say. "We'll take a walk into town, shall we?"

He laughs and points at everything: the soldiers, the gate, the grey swirl of the sky. The soldiers look interested, but no one stops us. I wonder how often he leaves his room, and if they even know who he is.

"Where is your favourite place to go?"

He doesn't understand. But when he sees a horse, a big stallion led through the gate, he claps his hands and gibbers some more.

"Horses? You like horses?"

Through the gate I've caught a glimpse of the town—people, horses, the monstrous houses that so offended my nephew—and I realize my heart's not ready for it, so I'm happy enough to lead him back to the stables. In the middle of a long row of stalls I find our animals, Tweak and Tar and Lady and Gem and the others. Arrhidaeus is painfully excited and when he stumbles into me I wonder from the smell if he's pissed himself. The other horses look sidelong, and only big black Tar takes much of an interest in us, lifting his head when he recognizes me and ambling over for some affection. I show Arrhidaeus how to offer him a carrot from his open hand, but when the horse touches him, he shrieks and flinches away. I take his hand and guide it back, getting him to stroke the blaze on Tar's forehead. He wants to use his knuckles, and when I look closely I see his palm is scored with open sores, some kind of rash. I'll have to find him an ointment.

"Do you ride?" I ask him.

"No, sir," someone calls. It's a groom who's been mucking out the straw. "That other one brings him here sometimes and lets him sit in a corner. He'll sit quiet for hours that way. He hasn't got the balance for riding, though. Doesn't need another fall on the head, does he?"

I lead Tar out into the yard and saddle him. It's raining again. I get Arrhidaeus's foot in my cupped hands and then he's stuck. He's stopped laughing, at least, and looks at me for help. I try to give him a boost up, but he's too weak to heft himself over the horse's back. He hops a little on one foot with the other cocked up in the air, giving me a view of his wet crotch.

"Here," the groom says, and rolls over a barrel for the boy to stand on.

Between the two of us we get him up alongside the horse and persuade him to throw a leg over the animal's back.

"Now you hug him," the groom says, and leans forward with his arms curved around an imaginary mount. Arrhidaeus collapses eagerly onto Tar's back and hugs him hard. I try to get him to sit back up, but the groom says, "No, no. Let the animal walk a bit and get him used to the movement."

I lead Tar slowly around the yard while Arrhidaeus clings to him full-body, his face buried in the mane. The groom watches.

"Is he a good horse?" he calls to Arrhidaeus.

The boy smiles, eyes closed. He's in bliss.

"Look at that, now," the groom says. "Poor brained bastard. Did he piss himself?"

I nod.

"There, now." He leads Tar back to the barrel and helps Arrhidaeus back down. I had expected the boy to resist but he seems too stunned to do anything but what he's told.

"Would you like to come back here?" I ask him. "Learn to ride properly, like a man?" He claps his hands. "When are we least in the way?" I ask the groom.

He waves the question away. His black eyes are bright and curious, assessing, now Tar, now Arrhidaeus. "I don't know you," he says, without looking at me properly. He slaps Tar fondly on the neck.

"I'm the prince's physician." I rest a hand on Arrhidaeus's shoulder. "And his tutor. Just for a few days."

The groom laughs, but not so that I dislike him for it.

EURIPIDES WROTE THE *Bacchae* at the end of his life. He left Athens disgusted by his plays' losses at the competitions, so the story goes, and accepted an invitation from King Archelaus to come to Pella and work for a more appreciative (less discriminating) audience. He died that winter from the cold.

Plot: Angry that his godhead is denied by the Theban royal house, Dionysus decides to take his revenge on the priggish young King Pentheus. Pentheus has Dionysus imprisoned. The god, in turn, offers to help him spy on the revels of his female followers, the Bacchantes. Pentheus, both fascinated and repulsed by the wild behaviour of these women, agrees to allow himself to be disguised as one of them to infiltrate their revels on Mount Kithairon. The disguise fails, and Pentheus is ripped to pieces by the Bacchantes, including his own mother, Agave. She returns to Thebes with his head, believing she has killed a mountain lion, and only slowly recovers from her possessed state to realize what she's done. The royal family is destroyed, killed or exiled by the god. The play took first prize at the competition in Athens the following year, after Euripides's death.

We all love the Bacchae.

The actors huddle together downstage, except for the man

playing the god, who stands on an apple crate so he can look down on the mortals. He's not very tall. For the performance they could dress him in a robe long enough to hide the crate. That's a good idea.

"Pentheus, my son . . . my baby . . . ," the actor playing Agave says. "You lay in my arms so often, so helpless, and now again you need my loving care. My dear, sweet child . . . I killed you— No! I will not say that, I was not there!" an actor says. "I was . . . in some other place. It was Dionysus. Dionysus took me, Dionysus used me, and Dionysus murdered you."

"No," the actor playing the god replies. "Accept the guilt, accuse yourselves."

"Dionysus, listen to us," the actor playing Agave's father, Kadmos, says. "We have been wrong."

After a moment's hesitation, the director calls, "Now you understand."

"Now you understand, but now is too late. When you should have seen, you were blind," the actor playing the god says.

"We know that. But you are like a tide that turns and drowns us."

"Because I was born with dominion over you and you dispossessed me. And I don't—"

The director interrupts, calling, "Kadmos!"

"Then you should not be like us, your subjects. You should have no passions," the old man upstage says reprovingly.

"And I don't," the actor repeats, and when no one interrupts him, continues, "But these are the laws, the—the laws of life. I cannot change them."

"The laws of life," the director calls.

"The laws of life," the actor repeats.

"It is decided, Father," the actor playing the woman, Agave, says. "We must go, and take our grief with us."

There's some business with a sheet of cloth, allowing the actor playing Dionysus to slip offstage, unseen by the audience, leaving the crate behind. I amend my idea to stilts.

When the actor playing Agave takes a deep breath and says nothing, the director calls, "Help me. Take me to my sisters. They will share my exile and the years of sorrow. Take me where I cannot see Mount Kithairon, where branches wound with ivy cannot remind me of what has happened. Let someone else be possessed. I have withered. Fuck me, but I have withered."

Afterwards, over wine backstage, the director shakes his head and says, "Amateurs."

"You won't get professionals here," I say.

He's an Athenian, this Carolus, with a drinker's genial blob of a nose and a husky, hectoring way of running the world. I speak dialect with the actors but not with him. His diction is high and elegant and a bit prissy, but he's learning, slowly. "Fuck me"—I taught him that.

The actor playing the woman, Agave, at a livelier table across the room, makes a leggy chestnut mare.

"That one looks the part, at least," I say.

"He does indeed," Carolus says. "That may have been my mistake."

At the actors' table there's much merry jostling of chairs to make room for me, though I refuse to sit down. They're still in their costumes and are enjoying themselves voraciously.

"Better every time," I say.

I've taken to haunting rehearsals ever since I stumbled on them the day we arrived. When I returned later that day to apologize to Carolus for the interruption, he too was apologetic. He suffered headaches and insomnia and his cast was made up of locals, mostly clowns and jugglers, acrobats, and one or two musicians. "I think of Euripides seeing this and I die," he told me. "I die and die again." When he discovered I knew the play, had seen it in Athens in my student days, we compared notes and realized it was his own Dionysus I had seen. He had been young enough then, still, to get away with it: dark-haired instead of white, thrilling-voiced, intense. The boy he's got for the role now is pretty enough, but dense and oddly prim. He has to be taught to walk like a cock and not a hen. Aging Kadmos, trained as a clown, fancies himself a professional, though he's never done tragedy, and considers himself the actors' spokesman. He takes their complaints to Carolus and delivers them long-windedly, pleased with his own diction. Agave looks nice in a wig but simpers and minces and forgets his lines. Pentheus often misses rehearsals, with no explanation. He's away today.

The actors are playing a drinking game, tossing the ball of rags they've been using for Pentheus's head amongst themselves; whoever drops it has to stand and drain his cup while the others hoot and jeer. I rejoin Carolus. I like him. I like having a friend near enough my own age. Older, actually, but not old enough to be my father, and I like that, too. And still the embers of a sexuality not quite spent; you can see it when he gets angry. He likes men, told me so early on, and didn't mind when I told him I didn't. We talk about plays and theatre generally, tell each other about productions we've seen. I don't have much to offer that he's unfamiliar with.

I ask him what makes a good tragedy. He thinks about this

for a while. A companionable silence between us while the actors slowly drift away, bidding each other stagy goodbyes, and the rain increases, drumming at the roof like fingers. He's got good wine from somewhere, not the local.

"Funny question," he says. "A good death, a good pain, a good tragedy. 'Good' is a funny word."

"I'm writing a book." The response I default to when my subject starts to look at me strangely. And maybe I am, suddenly, maybe I am. A little work to bring me back here when I reread it years from now, to this rain and this cup of wine and this man I'm prepared to like so much. The comfort here, this little sanctuary.

"Gods, man," he says. "Are you crying?"

I tell him I'm unwell.

"What kind of book?" he says.

"An analysis." I'm thinking through my mouth. "In two parts, tragedy and comedy. The constituent elements of each, with examples."

"Tragedy for beginners."

"Sure," I say. "A gentle introduction."

"How are you unwell?"

I tell him I cry easily, laugh easily, get angry easily. I get overwhelmed.

"That's a sickness?"

I ask him what he would call it.

"Histrionics," he says. "What do you do for it?"

I tell him I write books.

He nods, then shakes his head. "My father had the same. I wish he'd written books. He was a drunk."

I wait for more, but there isn't any.

"A good tragedy," he says. "I think you're a dabbler."

I lean forward. I tell him that's exactly what I am. I suggest the stilts.

He laughs, then falls silent again, long enough for me to wonder if our conversation is over and he's waiting for me to leave. I clear my throat.

"It's the whole course of a character's life," he says. "The actions he takes, decisions, the choices that bring him right up to the present moment. Having to choose." He points at me. "That's what I want to say. You're surrounded by evils, a banquet of evils, and you have to choose. You have to fill your plate and eat it."

"And comedy?"

He looks at me like I'm stupid. "Comedy makes you laugh. A couple of slaves buggering each other, I'll have that and thank you very much. How would you say that here?"

I think for a minute. "Ass-fucking," I say in dialect.

He grunts. He likes it.

"That's it?" I ask.

Carolus shakes a reproving finger at me. "I won't have you slighting the comedies. They were my living for the first few years. *Lysistrata* without the props, if you know what I mean. I got a reputation for that one. I was just a teenager then."

"You started young."

"I did, man." He grasps himself between the legs and we laugh. "It was the family trade. My grandfather was Tiresias in the first production of *Oedipus the King*."

"No."

"He was. After him, my father took up the role." He looks at me and says nothing for a moment. Then: "I kept the mask he wore that night. I'll show it to you sometime, if you like."

"They let you?" I mean the company. Good masks are expensive, irreplaceable.

"He stole it."

I nod.

"No masks for this crew." Carolus waves a hand at the table the actors have lately abandoned for a dive in town. "I haven't the time or the money. They're all so stiff anyway, I doubt anyone will notice the difference."

"You're too hard on them. Dionysus is improving, with your help."

His mouth goes bitter. "Don't patronize me," he says. "You think I wanted to end up here?"

"It's funny how often I hear that about Pella."

He's not interested. "You know who's going to be all right? The only one? Pentheus. You know why? Because I'm going to end up playing him myself if he misses one more bloody rehearsal."

"Fucking," I say.

"One more fucking rehearsal. You'll have me passing for a native by Friday. Where is that cunt, anyway?"

Something lands on the table between us: the ball of rags the actors used for Pentheus's head. It's come unwound, trailing a rag-tail like a shooting star. The grubby, soft white bundle lands almost soundlessly, not even overturning our cups. The paint on it, eyes and mouth and some pinky gore, is smudged like a child's drawing.

"That wouldn't scare anyone." The boy steps from the shadows. I wonder how long he's been listening to us.

"It's you, is it?" Carolus winks at me. "Monkey. What would scare us, then?"

The boy looks up at the ceiling. "A real head," he says.

Childish bravado, but Carolus is nodding, eyebrows raised. A show of seriousness; I'll play along.

"And where would I get one?" the director says.

The boy looks blank, as though the question is so stupid he wonders if he's missing something. "Anywhere."

"Logistical problems," I say. "You'd need a new head for each performance. I doubt they'd keep."

"We're doing only the one night," Carolus says.

"Lot of blood," I say. "Messy."

"Messy," Carolus says to the boy.

"Well, sure," he says. "Don't you want it to look real?"

"We use the costumes over and over," Carolus says. "Pentheus today, Creon tomorrow. You want us to do everything in pink? Real, but only just real enough, if you see what I mean."

"You could cauterize it," I say. They look at me. "Cauterize. You heat a metal plate over a brazier. Then you press the cut end to the plate to burn it. Seals it right up, stops the blood."

The boy frowns. "Like frying meat."

"Exactly."

"Well." Carolus claps his hands together once. "Problem solved." He tosses the ball of rags back to the boy. "I'm putting you in charge, then. Pentheus's head is now your department."

The boy looks pleased. He leaves, tossing the ball in the air and catching it as he goes.

"Interesting," I say.

"He likes to watch rehearsals, like you," Carolus says. "Stays out of the way, doesn't say much. The actors seem to like having him around. Bit of a pet."

"He's got a flair for the dramatic, anyway."

Eyebrows up again: "He's got a flair for something," Carolus says.

The boy is back. "By the way," he says. "I know where Pentheus is."

I clear my throat, assembling a formal introduction. It's time.

"Brat." Carolus ignores me. "Where, then?"

"He's sick," the boy says. "I heard the actors talking about him. He can't eat and he can't shit and some days he can't get out of bed."

"Fucking ass-fucker," Carolus says, pleased with himself. The boy turns, waves the rag head above his own, and is gone for real.

I'VE LEARNED IN THE past week that I can get Arrhidaeus to do anything if it has to do with horses.

"How many?" I point to the stalls.

"One, two, five," he says, and sure enough there are five horses inside this day, including his favourite, my big Tar.

"What colour?" I say of Tar, and he giggles and rocks and claps his hands and reaches for the bridle hanging from a nail in the wall. "No." I pull his hand away. "Soon. Not yet. What colour is Tar?"

"Back, back, back," he says.

"Black."

"Buh-lack."

"La, la, la," I say. "Blah, blah, blah. Black." He laughs at me; fair enough. I give him a stick and tell him to draw me shapes in the muck: circle, triangle. He struggles with square, and I see his attention is almost gone, like oil almost burnt out in a lamp. He has a kind of feral intelligence, knows more or less how to get what he needs—food, drink, basic companionship, the piss-pot—but try to draw him up a level and he's quickly exhausted. Literally: red rims his eyes, he yawns, even his skin seems to go more grey.

I leave off the shapes and have him jump up and down ten times while I count for him. Of this, too, he tires quickly, though already he's stopped crying whenever he doesn't want to do something. I've asked the groom to find some jobs for him around the horses, sweeping and so on, something to get him out in the air and moving. Before I go, I'll ask Philip to get rid of the nurse and find someone more congenial, more willing to recognize improvement and contribute to it. There must be someone.

"Is it time to ride?" I ask. He mounts more easily now and sits up tall. Mounted, he's more coordinated, with better balance than on his own feet. This amazes me and I can't think through a reason for it, though the groom tells me he's seen it before. He strikes me as the kind who's seen everything before and doesn't want to be told much of anything, or at least isn't willing to show surprise, but he's genial and alert and helpful without getting in the way, and hasn't asked me why I bother. He says he's seen children who are awkward and ungainly become graceful on their animals. He's seen it too with injured soldiers who have to learn all over again how to ride. Sometimes it might be an injury to a leg or the pelvis, but he says he's seen men with no outward impairment who've suffered some damage to the head and can't remember how to raise their hands until they're given reins. I ask him what he makes of all this. He shrugs.

"People like horses," he says. "It's a part of our nature. I'm happiest on a horse, aren't you? I could forget everything and still remember how to ride. My father was like that. Babbling idiot by the end, not far off this one"—he gestures at Arrhidaeus—"but he sat like a general. Aren't you happiest on a horse?" he demands again.

I haven't the heart to tell him not really. I wonder where the rest of his life takes place when he's not in the stables: what room, what meat, what sleep, who he rides in his bed. I remind Arrhidaeus to keep his heels down and watch the groom walk him around the ring on a lead. Walk on, the little man's taught him, and stop; a major accomplishment in just seven days. From the back Arrhidaeus looks grand, and I love to hear his voice giving these commands. I've ordered his nurse to bathe him daily and keep his laundry cleaner; I've told the little snit I'll make them exchange clothes if what the prince is wearing isn't suitable. I take good care to refer to him as "the prince." I love to hear my own voice giving these commands, and wonder sometimes why I have conceived such a dislike of the nurse. He has a job I would abhor, and it's natural enough for him to despise me, who plays at his life's work for an hour or two each day. I wonder what ambitions he would have were he not yoked to an idiot every hour of the day. I wonder what he does when I relieve him. I'll have to sneak up on him sometime and find out.

After Arrhidaeus's ride, I show him how to curry his animal. He's rough at first and I have to teach him about the grain of the horse's hide and the tender places on the animal's body. He's still nervous feeding Tar from his own hand, and the scabbing and peeling of the skin haven't improved, despite the mixtures I've given the nurse.

"He eats them," the nurse says, when I return Arrhidaeus to

his rooms today. "Licks them right off. Do you put honey in? That will be why."

He's tidying the room, sweeping, snapping blankets; or at least had enough warning of us coming to put on a little show. He has food already laid out for Arrhidaeus, who sets to with both hands, immediately ignoring both of us.

"He gets it every winter," the nurse continues, before I can say something scathing. "I've tried a honey poultice before. On his feet, too. Heals right up when the weather turns warm. I bind it when it bleeds, but otherwise I leave it to air. The feet, too. That's why the sandals, and I let him go barefoot when I can. Fresh air seems best."

"Do you read?"

He stiffens. "You already asked me that. I've been working on his letters with him. Ask him and see."

"I mean for yourself."

"Books?"

I nod.

"Why?"

And there is my prize. He's suspicious, painfully, because he wants painfully what he's not quite sure I'm offering.

"I've brought my library with me," I say. "I wondered if you might want to borrow something while I'm out with the prince."

"I've been wondering if I shouldn't be accompanying you," he says. "So I'll know how to continue once you've gone."

At last. We have exchanged courtesies, now, finally, and can begin to get a hold of each other.

"I'm here for a few days yet," I say. "Let me bring you something tomorrow. What do you like best? Poetry, history, the habits of animals?"

He laughs at this, contemptuously; thinks I've made a joke at Arrhidaeus's expense and is looking to play along.

"Something on education, perhaps," I say.

He wipes the look off his face. So much for a truce.

"I don't understand," he says, seeing the moment slip away. "He's worthless, useless. You of all people should understand. I thought you of all people would. I know who you are. How can you stand to spend time with him? How can it not hurt you? You who understand all a human mind can be, how can you bear it? I don't have the hundredth part of your mind and there are days when I think I'll go mad. I can feel it. Or hear it. It's more like hearing something creeping along the walls, just behind my head, getting closer and closer. A big insect, maybe a scorpion. A dry skittering, that's what madness sounds like to me."

Verse, then. A young man still, after all, in love with his own melancholy, forced to brood on his own wasted intelligence. But then I see he's weeping, his eyes glittering with it. He turns away so I won't see him in his depths. I ask how long he's been the prince's companion. He takes a shaky breath and says it doesn't matter.

"How old are you?"

"Twenty."

As old as my nephew. "Where do you sleep?"

He shrugs. "Here." Then: "There. On the floor." He points to a wall. He must unroll a pallet at night and put it away during the day to give the prince more play-space. Already the tears have soaked back into him, the eyes and nose, and he's back to being sullen. I am familiar with such easy fits of tears, and the odd disjunction between what the face does and what the mind might be doing. I myself can weep while working, eating, bathing, and have woken in the night with the snail-trails of it on my face.

Arrhidaeus has finished his feed and is tugging at the nurse's arm. The nurse obediently gets down on his knees and fishes the pot from beneath the bed. He places it behind a screen for Arrhidaeus, who's already bared himself and goes at it as noisily as he does his food, grunting and grumbling to himself, audibly straining. The stink is rich. I'm ready to go.

"Pythagoras," the nurse says.

I nod; my own blackness is lapping at me now and I need to leave. I'll bring him my Pythagoras.

"I wanted to study—" he says.

But I can't listen to any more. I'm out of the room and off down the hall, walking fast and faster, concentrating on the pattern of the tiles, thinking about the geometry of star-shapes.

I AM GARBAGE. This knowledge is my weather, my private clouds. Sometimes low-slung, black, and heavy; sometimes high and scudding, the white unbothersome flock of a fine summer's day. I tell Pythias sometimes, an urgent bulletin from the darklands: *I'm garbage.* She says nothing.

I WAS TO HAVE been Philip's guest at the performance, but Carolus asks me if I'll stand backstage with him, hold his copy of the text, help with the props, and generally be a calming influence. "On them, not me," he says. "They're used to you now. Tell me, why are even bad actors so high-strung?" I open my mouth to reply but he says, "Oh, shut up. That was a rhetorical question. You do like to talk, don't you. Here, hold this."

It's Pentheus's head, a second rag ball since the boy went off with the first and didn't come back. This one's been tied tighter, at least, and shouldn't come undone, though the face is still crude: staring black eyes, two-thirds of a triangle for a nose, red mouth, single red gash at the throat.

"These, too." Carolus gives me a handful of sticks wound with ivy. He himself is dressed in Pentheus's robes; like the boy, the actor has disappeared, and no one seems to know what happened to him. What Carolus really wants me for, I think, is to prompt the actors when he's onstage. Philip at any rate is occupied with his latest guest, Olympias's brother, Alexandros. He spent years as the king's ward in Pella, while Philip waited for him to come of age. Now Philip has just had him kinged in Molossos, and this is his first state visit to the court he called home for so long. He's coloured like his sister—rosy, rusty, dark eyes—and Philip likes him. From behind the flies I can see them drinking steadily, heads together in conversation, often laughing. I doubt they'll give the play much attention.

I tuck the head under my arm and stand ready to hand the sticks to the chorus as they file past. My palms sparkle with excitement; I've been giddy all day. I love this vantage point, the play from behind, and seeing all that's gone into it. I love to be on the inside, the backside, the underside of anything, and see the usually unseen.

"And." Carolus raises a hand, then brings it down. The music starts.

I'm not sure when exactly the boy slips in beside me. I look over and he's simply there, watching the stage, rapt as I am. He notices the movement of my head, looks at me, and we both smile. This is the real thing. He takes the head from beneath my arm, helping, and I nod, as much as to say I'll give him the signal when it's time to hand it to the actor.

"Look, she's coming," the actors playing the chorus say in unison. "Agave, his mother, running back home. Her eyes! Look at her eyes! They're staring. She is possessed. Take her into our midst, she is full of the god and his ecstasy."

I nod. The boy gives the head to the actor playing Agave, who rushes it onstage. Then, for a moment, silence. A faltering. Carolus, beside me, looks up sharply from the text and hisses, "Women of the east."

I look at the boy. He tosses the rag head he took from me in the air, catches it, and looks deliberately at the stage.

"Women of the east," Carolus hisses, louder.

"Women of the east—Bacchae," Agave says.

I remember the actor playing Pentheus had straight hair but a curly beard, and a mole beneath the left eye. I remember because I'm looking at his head now, cradled in the arms of the actor who plays Agave.

"Do you know us?" one of the chorus says. The others, staring at the head, have forgotten to speak. "Do you know who you are? Our true nature?"

"Look. It is a lion cub. I caught it. I caught it without nets. Look," Agave says. His voice has gone shrill and his eyes are glazed. He's drugged with shock.

In the audience, Philip has stopped talking to his guest. His eyebrows are up, he's watching the stage. He's interested now.

Afterwards, Carolus can't stop shaking his head. "That was

the best fucking performance I have ever seen in my entire miserable fucking life."

The head is gone; he's had a stagehand wrap it back up in the cloth the boy brought it in and dispose of it somewhere.

"I cauterized it, like you said," the boy tells me. "It worked."

"Fucking monkey monster," Carolus says.

"I thought they might not do it if they knew ahead of time," the boy says. "I was thinking of what you said about things looking real enough, and how you were always complaining about them all being such bad actors. And I thought, what if they didn't have to act? What if they just had to be themselves?"

The actors have long since fled. Backstage smells of piss and vomit: pity and fear. Carolus will have laundry ahead of him after all.

"He died last night," the boy continues. "I told you he was sick. I think things happen for a reason, don't you?" For the first time, he looks—not doubtful, maybe, but impatient. "What?" He looks from Carolus to me, back and forth. "You know it was perfect. What?"

THIS MORNING, before the performance, Philip had sent for me. I found him in a courtyard surrounded by assorted lengths of wood, tilting at a soldier who parried with a shield. I'd noticed the guards' enormous lances, which I had assumed were ornamental, but here was the king wielding roughly trimmed boughs of a similar length.

"My own invention," he said. "The sarissa. Look, you see, here's a Thracian lance, and an Illyrian, and a few others. The sarissa is longer again by a third. You see the implications?"

I did see, but was more interested in the physics. I hefted one. "It's heavier."

"Not by much. You adjust for the weight with a smaller shield."

I took a few thrusts while he watched.

"You're rusty," he said finally. "At least you've changed your clothes."

He introduced me to the soldier, who turned out to be one of his older generals, Antipater. Short hair, short beard, tired eyes. When Philip was off at war, Antipater was regent. The three of us sat under the colonnade, while the first rain of the day speckled the courtyard, and drank wine mixed with water. While we spoke, I thought about Philip as a boy. We had played together, in this very courtyard perhaps. I seemed to remember a wrestling match, smells of sweat and grass; fierce, private, sweet. I couldn't recall who had won.

"He offers you his loyalty, and asks for your help," I said now, of Hermias.

Philip reread the treaty I had brought him, slowly, while a page gathered up the assorted lances and took them in out of the drumming rain. I imagined Philip on various battlefields, squinting about for a new piece to add to his collection and promptly killing the bearer when he found one. Wasn't that, too, a kind of science?

"Drink," Philip ordered without lifting his eyes, when I shifted in my chair.

I drank. A scholar surrounded by scholars, I had forgotten how slowly some people read. After a long while, Philip began to talk about his ambitions.

"I like your friend here," he said, waving the treaty. "He's shrewd, a survivor."

"I will be pleased to relay that message to him."

"Someone will. Not you. I'll be needing you now."

I watched the page, a dark-skinned boy with tight curls and yellow palms. He had come from far away, Egypt, perhaps, or Ethiopia. He might have changed hands many, many times before landing here with these spears and dummies. Philip was talking about Athens. Athens was old, Athens was decayed, Athens was dying, but Athens was also key. Antipater sat with his feet flat on the ground, his palms flat on his thighs, staring fixedly at the air between his knees. I wondered, though he had parried nimbly enough, if he was in pain. Athens, though— that was all right. For a moment Philip had frightened me, saying he needed me.

"We had hoped," he said, "after Plato's death, the Academy would go to you. Then you would have had some influence. I don't like this Speusippus who's there now."

I was confused; Plato, my master, had died five years before. Philip had been watching me five years ago? "Speusippus is his nephew," I said. "I don't like him either." With his little hands and his mild manners and his mild little mind. He wrote dialogues, like his uncle, in which the challenger was always crumbling into confusion before the questioner's blithe prob- ing. I told him once not to be afraid to enter an argument he couldn't immediately see his way out of. I had thought to be helpful, but he counted me an enemy, in his mild way, after that.

"He writes me letters," Philip said. "Counselling me. He compares me to Heracles. Astounding parallels he finds between us."

Antipater and I smiled identical smiles, small and dry; we caught each other's eye and looked away. Friends, that quickly.

Philip, a deft enough wit to move swiftly past his own jokes, shook his head. "They'll consider you again, though, when Speusippus dies. He's elderly, yes? Because that's the sort of power I need. You can't do it all with spears. They look at me and see an animal, but they look at you and see one of their own. Military power they'll fight and fight like a butting goat, but you could get under their skin. Head of the Academy, that's the kind of thing they respect. Plato used the office like a diplomat, power-brokering, influencing policy. Kings listened to him."

"As you listen to Speusippus?"

"You're not an effeminate clown. Well, you're not a clown. They'll listen to you, too, when the time comes. Meanwhile I've got a job for you here."

No. "Here."

"You can tutor my son."

The rain paused in the air, then continued to fall.

"That's beneath you?"

"Of course it's beneath me," I said. "I've got work to do."

"But he likes you already. He told me so himself."

"Arrhidaeus?"

Antipater raised his head.

Philip looked wondering for a moment. Then his face cleared. "No, you dumb shit," he said. "Alexander."

AFTER THE PERFORMANCE, I lie in bed watching my wife remove the long gold pins from her hair and the sharp clasps from her tunic. What a lot of spikes it takes to hold her together. While the men were at the theatre, she spent the evening with Olympias and her women, weaving. She says the queen kept a basket by her foot, and when she saw Pythias looking at it, waved her over to see. Inside was a black snake no bigger than a bracelet. When the meal came Olympias fed it from her own plate, meat sliced fine, like you would give to a baby. The women spoke enthusiastically of the meal, and of different ways of preparing beans and meat. They demonstrated their favourite cuts by slapping themselves on the rump and legs, laughing, until my poor Pythias had to push her own plate away. The only pleasant moment of the evening, as she tells it, came early, when the boy Alexander stopped by to kiss his mother. That must have been before the performance. Introduced to Pythias, he greeted her warmly, with great courtesy and charm, and smelled, she said, most cleanly and pleasantly of spice. I haven't been able to tell her about the head. Maybe she'll never have to know.

"We'll do what we'll do," she says again.

"You can't have no opinion. It can't be nothing to you. If we stay, it might be for years."

"You've got a choice?"

I say nothing.

"They're rude," she says. "All of them. Their bodies stink. The women do slaves' work. Their wine is bad. The queen"—she glances back over her shoulder at me—"is insane."

"They will rule the world."

"I don't doubt it." She gets in beside me and lies on her back.

I rest on an elbow to look at her. "I wanted to take you to Athens," I say. "You'd have been at home there."

"I was at home in Mytilene."

Because her tone is petulant I don't answer, but touch her hip. She spreads her legs. Dry, again. She flinches when I touch her. She says something more about my decision, asks some question.

I put my tongue just there, on the pomegranate seed, and the tendons in her groin go taut as bowstrings. Pity and fear, purgation, relief. My tongue, working. A substance like the white of an egg.

THAT NIGHT, I DREAM of Stageira. When I wake, I sit for a long time by the window, wrapped in a blanket, remembering. I was a miserable child, lonely, and frightened when my father was called away at night or travelling, which was often. He was the only doctor for many of the little coastal villages, and as his reputation grew he was called ever farther away, to ever bigger towns. The twins were still allowed to sleep with our mother, but I had no one. I suffered night terrors until my mother taught me the trick of concentrating on whatever was closest to me—the length and texture of the hairs on the fur I slept on, or counting the threads of the pulse in my wrist, or feeling the tide of the breath in my body—and so distracting myself. She said this trick had helped her with the same problem. Soon I was practising it everywhere I went, observing and analyzing and categorizing compulsively, until no one wanted to talk to me because of the questions I asked and the information I spilled. Have you ever noticed? I would ask boys my own age. Can you tell me? I would ask adults. Soon I was spending all my time alone, swimming with my eyes open, trapping insects, reading my father's books, cutting myself to observe the blood, drawing maps, tracing leaves, charting stars, and all of it helped a little, and none of it helped a lot. On the worst days I stayed in bed, unable to speak or eat, until the blackness lifted.

"He's a strange boy," I overheard my father tell my mother, on one of his increasingly rare visits home. "He worries me. Not his health, but his mind. I don't know if he has too much discipline or none at all. He goes places I can't follow, inside himself."

"He misses you," my mother said.

I WATCH ALEXANDER MORE closely now. On the eve of Philip's departure for Thessaly, one early summer dawn, we ride out to hunt. I arrive in second-best clothes, unarmed, on slow, reliable Tar. Philip and his entourage of pages and purple-cloaked Companions are in full battledress. The ground beneath their mounts roils with dogs. After some insults—it's suggested I be made to wear a halter around my waist, like a boy who hasn't had his first kill—I'm handed a spare pike and shield and left to keep up as best I can. We ride to the royal park, where the day's festivities begin with the sacrifice of a screaming, spurting piglet. It's a day of pomp and etiquette that I see as a succession of frozen images, like a series of coins struck and over-struck, glinting in the sun. Philip in profile, helmeted. A dog rearing up on hind legs as its owner unclips its lead. A spear balanced on a shoulder. A boar crashing through a clearing. Alexander, unstraddling his horse, knife unsheathed. The boar shaking off a spear sunk too shallow in its side, kicking in the skull of a dog, crashing off again. The dog, one leg spastic. The dog, dead. A wineskin passed from hand to hand. Alexander looking for his mount.

Philip begins to tease him, offering him a skittish horse, daring him to ride it. Ox-Head, the animal is called, for the white mark on its forehead. The boy turns it toward the sun, blinding it, and mounts it easily. Philip, drunk, makes a sarcastic remark.

From the warhorse's back, the boy looks down at his father as though he's coated in filth. That's the coin I'll carry longest in my pocket, the image I'll worry over and over with my thumb.

I could help him, just like his brother. I could fill my plate. I could stay.

TWO

🔁

WHEN I WAS FOURTEEN, my father came home to announce we were moving to the capital because he had been named personal physician to the king. Abruptly his travels stopped, and for a final few weeks he stayed in Stageira, treating only local cases, preparing for the move. As my mother and sister and the servants busied themselves packing up the carts, I indulged in precocious fits of nostalgia, wandering from cliff to shore, swimming, and wondering when we would return. I was afraid of Pella, of the lack of solitude, of a landscape I wasn't intimate with, of being under my parents' eyes much more than I ever had been in our village. I was afraid of my father. Though as a small boy I had missed him terribly, now I found him strict, remote, and often disappointed in me. His encouragement came in mean doses, and often at random; why was it fine to want to watch the birth of a litter of puppies but idle and wasteful to work out the mathematical relationship between the length of a lyre string and the tone it produced?

He liked me best when I accompanied him in his work and helped him at bedsides, when I spoke little and remembered from one visit to the next which powder was used to treat which illness, and when I correctly recited the aphorisms he made me memorize: use a fluid diet to treat a fever; avoid starchy foods in summer; it is better that a fever follow a convulsion than a convulsion follow a fever; purge at the start of an illness but never at its height; teething can cause fevers and diarrhea; drugs may be administered to pregnant women most safely in the fourth to seventh months of gestation, after which the dosages should be reduced; sandy urine indicates a stone forming in the bladder; eunuchs do not suffer gout; women are never ambidextrous; and on, and on, and on.

My father was a man of causes and effects, impatient with amateurs who tried to pray or magic sicknesses away. He would accept a stone bound to a wrist to ease a fever, say, only if the stone had proven itself on two or three other patients in the past. He believed in the medicinal properties of opposites: cold to cure heat, sweetness to cure bile, and so on. He used herbs, and sacrifices were of course conventional, though he opposed ostentation of any sort and once refused to treat a feverish man whose family had ruined itself to buy and slaughter an ox on his behalf. The hysterical waste of it revolted my father, and (probably more to the point) made him doubt they would follow any less glamorous, more pragmatic instructions of his. The man died. My father disliked, too, the procedure known as incubation, where a patient would be made to spend a night alone in a temple in the expectation that the god would send him a dream of how he was to be cured. My father said this was blasphemous. He taught me to keep case studies, charting the progress of an illness day by day in the modern manner, though he seemed to prefer problems that needed only a single visit. "In and out," he would say with satisfaction after some spectacular single treatment; I once saw him pop a separated shoulder back into place in the time it took to greet the man. He had a gift for childbirth, though he particularly despised women healers, and tolerated midwives only grudgingly. They practised witchery for the most part, he told me, and were irrational, untrustworthy, and liable to do more damage to a woman than if she were left alone and allowed to follow her own crude animal instincts. He spoke of women in these terms generally—witches, animals. Still, he was at his softest with a labouring woman, speaking gently, cajoling but not babying, and greeting each dripping purple arrival with quiet joy, lifting it to the light in a private ritual only I recognized as such, having seen it again and again.

The first surgery I ever witnessed he performed on a local village girl who had been labouring for two days. She was only half-conscious by the time we got to her, though we lived only a few minutes' walk away, and the family had already begun to prepare the house for her death: neighbour women had gathered by the front door, hoping to be hired for the mourning, and we stepped past a tray of anointing oils and white cloths outside the sickroom door, as well as a coin for the ferryman to be put in her mouth once she was dead. My father examined her quickly, palpated her belly, and said the baby had started to come feet first and was stuck. Quickly he stripped the bed and the girl and called for clean sheets. I stared at the great mound of her belly, trying to picture the arrangement inside. I was ten, and had never seen a woman naked before. "Can you see it?" my father said, unexpectedly.

I thought he had forgotten me. I knew he meant could I imagine the position of the baby through the flesh, and I said I wasn't sure. The wet sheets were replaced with new.

"This is so I can see the progress of the fluids, the colour and quantity and so on," my father said, just to me, calmly, as though all this—the dying girl, the weeping family, the husband already wordless, motionless in a corner chair, grief-stricken—was for my private instruction. "Did you bring my knives?"

A rhetorical question. It was my job to prepare his kit every morning before we set out and to clean it every evening when we got home, and though we generally had some idea of the patients we would be visiting in the course of a given day—say, a child-birth, a fracture, a couple of fevers in the same house, a baby with spots, an old one bringing up blood—my father told me never to bring only what I thought we would need, because inevitably we would be surprised by something and find our-selves lacking. The resulting kit of everything strapped to my back was too heavy for me to walk upright, but I knew better than to complain. Wraps and bandages, woollen pads, splints, sponges, plaster, bowls and ampoules for collecting fluids and other excretions, metal wands for cautery, a tablet and stylus for note-taking, a selection of herbs and medications for the most common remedies (he kept a larger apothecary at home), tongue depressors, tourniquets, scissors, razors, bronze pipes for blood-letting, and a small amphora of marsh-water and leeches. Also a purse of assorted coins to make change when we were paid.

I unrolled the pack now and produced the leather sleeve of knives I whetted regularly and had yet to see him use. "Third from the left," he told me over his shoulder. He had called for four men and was showing them how to hold the girl down, one at each limb. I unsheathed a knife not much smaller than a table knife, though not the very smallest blade, and gave it to him. ("Eyes and ears," he had told me of the first two when I asked him once.)

The girl woke with the cut, a stroke the length of my hand
from navel to pubic hair. It looked like a scratch at first, and then
it started to bleed. My father probed it with his finger, and
then ran the knife a second time along the same line, deepening the
cut. The girl was screaming now, get it out, get it out.

"Quickly," my father said, glancing up at me. "If you want
to see."

I did want to see. Through the blood and the yellow fat I saw
the head, and then my father reached in and lifted out the baby.
It wasn't moving. The umbilical cord was thick and ropy, an
unfleshy grey. My father was holding the baby with one hand
and pointing back inside the girl with the other, naming parts I
couldn't properly make out for the gore. A midwife appeared at
his elbow with a clean cloth; he gave her the baby so he could
cut the cord. Fortunately he had encountered her before—a
competent, unemotional woman near his own age. It was she
who had persuaded the family to send for him when her own
skills had proved insufficient. She didn't wait for his instruction
now, but swiped the baby's mouth out with her little finger and
then put her face over its nose to suck out the blood and mucus.
Her own lips now red with blood, like a predator at feed, she
slapped its purple bum smartly and it began to choke, then
scream.

"Good." My father, surprised, glanced up from the cord,
which he had tied off to stop the bleeding. "There's a little
sewing kit, like your mother uses," he told me, but I already had
it out. He closed the lips of the girl's belly with small, tight
stitches, a painstaking process made worse by her screaming and
writhing. In the corner, the husband was vomiting a thin yellow
gruel onto the floor. My father had me hold a wadded cloth to

the incision to sop up the blood that continued to seep through, and held his hands out for the baby. This had all taken a matter of minutes.

"Boy," the midwife said, and handed it over.

"A lovely boy." My father held the swaddled bundle up to the light, and then down to the mother's head, so she could see. Her glance slid to it and stayed there. My father nodded at one of the slaves, who released her arm so she could reach for it and touch its hair. When we left, she was still bleeding.

"The baby will live," my father said as we walked home. We were both bloody, my father especially, and I carried the bloodied tools in a separate bag to keep the rest of the kit clean. "The mother will die, tonight or tomorrow. Usually like that you lose them both. That was a good day's work."

"What if you sealed the incision with wax to stop the bleeding?" I asked.

My father shook his head. "You have a good head for this. I was proud of you today. Wax would get into the wound and clot the veins, kill her from the inside. Did you see the afterbirth?"

I had: a slab the size and texture of a beef's liver, with a membrane dangling from one side. My father had pulled it out before he closed the incision and had given it to another woman, who took it away, wrapped in a cloth.

"You must never forget to remove the afterbirth," he said. "Through the belly, as we did today, or through the vagina if it is a normal birth. It will rot if you leave it inside and kill her that way. Sometimes you can cut a slit to make the vagina bigger, but that works best when the baby's head is already coming. That wouldn't have helped us today." We were home. "This way." My father led me around back. "We'll clean up before your mother sees us. That's good manners."

That evening, my father saw me attempting to draw the inside of the girl's belly. "The blood made it hard to see," I said.

My father looked at the drawing but offered no correction. "You learn to do it by feel. The position of the baby, the depth of the incision, the bits of the afterbirth if it's torn apart. Your fingers become like your eyes."

"Have you ever cut in the wrong place?"

"Certainly," my father said.

"But we are all the same inside." I tried to approach what I wanted to say without sounding unfeeling, or blasphemous. "I mean, men are the same as men and women are the same as women. The organs are in the same places, aren't they?"

"Yes, more or less. I think so. The size can vary. You know a field slave has bigger muscles than a lady like your mother. Similarly, the organs can vary in size depending on use. The stomach of a fat man and the stomach of a starving man will not look the same."

"Still, the location will be roughly the same."

My father looked uncertain.

"You don't know?"

Now he looked displeased, but I was too close to my thought to keep it in my mouth.

"If you could cut open a person's body," I said, "a dead person, to see inside, you could make a drawing of all the parts, and then know. You could refer to it when you had to perform a surgery on a live patient, and reduce the risk of mistake."

"No." My father was looking at me the way he did sometimes, as though black birds had flown out of my mouth. "We don't treat the dead that way."

I knew we didn't treat the dead that way. I thought of the girl whose baby my father had delivered that day, who would die, or was dead, and the map of her all sealed up in her skin. We had killed her by breaking that seal.

"She would have died either way," my father said, responding to something I was not aware of showing, and then he called for my mother, whose face puckered into concern when she saw me.

The next day I was excused from accompanying my father on his rounds, and spent the day swimming while my mother and her woman watched me oh-so-casually from the picnic site they had set up on my favourite beach.

"It's not fair," my sister Arimneste said. She was eight to my ten, and had recently been forbidden to swim; she had reached the age when she must keep her clothes on. She walked barefoot at the edge of the surf, skirts held up sloppily and often trailing in the water, purposely, to show her disappointment. I paddled a few feet farther out. "I want to come watch, too."

"You'd puke."

"I didn't when Ajax and Achilles were born." Her kittens. "I think it's interesting."

Tall for her age, like me, and my eyes. Her twin, Arimnestus, had taken to rampaging around with a gang of village boys, setting fires, torturing livestock, and pretending he and Arimneste hadn't once been inseparable. A tomboy, she disdained the village girls and would have gone with him if she could. My father had come to an understanding with a colleague of his, a promising young physician named Proxenus, but the wedding was still a few years away. I knew she was lonely.

"You're the one who puked, anyway," she said. "You should have seen yourself last night. You were green."

"People don't turn green," I said.

"Green right here." She touched her cheek.

I was more curious than tender, though, and it was not long before I was back to carrying my father's kit for him.

Despite his disapproval, small animals were not safe from me. I had already dissected numerous crustaceans, fish, mice, and once a dog I found lying dead on the beach. I hid my drawings, wrapped in an oilcloth, in a hole under a rock above the high-water line. The dog had been the best: there had been food in the gut still and shit in the bowels. I burnt the carcass when I was done so no one would find it mutilated and know it had been me.

The last surgery my father performed before our move to the capital was on a man who suffered headaches and seizures preceded by intensely heightened vision. At the highest pitch of the sickness he would fall to the floor, kick his legs, flail his hands, clench his teeth, and foam at the mouth. Afterwards he would have no memory of the attack. His family had tried the conventional treatments: ritual purifications, chants invoking the gods, charms thrown into the sea, no baths, no wearing black or goatskins, no highly flavoured foods, and no putting one hand or foot on top of the other.

"Bullshit," my father said. "They want to avoid the only true cure. Not that I blame them, but I ask you." He slapped one hand on top of the other to demonstrate the forbidden position. "Absolute bullshit. There's a woman behind it, you wait and see."

"What is the cure?" I asked.

"Mucus," my father said. "In you and me, it flows naturally down from the brain and is dispersed throughout the body. In men like this, though, the normal passages are blocked and it enters the blood vessels, where it prevents the flow of air to the brain. And it is cold, you see, and the sudden cooling of the blood vessels brings on the attack. If there is too much mucus, the blood will congeal and he will die. Or if it enters one vessel but not another, one part of the body may be permanently damaged. The patient will suffer worse in the winter, when there is cold outside as well as in. The winds, too, must be taken into account. The north wind is the healthiest because it separates out the moisture from the air. The south wind is the worst. It dims the moon and the stars, and darkens wine, and brings damp. No wind today, so that is not a factor."

I knew he was rehearsing what he had read the night before, reminding himself as much as teaching me. The sacred disease, it was called, though my father agreed with the author of the treatise that the gods were no more responsible for this than for a runny nose. Bad healers claimed so only to excuse their own incompetence, or inability to effect a cure. It was, my father acknowledged, one of the most difficult diseases to treat.

"What is the cure?" I asked again.

"The mucus must be released."

At the house we were met by the man's brother. "Will he suffer?"

"He is already suffering," my father said.

In the man's bedroom he laid out his instruments. These were three stone tools I had never seen before, not part of his regular kit.

"I know," he said, reading my thoughts. "But they're too heavy to carry around every day, and you never do this without preparing for it first."

"You will release the demon," the man said from his bed, with relish. He looked like his brother, a big barrel of a man with a shaved head and a genial face that was probably good, in happier times, for amusing children. They shared a sympathetic, humorous look, more pronounced in the sick man, who also slurred his words slightly. Damage from the seizures, I guessed, but my father knew better.

"I hope there will be a release." For all his impatience and sternness, my father was careful never to contradict a patient or do anything to disturb him unduly. "Will you excuse me?"

In the hall, I heard him ask the brother if the patient had been drinking.

"Not at all!" the big man said.

"I smell it on his breath," my father said. "I gave you specific instructions."

"For the pain." I could tell the man was crying.

My father told him to wait downstairs.

Back in the room, he pulled from the large bag that he had carried himself something that looked like a vise.

"Oh dear," the sick man said.

With the help of a slave, my father positioned the sick man's head in the grip and tightened it very slowly. "Shake your head," he kept telling the man, and when he could no longer do so, my father was satisfied.

"It's tight," the man said.

My father placed a leather bit in the man's mouth and told him to keep it there. He took the knife I held out to him and made a quick X on the man's shaven scalp. The man screamed. My father took one of the stone tools, a bore, and placed its tip in the centre of the X, where he had peeled back the flaps of skin.

"No, no, no!" the man screamed.

My father pointed to the floor, and I retrieved the bit and put it back in the man's mouth. He gnawed fiercely at it, snorting through his nose, his eyes rolling in his head.

It took long, longer than I want to remember, even now. My father had time to tell me the name of the tool, a trepan, and to praise the antiquity of the procedure, practised even by the ancients. The blood was profuse, as with all scalp lacerations, and the man shat himself more than once.

"You must tell me if you feel the sickness coming on," my father told him, but the man was past talking at that point.

I knew my father hoped to release the mucus in a dramatic stream, but by the time he withdrew the button of bone it was clear that would not happen. We both peered hopefully into the little black cavity, though my father was unwilling to bring a candle near so we might see better, and risk heating the brain. Heating and cooling in rapid succession were known to bring on the seizures, he explained. He seemed uncertain for a moment, still expecting that sudden gush, but then roused himself and pointed hopefully to the glossy quantity that had flowed from the man's nose during the procedure. He instructed the slave who had sat on the man's legs on the dressing of the wound, retrieved the bit, and patted the man's shoulder affectionately before leaving the room.

Downstairs we found the brother passed out on the kitchen table, a wine cup by his head. A woman stood nearby, her arms crossed over her chest. Her hair was hennaed orange and she wore a fine linen dress and a lot of jewellery. Her eyes were hard.

"We are finished," my father said, unnecessarily.

"Did you see the demon?" I guessed she was the well brother's wife.

"We did not," my father said.

She gave him a small, clinking pouch: his payment.

"Come," he said to me. He had found his woman.

"He won't have died on my watch, anyway," she said, seeing his dislike of her and needing to swat him back.

My father didn't answer her or look back, but put his arm around my shoulders and walked me out of the house. The sick man was still alive when we left the next morning.

WE ARRIVED IN THE CITY on a late-summer afternoon three days later, the air swimming with heat and, we would learn, fever. My mother and Arimneste drew veils across their noses and mouths against the stench. My mother closed her eyes; Arimneste kept hers open. Arimnestus refused to sit with the women and rode with my father and me, annoying us with his constant burping. He was practising.

The streets were empty; no one came out to see us rattling down the cobblestones in our few carts piled high with the stuff of home. I had never seen a settlement bigger than a village, let alone a city, let alone a royal capital, and felt like a country rube with my eyes popping out and my jaw hanging down. There were animals lying in the streets, rats mostly and some mangy dogs. I hopped off the cart to look closer.

"Plague," my father said, looking up from his book. I knew I had expressed an interest of which he approved. He caught my eye and I saw the encouragement there—*look, look, tell me what you see.* I picked up a rat by the tail and the flesh streamed from it, running with maggots. It had gone soft as a bad fruit on the side it lies on. I gave it a shake just to see the body drip from the little cage of rib bones.

"Would you think that could happen to a man?" my father asked.

I smiled despite myself, a smile he extraordinarily returned. We both shook our heads. The wonder of it!

Our house turned out to be smaller than our home in Stageira, and poshly appointed. My father had bought it from the son of a government official who had recently died in the epidemic. I wondered in which room his body had dripped from his bones when they lifted him onto the plank to carry him out. My mother, grim-faced, withdrew with her women to the kitchen and emerged ten minutes later, smiling. Quality pots, she informed us. My father took the largest room for his dispensary and study and allotted the twins and their nurse a pair of sunny rooms overlooking the flower garden, me an alcove off the kitchen. He said I would thank him in winter for letting me sleep so close to the hearth. My mother gave me a look to say we would find a place for my things and probably rig up a curtain for privacy; a lot for one look, but we had spent many years more or less alone together and often understood each other quicker than words. I was too excited about the prospect of exploring the city to be disappointed with the sleeping arrangements. For supper that evening we ate the last of our travelling food, dried this and that. The women would go to the market in the morning.

I announced my intention to spend the day alone, walking. My father corrected me.

"You boys will attend the king with me," he said. "We're expected."

"But," I said.

My father looked at me, full of sadness, took my plate, and sent me to my alcove, where I lay listening to the bustle of unpacking that lasted well into the night. I heard my father's querulous voice submitting to my mother's arrangements, and luxuriated in hating him for a few hours. My mother had that effect on him, rendering him feckless and feeble and needing to be led. His hands seemed to go slack from the wrists in her presence, so that he couldn't even lift a book unless she'd brought it to him first. If she asked him for something, he would go stupid. Is this soap? he would say, bringing a vial of oil, and couldn't suppress an animal grunt of pleasure when she brought the correct object herself. The twins and I agreed this behaviour was supremely irritating and ourselves relied on our mother for as little as possible, seizing our independence early. Poor woman. She was harmless, though fiercely organized, clean and tidy, and loved her little queendom. She wanted us all to be helpless without her, which only our father offered. We children preferred to be cruel.

The next morning I woke early. I lay in my alcove for a while listening to the street-vendors who'd seen our newly arrived carts and paused just outside our gate—*fresh bread, goat's milk, best milk*—then got up. My mother's bronze, not yet hung in her room, leaned against a wall amidst the jumble of furniture and unpacked crates. Unused to seeing myself, I stopped to strike a few poses: one foot forward, hand on hip, chin high, higher. Was this a sophisticated city boy? Maybe this?

My father's shove propelled me into an iron sconce. I hadn't heard him come up behind me.

At breakfast my mother took one look at me and gasped.

The bleeding had stopped, but the eye was puffy and already bluing.

"It's nothing," I said. "I tripped."

"Come, boys." My father pushed his breakfast plate away.

He hadn't eaten; neither had I. From the way he had stared at his food without touching it, I knew he hadn't meant to hurt me.

"Kiss your mother."

"And me," Arimneste said. When I leaned close to her she whispered, "Take me out later. Mother will let me go, with you."

I didn't answer.

Arimnestus immediately ran ahead of us, happy and excited, sniffing at everything like a little hunting dog.

"Nervous," my father said to me, just the one word during our walk up to the palace. A statement, a question, an apology.

I took his arm to steady myself as I searched for a non-existent stone in my sandal. He looked at my foot, then discreetly away as I fingered out the little fiction.

The king, Amyntas, smiled when he saw my father. It was like seeing a piece of granite smile. I saw that this particular movement of the face hurt him, saw the flare of pain in his eyes. I saw that almost every movement he made hurt him. He had been wounded all over his body at various times, and was suffering constantly now. My father knelt and began to unpack his kit.

"And these are your sons," Amyntas said.

"My sons," my father confirmed.

"Trained, yes?" Amyntas said. "They'll fight?"

My father sent us then to play with the pages.

Arimnestus ran off immediately with a few boys his own age as though he had known them all his life. That was his gift.

"Where'd you get that?" the older ones wanted to know, of my black eye.

"Fight," I said.

Raised eyebrows, half-smiles.

"Leave him alone," a voice called. "My father likes his father."

Philip was less than a year younger than me, short, strong, with a high colour and clear, open eyes. The pages separated to let him through. He reached up and flicked me companionably across the eyebrow with his finger. "Hurt?"

It occurs to me now that I had the one eye then and he the two; a joke across the years. I want to have flicked him back or hit him or said something withering, but I just stood there, eye watering like a mouth until I couldn't see from it but could feel tears running down the one cheek. He laughed happily and invited me to the gymnasium with his companions.

"My father told me to wait here," I said.

What a lot I am claiming for the eyes—my mother's eyes, my father's, and now his—but I swear he looked at me as much as to say that he too had such a father, and understood, and would help me. He flicked me again, roughly in the same place, with his knuckles this time, enough to open the wound there and start it bleeding again.

"Come on," he said when I hesitated. "Come on. Have to clean that up."

The other pages were already ahead of us. I was seeing through a red scrim.

"It's just over there," he said.

I had never been in a gymnasium. The attendant wanted to bandage my eye, but my father believed in clean water and open air. He said covering allowed a wound to fester. The attendant dabbed hard until the bleeding stopped, and told me to avoid anything vigorous or risk opening it again. The other boys were already hard at it, my brother too, wrestling and tumbling on the mats, their voices echoing off the high stone ceiling. The few old men who had been there when we arrived sighed and left for the baths. Philip looked around his world in approval.

"You've never been in a fight in your life," he said. "You don't have another scratch anywhere, and when I hit you, you didn't flinch. You didn't even see it coming. And you didn't try to hit me back."

"Can you swim? I need a place where I can swim. Every day."

He asked if I was fast and I said no. "No kidding." He laughed. "Maybe one day you'll be my physician."

"No. Do you swim or not?"

"It's like you're retarded. I can swim. Do you fuck girls or boys?"

"Both," I said.

"That your father?"

He was in the doorway, waiting.

"Tell him I hit you for no reason," Philip said. "I want to see what he does."

I could tell my father was staring at my brow as I walked over to him, and only at the last second looked at my eyes. "All right?"

"I hit him for no reason," Philip said. He had come right along behind me.

My father took him by the elbow and raised his arm once or twice like a wing. "Show me."

Philip pulled the clothes from his shoulder and let my father dig his fingers under the collarbone. I looked over my father's shoulder to see the scar.

"Excellent," my father said. He cuffed Philip lightly on the head and turned away. I followed him.

"I'm going swimming tomorrow," Philip called after us. "Can he come?"

My father raised an open hand without looking back, *yes*.

The scar had been a smallish white clot, indicating a penetration rather than a tear. My father told me, when I asked him, that it was from a training session, a spear wound, and Philip was lucky it hadn't been a finger or two off in any direction—joint, throat, heart.

OURS WAS AN ODD friendship, with respect and contempt barely distinguishable. I was smart and he was hard: that was what the world saw, and what we saw and liked and disliked in each other. I was not his first friend by any stretch, but he was interested enough in me that I became known around the palace, and I did eventually have a few more encounters with his father. Soldiering had hammered Amyntas down, scarred him ugly, wrecked his knees, hollowed his eyes. He said (as everyone did) that he saw my father in me, which I took to mean tall, serious, quiet, forbidding, sad. Philip claimed I never shut up. I taught him to swim with his face in and his eyes open, and he taught me to use my height against him when we wrestled. He was never devious in combat.

My father, strangely, liked him. Strangely, because Philip was no kind of scholar, loved violence, and had a crude sense of humour and a precocious sexuality he didn't bother to hide.

"Watch him," my father said more than once. "You have a unique opportunity to observe at close quarters the moulding of a king." He could be pompous like that. He approved of our friendship and encouraged me to spend time with him. I didn't mind, mostly. My father was busy in the city, his cachet as the king's man securing him work amongst the courtiers and administrators too, and I was usually left to myself. Arimnestus took his schooling with the pages. Arimneste spent most of her time tending her flowers, or whispering with two or three other well-born girls my mother had found for her to weave with, preparing their dowries. They had their dolly picnics in the courtyard and shrieked with laughter when I walked by, Arimneste's glance lingering on me a little longer than the others. I never did take her out.

I spent a lot of time wandering alone, and sometimes I thought of writing, though I wasn't sure what I would write, where to start. When I confessed to my mother that I had thought of writing a great tragedy, she stroked my hair and told me I must. She must have spoken privately with my father, because not long after that I was summoned to his room for a talk. Or, rather, a listen.

"I have found you a tutor," my father said.

That sounded possibly pleasant; someone to talk to about the things I was interested in. Though it gave me a sick feeling, too. Someone chosen by my father would probably be someone very like my father, and I didn't want anyone else controlling my time. I didn't want to be guided.

"You're not cut out to be a soldier," he continued. "We have to think what to make of you."

At this I was a little offended. I was tall and rode well and

Philip's wrestling lessons had improved my coordination. I could hold my breath under water a long time, and my eyesight and hearing (then, anyway) were pure and sharp. I was not sure how holding my breath was relevant to soldiering, but it was an athletic feat that I thought deserved some respect. And then, if I wasn't meant for soldiering, wasn't I supposed to become a physician, like my father? What failing, I wanted to know, had suddenly disqualified me from that?

"No failing." A trick of the light, maybe, but my father's face softened a little into that sadness that sometimes kept him too long in bed, the way it did me. "You are well on your way to becoming what I am. Only I thought it bored you."

And I was ashamed, because it did.

"His name is Illaeus," my father said. "He had a play in the festival in Athens, once. Your mother tells me you have an interest that way."

And that of course made it official: I would become a tragedian and have plays in the festivals in Athens. The only way to overcome the shame of his knowing this ambition of mine (half-formed at best) was to embrace it wholly.

"He expects you tomorrow afternoon, and says not to be early. Apparently he does his own work in the morning."

I saw approval withheld, but disapproval too. It dawned on me that my father didn't know what to make of this Illaeus, and wasn't at all sure of himself in sending me to him. What other avenues had he exhausted without my even knowing of them, I wondered, that he would take such a risk?

Fall was then hardening into winter, and the next day came up soft and grey, a low sky with a whisper of snow. I liked it; it was a change from rain. If the man did his own work in the morning, then I decided I must too, and sat in a corner of the kitchen with a tablet and stylus. I wrote nothing. After lunch I put on my warmest clothes and went out to find the house my father had directed me to. It was in a poor part of the city, a long walk down the hill from ours. I passed a man in rags shitting in the street who laughed at me when I looked at him and then when I looked away. Steam rose from the little pile. The houses here were small and mean, and I knew the families inside slept in single rooms with their children and their animals too. My mind went inside their doorways, to the rich noises and smells of that shared sleep. There had been farmers in Stageira who lived that way in the wintertime. I had never shared a room with anyone.

I asked a child for the house of the scholar, Illaeus, and she pointed to a stone hut like the others.

"He'll eat you," she said.

I had seen her appraising my woollen clothes and knew I should toss her a coin, but I had come out with nothing but the pouch my father had given me for the scholar.

"Cunt," she said when I turned away from her. She might have been five.

I rapped my knuckles on the wooden door jamb, pushed aside the heavy curtain, and stepped in. It was dark but for a single oil lamp on a table in the far corner (and that not so far, really, only a few paces away). A man sat there. I could see the outline of him but no details, nor of the room. My eyes had not yet adjusted to the dark.

"Here is star bright," the man said.

I asked where I would find the scholar Illaeus.

"Now, isn't that interesting. You know you've found him but you ask anyway. Is that a good way to start relations?"

I realized my father had never met this man, or I would not

be here. I wondered who had been the go-between. Was that person playing a joke on my father, on me? I saw now the table in front of him was empty. He was drinking unwatered wine from a cup he coddled in his groin and never put down. The room was warm enough. The walls were heavily swathed in cloth to keep the heat in, and the bed and chairs were lapped with more cloth and bolsters. Dim warmth and softness on every surface: a drinker's cocoon. A corner hearth, which I had taken for dead, glowed faintly, a spidery heat outlining the embers in white.

"Will you stay, star bright?" he asked. "Or have I emptied my piss-pot for nothing?"

I could see now that he was not as old as my father, though his face was sternly lined, especially around the mouth, like a shirring, and his hair was a bristle-brush of white. It was the skin of his cheeks that gave him away; my father had taught me to look for that; smooth, pink. In a woman of his age it would be a last remaining vanity. His voice was deep, not loud. I sat on a chair.

"Does he talk?" he asked his cup, and drank again.

"My father might have misled you. I'm not writing a play."

"That's a relief."

"What is your work?"

"Chatty," he remarked to his wine cup. "He's chatty now. He likes the idea of work, I think."

I nodded.

"Wants his own work. A problem to solve?"

"Maybe. Not exactly. I'm not sure."

"Why did you think you were writing a play?"

I told him I had trouble sleeping because my mind was so

full, and I had thought it might relieve me to write something down, get it out of my head.

"But there are other things to write," he said. "Not just plays."

I told him I thought maybe it would be better for me to write one of those other things.

"Excellent. And did you bring something to write on?"

I pulled my tablet from under my clothes.

"Describe this room, everything in it. Me, if you're ready for that. Don't leave anything out."

"Why?"

"No one will read it but you. You're still nervous. I want you to calm down. We'll start properly next time. We'll get some of the busyness out of your head so that next time you're here you can concentrate. Some of what keeps you awake, yes? Maybe you're thirsty?" He half-offered me the wine cup.

"No."

"Fine young man." He nestled the cup back in his groin. "We begin."

I wrote for a long time, until, even in the windowless hut, I could tell it was getting dark. My stomach growled.

"Tomorrow you might even take off your cloak." He had lit one or two more lamps and woken the fire, and there was a simmering pot now, beans from the smell, hanging from a peg above the flames. I had been oblivious to everything.

On my way out, he handed me a coin from the pouch I had given him. "If there's a boy in the street out there, give him this and tell him Illaeus is hungry. A young one, mind you. Not if the voice has broken, like yours."

In the darkening street I found a boy my brother's age playing a game on the ground with pebbles, tossing them into piles and allotting himself more pebbles as prizes when he scored. "Do you know Illaeus, who lives in that house?" I asked, pointing.

He held out his hand. I gave him the coin and walked away, back up the long hill, without looking back.

I went to him for three years. I learned more about him—that he had lived in Athens, studied with a great man there named Plato, had been a star bright himself, briefly—and I learned nothing more than I had learned that first day: that he was a drunk with a tooth for young boys, who didn't like me or my father but badly needed our money for wine and sex. He needed these so much. Some days he was too drunk to teach, and I stayed in the shadows and let him ramble on about his glorious youth and every petty remembered grudge and grievance, tits he had nursed at for years, that had led him to this time and place, where he would die. Other times he spoke of Plato, still in Athens, still nurturing young men such as he had once been, young prodigies. "Maybe one day you'll go to him, star bright," he said, and the idea seemed to take root in him as he spoke it, for he mentioned it again once or twice when he was more sober, said he would write to recommend me, said the man would remember him and would take him seriously. "I can't do this for-ever," he would say, which I believed—he had some sickness in the chest and by the end kept two cups on the table, one for his wine and one for the wine-coloured clots he spat up. He was never so drunk, though, that I could slip away without him giv-ing me a coin and having me procure a child for him. Once he even asked for a girl. "Variety," he said, laughing at the surprise on my face. "You must taste all the fruits of the world. Curiosity is the first sign of an intelligent mind."

I found a prostitute my own age, fifteen or so by then, whose face opened up when I approached her and closed again when I explained the situation. She said the coin wasn't enough. I turned to walk away.

"Not enough for that old bag of blood, I mean," she said. "It's enough for you."

My sister had married Proxenus a few months before and gone to live with him in Atarneus, where she was now, at thirteen, expecting her first child. Arimnestus's training with the pages had given him biceps and soldier's slang and a flop of hair over the eyes and a lazy grin. People liked him. People, girls.

"Where?" I asked.

She led me into another hut a few doors down. An old woman poking at the hearth with a stick got up and left when we came in. The girl sat me on the bed and sucked on me until I went weak and the room tipped over into sweetness. My father had told me that touching myself would turn my fingers black and my mother would know what I had been doing, and I had believed him. For long moments I thought this girl was murdering me in a way I had never heard of. I thought I was dying, had died. When I finally sat up, the girl smiled, grudgingly, with one side of her mouth.

The next day, Illaeus said nothing about the missing girl or the missing coin.

I haven't said what he taught. At first history, geometry, a bit of astronomy. He had books that he kept hidden, in a hole in the floor or behind the cloths on the walls or in some other place altogether, I couldn't tell. I would arrive and he would have one or two sitting on the table in front of him. He would assign me to read and then summarize what I had read. Exercises of memory, I said once, dismissively (I was good at them), and he corrected me: exercises of attention. Once he asked me if I agreed with a particular passage from Herodotus, about the battle of Marathon. I told him I didn't think it made sense to agree or disagree; it was history, facts.

"Of course." It was a year before he asked me the same question again, about the same passage.

"An exercise of attention," I said.

"Don't be such a braggart smartass. I get so sick of you I want to puke."

"No, you don't." I knew he had come, if not to like me, at least to tolerate me. He got angry when I was late and smiled when I was quick with an answer.

"No, I don't," he agreed. "I get tired is what it is. I didn't think my life would end this way. I don't mean you, you're a good boy."

I could see the lesson was ending, and hesitated, my hand grazing the Herodotus.

"Yes, yes, you can borrow it. I loved books, too, when I was your age. You know not to eat when you're reading?"

I did; my mother had taught me that during one of my father's long absences, when she reluctantly allowed me into his library for the first time. No eating, no creasing, no taking books outside; clean hands, not too close to the lamp, and everything back exactly where I found it.

It was my father who noticed the inscription.

"Look at that," he said. "Plato. You have to be one of ten or twenty in the world to be allowed to study with him. This Illaeus, does he speak much of his time there?"

"A little," I said. "Not really. He seems—bitter."

My father frowned. This wasn't what he wanted to hear. "Perhaps you should ask him. Draw him out in conversation. Ask him about his own work. Flatter him a little. You can be quite unfriendly at times, and perhaps he senses that."

"I am not!"

"Bitter." It was as though the word had only just caught up to him. "I wonder why he left the school. Those who study there often stay on to teach, I'm told. Would something like that appeal to you?"

"Teaching?" I was appalled.

"I didn't think so." He handed me back the book. "Take care of this. I don't want him coming after me for a replacement because you dropped it in a puddle."

"I can take care of books!"

"Don't raise your voice to me," my father said. "Bitterness is caused by an excess of gall. Perhaps he needs to drink more milk to counteract the effect of that humour. I think I will prescribe the same for you, so you don't end up with a similar personality. I see the beginnings of it in you, already."

I drank goat's milk every day from then on, brought to me by a slave on a small tray every afternoon, usually while I was studying. It became one of the household rituals. I was to take it out into the courtyard, drain the cup, eat the accompanying walnuts (little brains for my big-little brain), and give the tray back to the slave, who would take the empty cup straight to my father, to prove I was following orders. Our household was sewn up in such solemnities, the absurdity of many of which was gradually coming clear to me.

Fortunately I could visit the palace when the smallness of my parents' world threatened to overwhelm me. No one made Philip

drink goat's milk to forestall bitterness, and a black cloud of disappointment did not hang over his rooms if he put a book back
on the wrong shelf.

"You're just in time," he said, the next time I went to see him.

I was allowed to use the palace gymnasium because of my
father's standing at court, and often went there as a pretext when
I was hoping for company. He had found me doing squats with a
weighted ball, without much enthusiasm, but he had a soldier's
respect for athleticism of any sort and waited for me to finish my
set before he spoke.

"My new armour's ready. Come see when you're done."

"I'm done."

He took me to the armoury, where his new gear was laid out
on a table: helmet, breastplate, sword, shield, spear, greaves, sandals. There were starbursts worked into the breastplate and
shield. A gift from his father, he said. He had outgrown his
practice gear anyway. I watched him lace and strap himself up,
everything fitting just so. I wanted to make a joke about it, how
he must have had to stand still for hours while they measured
him, like a woman being fitted for a dress, but I knew he
wouldn't laugh.

"It's magnificent," I said, and meant it. He looked the warrior,
with the helmet pulled down and the nose piece riding perfectly,
everything glinting, the new leather creaking. His eyes were dead
level, and I wondered what enemy might next stand this close to
him in his finery, and the last thing he would see would be those
eyes: calm, measuring, not without a kind of patient humour. He
was looking at me like that right now.

"You don't like to fight, do you?" he said. "You wouldn't want
all this. You really wouldn't."

"I wouldn't know where to begin with it. It would be like play-acting for me." I was on the verge of offending him, I knew. "Can you see me wielding a sword? The only person I'd be a danger to would be myself."

"That's true enough." He gently removed the helmet—gentle with the helmet, I mean, rather than his own head—and laid it back on the table. "The future's coming fast, do you know that?"

Such an extraordinary thing to say that I immediately suspected he had recently had it said to him, and was merely repeating the wisdom to me. His father? I knew there were ongoing skirmishes with the petty mountain kings in Illyria, who were trying to encroach south into Macedon. Philip was probably headed off to one of these in his bright new gear, to bloody it up a little and prove he was worth it. A life in meat, and never a doubt about it.

"And you?" he was saying. "What's coming for you?"

I didn't answer. I was a child next to him, or an old man, so crippled by thinking that I couldn't even make a sentence.

"You could still have a place in the army."

That was the curious kindness in him, the way he saw my distress and held the punch anyone else our age would have landed without thinking.

"You could be a medic," he continued. "Your father's trained you, hasn't he? Don't you still do rounds with him?"

"Sometimes. I think he wants me to be a teacher, though."

"Of what?" He dug a finger in his ear and rooted, looking either skeptical or pained by his own nail. He may not have been thinking of me at all, or listening to my answer. Sex and books, that was what I wanted from the future. An Illaeus in my heart after all, maybe.

"Everything," I said. "Swimming."

He laughed. "When are we going again?"

"Now."

He disarmed and we went down to the beach, a long walk, without speaking. I knew he was more comfortable surrounded by larger groups in higher spirits. We didn't often find a lot to talk about when we were alone, though he never avoided such situations, trying, I think, to be kind to me. I in turn tried not to talk too much, or to assume any intimacy, and test his patience that way. It was snowing again, very lightly, a high mindless drifting that would turn heavy that night and freeze everything but the ocean by morning. Everything was soft and grey and sounds were muffled and distended. Our breaths were smoky in the cold. The sun was a white disc, faraway, cool. At the usual rock I began to undress.

"Fuck, no," Philip said, but when I didn't stop, he undressed too.

The water was warm for a moment and then searingly cold, burning rings around my ankles, my calves, my knees, my thighs, every time I stopped to think about what I was doing. I hadn't been swimming in weeks. Just before the plunge I looked back to see Philip, naked, in to his knees, hands on his hips, surveying the horizon. We didn't stay in long. Afterwards we dried ourselves on our cloaks and walked back up to the city carrying them sopping over our arms, shivering.

The next time I saw him was in the spring, at games. Philip had recently returned from a brutal winter campaign in Illyria; I had recently finished writing my first book, a treatise on local varieties of crustacea. I had described and categorized as many types as I could find, attempting to group them into families, and written of their habits from long solitary hours spent on the winter beaches staring into rock pools, and included illustrations I had drawn myself. Those had been the hardest, but Illaeus had shown me the trick of using gridded paper to get the proportions right. He had also recommended a scribe to make a fair copy, someone whose handwriting and materials would be better than mine—a tiny, grinning, snaggle-toothed man in another dank hut—and they were. I presented the finished article to my father as a gift.

"That is lovely," he had said. "Lovely paper. Egyptian, is it?"

I was not discouraged. Illaeus had made me revise again and again until every sentence was concise and clear and necessary. He had asked me if I loved shellfish, found them elegant, and I had said I supposed I did. Then I must write elegantly about them, he had said, and that was our entire discussion about the validity of my project. He did not ask me for a copy of the book, but took a small spiral shell I had brought with me from Stageira, which I had put on the table in front of me while I was working one day.

"I'll keep this," he had said, and that was that.

It was tiny, whorled like an ear, pink like a nipple, with a creamy pouting lip; a perfect prize, and I didn't fight for it. Suddenly I had my book, and that was more.

The games were to honour Amyntas's recent death—from old age, an extraordinary feat in the house of Macedon—and to celebrate the accession of Philip's elder brother, Perdicaas. Philip and I were both sixteen by then, both looking it, in different ways. I had shot up past my father, who was not a small man, and grown a neat, tight fuzz of a beard my mother loved to pat. The swimming season had begun again in earnest a few weeks back and I had begun to put on muscle, though I was still gangly next to Philip. I watched him in the wrestling and the javelin, both of which he won.

Afterwards my father took me to the temple of Heracles to sacrifice for future military success, and then he suggested the baths. He wanted a look at the whole of me, I knew, with his physician's eye, something I'd increasingly been denying him. He wanted to see the tone of my skin, the hang of my joints, the set of my muscles, the size of my penis. He wanted to find something he could fix.

"You might have competed," he said, once we were stripped.

I sat with my back to him, scraping the dirt from my legs with a honed stone while he looked me over.

"Perhaps this summer."

"In what?" I meant the question rhetorically, scornfully. After the first moment I couldn't look at him; he was an old man now, pasty, sparse-haired, with an old man's tits and a frost-haired, drooping business between his legs that I didn't want to get a clear image of.

"Running."

"That's ridiculous. You've never even seen me run."

"You have the body for it. Not for a sprinter, no, but for distance. Perhaps that would be something for us to think about."

I foresaw another of my father's regimens, a training routine to go with my goat's milk and my nuts and my studies with Illaeus. "No."

"Think about it," my father said.

I thought about it; I thought about the fact that my father never used to value games, and that our time in Pella was making him increasingly ashamed of me. Arimnestus was all right; Arimnestus was brave and athletic and gave a shit about horses; Arimnestus would make a solid Companion. But I was not the kind of son men had here, and something in my father had given way, like a rotten floor, so that he could no longer see how very like him I was, and how inappropriate his plans for me were. He could only see that I was not like other Macedonian boys, and that was a problem. I realized for the first time that it might be necessary to leave Pella, to leave my father, if I did not want to end up a uniformed medic—trudging along at the ass-end of Philip's glorious army, diapering his shit—who had once placed fourth in a distance event before he became a bitter letch, a misanthrope, and a drunk.

Still, my world was small, and I could think only of returning to Stageira. I planned vaguely to farm and write and swim and find some girl to marry who would suck on me the way the prostitute had, for some regular relief.

I didn't think about Illaeus's boasting about the great teacher in Athens until my last day with him, which I didn't know would be my last day. He told me he had received a reply to his letter.

"What letter?" I asked.

Instead of answering, he gave it to me and told me to give it to my father. He had resealed the wax over a candle. "All right?" he said.

I saw his hand come up, for my hair or my shoulder, and I left quickly, before he could find a coin. I had asked him recently what his work was, as my father had advised, finally summoned up that courage, and he had said quite simply that he was writing a play, and had been writing the same play for as long as he had been in Pella: over a decade.

"It must be very long," I had said.

"Not really."

I wanted to ask him the name of it, or what it was about, but we glided onto other subjects and I never raised it again. It was a simple enough exchange, but things between us changed after that, as though we had been intimate in some way that left him vulnerable to me. It wasn't a feeling I liked. He did not always tidy his table, now, before my lessons, and sometimes I arrived to see the crabbed sheaves with their angry strike-throughs and scribblings. He would look up at me, shyly, acknowledging that he had allowed me to see, and then tidy them away with tender hands that made me a little sick.

At home, my father read the letter in silence while I watched him. Summer, again, and the dust turned in the dusky, golden air around his head. The plague was bad that year, the worst since we'd arrived, and my father was tired from long days with the dead and dying. He gripped the letter a little too hard. I understood the gist, by then: a place in Plato's Academy, room and board, a place in the shape of myself held for me in the fabled city.

"He shouldn't have written without consulting me," my father said. "It's out of the question."

The next day, he didn't get out of bed. I assumed it was melancholy.

"I want to go," I told my mother. I had found her in the courtyard, clipping herbs. "No one has any use for me here." She didn't answer. I looked closely and saw the fine skin around her eyes all ruined with crying. "What?"

"Daddy told me to collect these." She meant the herbs. "For

him. He has—" Her fingers fluttered under her arm. "Two of
them. Only two. Here, and here."

"What colour?"

"Red, like blisters."

"Seeping?"

She shook her head. "That's good, isn't it? No blood?"

I didn't know how to answer. She read my face and ran into
the house, into my father's room, with her fistful of greenstuff,
and forbade anyone to open the door. That same day I was sent
to the palace to sleep with the pages. Arimnestus, quarantined
with me, was bewildered. I pretended to be too.

Two days later, we were summoned to appear before the king.
Philip, I knew, didn't have much time for his elder brother. Perdicaas had been tutored in his own youth by one of Illaeus's classmates, a man named Euphraeus, who was still influential at court
and arranged what Philip called snot dinners, with pre-set topics
of conversation and minimal drinking. Perdicaas was taller than
Philip, thinner, paler, only adequate in battle, always drumming
his fingers on whatever book he was reading and wanted to get
back to. Eight years later he would die in Illyria in a rout, four
thousand killed, bequeathing Philip a royal mess.

"I'm sorry," the king said.

Arimnestus wept and asked for our mother.

"I'm sorry," Perdicaas the reader-king said again, tap-tap-
tapping on his Homer. I had to squint to make out what it was.

Arimneste arrived from Atarneus with Proxenus and their
baby son. She took charge of the household and of Arimnestus,
managing servants and meals and her twin brother's pain. There
was ash in all the corners from where my sister had burnt herbs
to purify the air of plague. It got on our clothes and in the food,

but that was good. You left the ash to disperse naturally or the cleansing wouldn't take. Arimneste was matronly now, plumper, busy and efficient, and wouldn't look me in the eye. Someone—one of the slaves—must have told her I hadn't wept. I lived in my father's study, now, surrounded by the smell of him—faintly spicy from his apothecary, faintly sour from his old body—and his books. Mine, now. I piled them around me, scrolls unspooling, single leaves falling in drifts to the floor, and read late into every night. There were books I had never seen before, medical books shading into smut, wild histories, and plays, raunchy satires I had never suspected my father had a taste for. Periodically I came up for air, visiting the kitchen for an apple or bread. The servants avoided me. Every time I started to feel something, I dove back into the books and stayed down for as long as I could.

"You don't grieve?" Proxenus asked me.

He was a decent man, a hard worker who treated my sister well and had revered our father. My dry eyes outraged him. I had returned from a walk—I still took walks, numbly, trying to tire myself enough to sleep—to find him in my father's study, in my father's chair. He wanted to tidy the mess I'd made, wanted me to help him. When I didn't respond, he waved a piece of paper I recognized.

"There's a letter here. As your guardian, I can't let you remain in Pella."

Escalating military losses meant Philip and forty-nine Companions would soon leave for Thebes as hostages, an elaborate diplomatic arrangement to ensure Macedonian docility. Philip would spend the next three years in the household of the great Theban general Pammenes, learning the arts of war in a city famous for its infantry, cavalry, and military leadership. He would watch their phalanxes drill on the training ground every day. I was high enough born and a frequent enough companion of the prince that I knew Proxenus feared to see me promoted to hostage number fifty-one. I was not hardened to military life and probably would not have survived my first winter there. If I wanted to live, I would be wise to leave Pella before the Theban escort arrived.

Arimnestus would stay with Proxenus and Arimneste, at least until he was of age. They would leave as soon as possible. I knew the twins didn't need me, and Proxenus didn't want me festering in his house, staring too long at people and taking over his library. It was time I became a problem to no one but myself.

I told him I wanted to go to Athens. "You would always be welcome to come to us in Atarneus," he lied. "Perhaps once your studies are concluded."

"I would like that," I said.

When I told Philip, he called me a piece of shit, and congratulated me, and told me not to leave without coming to the palace one last time. Suddenly everything was happening fast, and I was leaving much sooner than I was ready for. Not even weeks; days. Arimneste and her maids made clothes for me, summer clothes painstakingly embroidered. Then it was the day before the journey. Proxenus and the twins would ride down with me to see me settled and then continue on to their own home. Their preparations took far longer than mine, and on the afternoon of that frantic eve I went up to the palace.

"Got you something." Philip gave me a book of pornographic verse, illustrated. He had found it in the palace library, he said, and doubted his brother would miss it.

I thanked him, wondering where to hide it on the journey.

My trunk was already packed and stowed on the cart. I asked him, in our old manner for the last time, if he was sure he could spare it.

"It's a book, you dumb shit. You think I need it from a book?" He grabbed at his crotch. He repeated the gesture the next morning when we rode out—he and some pages had come down to wave me off—and smiled his disarmingly happy smile. I had finally stuffed the book deep down the throat of a giant amphora of sweet raisins with which my sister had lovingly provisioned me for the winter ahead.

THREE

PYTHIAS SAYS SHE doesn't mind living in the palace, but now that we're staying in Pella I want a house of my own. The flunky knows of a place, a modest single-storey house tucked behind the first row of mansions immediately south of the marketplace. We tour it behind the owner's widow, a sniffling young woman in an indigo mourning veil. She scurries ahead of us from room to room, trying simultaneously to straighten things up and keep out of sight. The flunky assures me she's got family to go to; I don't press him for details. The house has a gaudy entrance hall (the mosaic floor shows Zeus eyeing a nymph); a small courtyard and measly garden, surrounded by a colonnade; and, at the back, living quarters, including a room for my books, a room for the women, bedrooms, and a small shrine whose care I'll leave to Pythias. Callisthenes is old enough to find his own place. When I tell him this, he hesitates, swallows, nods. He'll be fine.

I stack the animal cages against a south-facing wall, though half my specimens—tender as playwrights—have already died from the wet cold. I attend court, and bring Pythias gifts from the marketplace: some fine black and white pottery, a bolt of pale violet cloth. I have bulbs planted in the garden, and furniture delivered to the house.

"We're settling down, then?" Pythias asks. Laughing at me with her gravest face.

At least she's happy about it, or less unhappy. She likes the house, which is bigger than the one we had in Mytilene, and she likes her status here too. Is shocked by it, I think: in Mytilene she was simply herself, but here she is in vogue. The royal wives fight over her for their sewing parties. Her advice on hair and clothes and food and servants is sought out and followed. I've taught her to explain, if anyone asks, that our slaves are like family: we've had them for years, care for them, would never sell them; you don't sell your own family. Very cosmopolitan, very chic, very fresh. The wives are impressed.

"You see," I tell her, "we will be a force for the good, you and I. A civilizing influence. When we leave, we'll have helped shape the future of a great empire."

"The prince, you mean," Pythias says. "I like that boy. There's something pure in him."

I hug my fashionable wife, hold on a moment too long, smelling her clean hair. That boy is my project now, my first human project. A problem, a test, a trust; a metaphor I've staked my life on. A thirteen-year-old boy. And Athens is a promise Philip has made me, payment in gold for when my time here is done.

"Sweet and pure," I agree.

The palace is quieter now with the army gone. In the Macedonian tradition, the king must be present at battle to win the favour of the gods. Tiring for Philip, no doubt, and eerie for those of us left behind. It's hard not to feel like a child left alone when his parents have gone to an important dinner and will be away all night. The familiar rooms echo differently, somehow, and time turns to honey.

Boys, each in the black and white livery of a court page, file into the hall I've been assigned. There must be thirty of them, all armed. I look at Leonidas.

"His companions," the older man says grimly.

Alexander is not among them. "What am I, a nurse?" I say.

Leonidas shrugs.

I ask which are the prince's closest friends. Leonidas singles out a pretty pink-skinned black-eyed boy named Hephaestion, a young man my nephew's age named Ptolemy, and a couple of others.

"Right," I say. "You boys to the left, please, and everyone else to the right." Athenian boys would tussle and tarry; these Macedonian boys are quick and silent, efficient as a drill team. "Right side is dismissed."

The boys on the right, including all the littlest ones, look from me to Leonidas and back again.

"Where do you want them to go?" Leonidas asks.

I shrug.

Leonidas points to the door and barks them back to the barracks. They run.

I'm left with the four oldest standing at attention. A philosopher with no military rank, I'm not sure I have the authority to tell them to relax. I put the cloth-draped cage I brought with me on a table. Leonidas withdraws to the back of the room.

"You can't start," Hephaestion says. "Alexander's not here."

"Who?" I say.

I remove the cloth. Inside the cage is the chameleon, but emaciated, barely alive after its three weeks in Pella. The dissection of a blooded animal requires careful preparation, otherwise the blood will flood the viscera at the moment of death. You have to starve the animal first, I explain, and kill it by strangling to preserve the integrity of the blood vessels. Fortunately this one hung on just long enough. I open the top of the cage, reach in with both hands, and grasp the leathery throat. It struggles feebly, opening and closing its mouth. When it's dead, I take it out and lay it on the table. The cage I put on the floor.

"Now," I say. I turn it on its back. Normally I would spread-eagle the legs with pins, but I want to keep the boys' interest. I nod for one each to hold a leg. "Let's find the heart," I say. With a sharp knife I cut through the belly skin, peeling back the flaps to reveal the viscera. The boys press closer, crowding me, but I don't ask them to step back.

"You see, here," I say. "The oesophagus, the windpipe. Feel your own."

The boys touch their throats.

"See the movement, the contraction around the ribs? In the membrane, here."

Movement in the back of the hall. I don't look up.

"This will continue for some time, even after death."

The boys part for Alexander, who walks up to the table.

"You see there isn't much meat. A little by the jaws, here, and here, by the root of the tail. Not much blood, either, but some around the heart. Show me the heart."

Alexander points into the chameleon's body.

I make a sudden fist and hold it up in front of his face. His eyes flare in surprise. Around me the boys go still. "Your heart is this big," I tell Alexander. With what I will always think of as the second blade from the left, ears—the ghost of my father's grip worn into the wooden handle—I detach the bloody nut of the lizard's heart and hold it out to him. He takes it slowly, looks at me, and puts it in his mouth.

"I'm sorry I'm late," he says. "I was with my mother."

Shorry, it emerges through the mouthful. There's blood on one corner of his mouth like a trace of fruit. He chews and chews and swallows with difficulty.

"That's all right," I say. "Are you going to vomit?"

He nods, then shakes his head.

"Shall we have a look at the brain?"

The animal's brain is reduced, through the boys' industrious prickings and slicings, to a substance like meal. Alexander has recovered from his fit of petulance or penitence or peckishness or whatever it was and is busy impaling bits of brain on his knife and smearing them on the arm of the boy next to him. Another boy flicks some brain into Alexander's hair. They're all giggling now, jostling, feinting at each other with their brainy knives, normal boyish behaviour I infinitely prefer to their creepy militarism. We move on to the lungs, the kidneys, the ligaments, the bowel, the lovely doll-knuckle-bones of the spine. Alexander sneaks glances at me and when our eyes meet we both look quickly away. Ours is after all a kind of marriage, arranged by his father. I wonder which of us is the bride.

"Who can tell me what a chameleon is?" I ask.

"An animal."

"A lizard."

I collect my father's scalpels from the boys and wipe them slowly, meticulously, as I was taught. "I had a master, when I was not much older than you. He was very interested in what things were. In what was real, if you like, and what"—I gesture at the remains of the chameleon—"was perishable, what would pass away and be lost. He believed that there were two worlds. In the world we see and hear and touch, in the world we live in, things are temporary and imperfect. There are many, many chameleons in the world, for instance, but this one has a lame foot, and that one's colour is uneven, and so on. Yet we know they are all chameleons; there is something they share that makes them alike. We might say they have the same form; though they differ in the details, they all share in the same form, the form of a chameleon. It is this form, rather than the chameleon itself, that is ideal, perfect, and unchanging. We might say the same of a dog or a cat, or a horse, or a man. Or a chair, or a number. Each of these exists in the world of forms, perfectly, unchangingly.

"My master's theory was ingenious, but it had many problems. For instance, how are we able to perceive the forms, if we are of this world and they are not? And if two similar objects share a form, then must there not be yet another form of which all three partake? And then a fourth form, and a fifth, and so on? And what of change? How can a perfect, unchanging world be the ideal form of *this* world, where change surrounds us?"

From outside comes the clang of a bell and the sound of many boys shouting, running, rallying to their next place of instruction.

"Master." The boys salute me, one after another.

When it's Alexander's turn I touch the corner of my mouth. He hesitates, then wipes off the dried blood with the heel of his hand. I nod and he leaves.

Leonidas steps forward from his corner. He's a tall old man with a craggy face, a warrior who has lived too long. He looks tired. "They liked the lizard."

Together we pack up my materials and scoop the guts into a bowl.

"You left them behind," Leonidas says. "I suppose you know that. All this metaphysics goes over their heads. I'm not sure it would be useful to them even if they did understand it."

"Nor am I."

"They've had trouble keeping tutors for him. He—"

"Yes," I say.

"He frightens people."

Yes.

Leonidas invites me to eat with him. It's a simple meal, austere even—bread and a small cheese, some wizened fruit, and water.

"I like soldier's rations," he says. "That's what I'm used to. Quite the feast, eh?"

I hear in the sarcasm a gruff note of apology.

"Plato would have approved. He ate fruits and vegetables only, no meat, and believed in Spartan habits: cold water, a hard bed, simple clothing. I was his disciple for a long time."

"No longer?"

"His nickname for me was the Brain. When I began to confront him, he said it was in the nature of the colt to kick at its father."

"Ha," Leonidas says.

After a moment, I realize this is an expression of genuine amusement.

As I'm leaving the palace for the day I look into the theatre, hoping for a drink and a debriefing with Carolus. Fortunately I've made no noise. Alexander is alone on the stage, mouthing words I can't hear. Abruptly he raises a fist to eye level, then lowers it. He performs this gesture again and again, each time with a different face: smiling, threatening, sarcastic, quizzical. He can't seem to decide which he likes best, which makes the most sense. My palms are sparkling like the night I stood backstage: for pleasure, excitement, shame at my own amateur theatrics?

Silently, I back out of the theatre.

I AM NOT HIS only master. There are the men like Leonidas who teach him the arts of war: weaponry and riding, combat, the choreography of battle. These are soldiers, athletes, and don't interest me much. But there are others, too: a musician, for gods help us but the boy is talented on the flute; a grey-faced geometer; and an all-around wit and wag named Lysimachus, younger than me and more charming.

At the end of our next lesson, as the boys leave, Lysimachus steps forward and introduces himself. I hadn't noticed him, and feel my face harden. He flatters me prettily: my books, my reputation, my oratory, my way with the boys, right down to the leather of my sandals, obvious quality, obvious taste. He perches his bum on the edge of the table where I'm sitting so he can look down on me. He has one toe on the ground and one foot in the air waggling languorously, letting his own loose sandal slip a little back and forth. It looks new. I wonder if I'm meant to return the compliment.

"The arts," he says, to the question I ask instead.

It's an answer he seems immensely satisfied to give. And a surprise: he's big and young and hearty, muscle-bound, and I've seen him from a distance, mounted, at war games with the prince and pages. He's no flower.

"Some theatre, poetry, history. I'm glad you bring it up. I'm glad you have the same concern I do. You've no idea how much that eases my mind. I had been afraid this conversation would be difficult."

"What concern is that?" I ask.

It emerges that he's worried about overlap: about us treading on each other's toes, pedagogically speaking, and the prince getting caught in the middle. A brilliant but challenging student, didn't I agree? Needing a little extra guidance, deserving a little something extra behind the scenes?

"I'm not aware of holding anything back," I say. "Ethics, politics, and metaphysics are my primary subjects. And whatever else I see fit. The king did not restrict me."

"Excellent!" he says. "You know, I was even thinking—stop me if this is presumptuous—I was thinking we might meet regularly, to discuss the prince's progress. To chart a course, yes? Plan our areas of influence? Divide and conquer, if you see what I mean."

"No. I don't."

"Absolutely," he says. "Absolutely. You think about it. He's at an impressionable age, the sap only just rising. Wouldn't want to confuse him, would we? One thing from me, another from you? We connect, he and I. He's always eager to hear what I have to say. Enjoyed your talk this morning, by the way. You're confident, aren't you."

So, an enemy.

I'm never sure how much Arrhidaeus understands, but decide to ignore his affliction when possible and speak to him as I would to any boy his age. When I tell him I'll be visiting him for a long time to come, he smiles his sudden sweet smile and I wonder if he's almost understood. We're readying Tar and Gem for a ride in the fields when a group of boys, including Alexander, enter the stables. The boys busy themselves with their tack, preparing for lessons of their own. Alexander looks at Arrhidaeus and away.

"What are you doing?" he says to me.

"Tutoring the prince."

He flushes, a trait he must get from his mother, along with the fair skin and rusty hair.

"Do you spend much time with your brother?"

"Don't call him that."

"Do you?"

Alexander won't look at Arrhidaeus, who's mounted now and clutching the reins, watching the younger boy with unconcealed pleasure, his mouth slackly open. "My brother died when I was three. He was five."

"I'm surprised no one told me," I say, trying to hook a laugh, but Alexander won't be caught. "Why don't you come riding with us? You'd be surprised, I think, at all he can do. He's not how you probably remember him as a child."

"How I probably remember him?" Alexander says. "I used to have my lessons with him. I know him better than you do. He drools, he shits. He walks on two legs instead of four—I've seen trained dogs do that too. Now you're teaching him more tricks. You know what? I don't think you're doing it to help him. I think you're doing it to prove you can. I think you've probably tried to teach your horse to talk. I think you probably have a trained bird at home. It hops over to you and you make it do a trick, nod or flap its wings, and then you give it a seed, and tell yourself you're a great teacher. I think that animal"—he points to his brother—"is another laurel leaf for you. A challenge."

He's flushed, he's breathing hard. This is the longest conversation we've had. Hatred, or maybe just disgust—let's say disgust, something I can work with—has lit a fire in him.

"Every student is both a challenge and a laurel leaf." I mean his own self, and mean him to know it. "I like a challenge. Don't you? And if he drools and shits like an animal in a human skin, wouldn't it be worthwhile to make him a little more like us if we can? To clean him up, teach him to speak more clearly, and see what he has to say?"

"What would a dog say? Feed me, scratch me." Alexander shakes his head. "He used to follow me around everywhere. I took care of him and taught him the names of animals, and songs, and things like that. I taught him to beg and fetch because it made people laugh, but it never made me laugh. He's never going to fight a battle or ride a horse properly or travel anywhere. He's going to stay right here until he's an old man, doing the same things day after day. Feed me, scratch me. It makes me sick."

Arrhidaeus grunts out some sounds. He's eager to be off and is telling me so.

"He doesn't seem to remember you," I say.

Alexander looks at him and again away, as though from something painful, the sun. "I told my father I didn't want him near me any more. Not for lessons, not for meals. I didn't want to look at him ever again."

"How old would you have been?"

"Seven," he says. "I know, because it was right around the time of my first hunt. Arrhidaeus, fetch!"

The older boy's head snaps up sharply, looking for the thrown object.

"He remembers me," Alexander says.

"You're a cruel little shit, aren't you?"

His eyes go wide.

"Leonidas says you frighten people. You don't frighten me, you make me sad. You're supposed to be brilliant. Everyone tells me so: your father, Lysimachus, everyone I meet at court who congratulates me on the honour of becoming your master. You know what I see? An utterly ordinary boy. I train birds, you pull the wings off flies. I haven't seen anything in you that tells me you're extraordinary in any way. Athletics, I wouldn't know or care about that. I'm talking about your mind, your personality. Just an ordinary boy with too many privileges. A violent, snotty little boy. How could you possibly know what your noble brother might or might not be capable of?"

Now we're both breathing hard.

"Stop insulting me," he says quietly.

"Stop insulting *me*. You're late to lessons when you come at all. You don't do your homework. I don't think you try to understand anything I teach you. Are you really as stupid as you seem, or are you just putting on a show?"

"You need to stop right now." He's almost whispering.

"Or what?"

"There are three cavalry officers about ten paces behind you. If they hear you talking to me like that, they'll kill you. Don't look back. Act like we're joking around."

Slowly I reach a hand up to tousle his hair.

"I don't understand your lessons," he says. "I don't understand what they're for. Maybe I am stupid. Smile. They're coming over."

"You're an actor, aren't you?" I murmur, smiling stiffly.

"I have to be."

The officers pass, saluting Alexander, squinting at me, ignoring Arrhidaeus, who sits oblivious through all of this, high up on Tar, plucking at his thick lips.

"Thank you," I say when they're out of earshot.

Alexander looks up at his brother on my horse. "I can't ask questions in front of the others. I can't let them know I don't understand. When I'm king they'll remember and they won't respect me."

"Private lessons, then. I'll arrange it with Leonidas."

He nods.

"Can I clear up one thing quickly, before you go? My lessons are to make you think in ways others don't. To make your world bigger. Not this world"—I wave a hand to take in the stables, the palace, Pella, Macedon—"but the world in here." I tap my temple.

"I thought you didn't believe in two worlds."

I point at him. He smiles for real now, pleased with himself, and runs off to rejoin the boys, who are now under the eye of one of the officers, their riding master. Alexander swings up onto Ox-Head and joins the file out of the yard and into the arena.

"Look, Arrhidaeus." I point after him. "Look how tall he sits, and how he keeps his heels down."

"Down." Arrhidaeus bumps up and down a couple of times, impatient for us to go our own way.

CAROLUS SAYS I'M WRONG. "It's not the father at all, it's the mother. Olympias takes up so much room in his head, I'm surprised her hands aren't sticking out of his ears. He gets a lot from her, no doubt at all."

We're in my house, summer ending, supper just finished, talking about the prince's weirdness. "It's like he already is king in his mind," I say. "Never showing weakness. The insolence, the dramatic gestures. The brains, for that matter. Philip's not stupid."

"Nor is Olympias." Carolus lies back on his couch, wine cup trailing from his long fingers. "Can you believe she used to be a beauty? Not all tight and dried like she is now."

"A dried apricot."

"It's difficult skin, red-haired skin." Carolus closes his eyes. "I've seen it in actors. The reds age quicker than others. Darker skin looks younger longer, for some reason. Do you know why that is?"

"More oils?" I guess.

"Alexander got her looks, anyway. I don't see Philip in him at all."

"You find him attractive?"

Carolus doesn't miss a beat. "I find them all attractive, friend. Though, yes, he's got a little something extra. Just who he is, maybe, the power he has, or will have. You can't help wanting to see that on its knees. You don't?"

I shake my head.

"You do," Carolus says. "You just don't know it yet."

"Lysimachus does. You know Lysimachus, his history master?"

Carolus nods. "Always go carefully around large animals in heat."

"It's all sex with you, isn't it."

He laughs. "Not just me. I was a bit of an oddity in Athens,

I'll grant you, but here I fit right in. It's in the air, the dirt, the water. It touches everything. Why am I telling you this, anyway? You're from here. You know."

I shake my head. "It was different then. Power changes things, maybe. Macedon wasn't the power it is today when I was young. I don't remember it being so—charged."

"Well, whatever the reason. They celebrate with it, they make people suffer with it, they do their business with it. They run the kingdom with it. You've heard about Pausanias's promotion?"

I nod. Pausanias was a soldier who serviced the king so thoroughly, gossip had it, that he made officer the next morning. Not the Philip I remember, but I've been away a long time. Who knows?

"Maybe because of how they lock their women away here," he says. "Where is that wife of yours, anyway? She didn't even eat with us."

"She thought you might prefer that."

"She thought wrong." Carolus sits up. "I miss talking to women. Haul her on out here and let's see what she thinks."

I send a slave to find her. "Thinks about what?"

"About our boy."

Pythias appears minutes later with a plate of sweets that she sets on the floor beside Carolus's couch. "Husband," she murmurs.

I pat the couch beside me. "We were just talking about the prince."

Carolus says, "We were talking about love."

She sits and lets me take both of her hands in mine. "I liked him very much, the once we met."

"Liked him why?" Carolus demands.

Pythias says, "He seemed frail."

Carolus and I snort, laughing.

"Frail and sad." She's frowning, distressed but determined too.

Carolus takes her hand and kisses it. "Forgive us, pretty one. We're just all barnacled over with meanness, the two of us."

"I'm not," I say.

"I'm sure he's very good at sports," Pythias says. "That's not what I meant. Will you laugh at me if I say lonely? He seemed like a lonely little boy, younger than his years, with that awful shrieking mother. I wanted to hug him and whisper in his ear, 'Come stay with me for a while. I'll take care of you.'"

"You did?" I say.

Carolus leans forward. "Did you, indeed."

I LIKE THE FEELING of combing out the tangles in things, of looking at the world around me and feeling I'm clearing all the brush, bit by bit. This bit reclaimed from chaos, and this bit here, and that bit there. Back in Mytilene, my focus was on biology, particularly marine life. Here in Pella, I want something new.

I feel the thoughts clustering, forming a constellation whose inner logic I've yet to perceive, the harmony of whose spheres I've yet to hear. It's that little book on theatre I sketched for Carolus: something about his father and my father, Illaeus's sickness and my own, and my two young princes, especially Alexander. He's a different boy in our private sessions: tense, intense. He rarely smiles. He asks incessant questions and writes down the answers. These sessions are generally late in the evening to keep them secret; he's giving up sleep for the pretense of effortlessness. He's angry, curious, pompous, charming, driven. He's a comedy or a tragedy, one or the other. Which?

My nephew, I've decided, is a comedy. He's found himself a house in the city, and his comings and goings are less my concern these days. I visit him there for an informal supper, and am surprised by the gap that has grown up between us, between his student-slovenliness and his elaborate care of me, his older guest. The place has a reek to it. He has, moreover, found himself a lover—so he tells me, while we eat, lying on couches in the courtyard in a drift of fall leaves—and is throwing gifts at the boy like he's a moving target.

"Three pairs of winter shoes!" Callisthenes brags.

"That's practical," I say. "At least you're not off writing poetry all day."

"Picking flowers," Callisthenes says.

"You did that?"

Callisthenes covers his eyes with his hand, laughing at himself.

"Pythias instructs me to ask you," I say, "before I forget, are you provisioned for the winter? She says to tell you to start thinking about your squash and your beans, about putting them up now, while they're still available in the market. I think she'll make a list for you, if you like."

"My squash and my beans," he says. "Dear Auntie. Has she had that beer yet?"

"Respect," I say.

He laughs again.

After we finish our meal, he wants to talk politics; gossip, I want to say, though politics is a kind of theatre too, and it occurs to me we might tease out something useful for the new work I'm contemplating. The personalities of the city-states, the logic of their confrontations, the simultaneous sense of both the contingent and the inexorable. Philip is still in Thrace. Athens clashes with Cardia, in the Chersonese, where the Athenian corn ships must pass. Philip will back Cardia when the time comes, ever so reasonably and regretfully. Demosthenes rants as much, fumes and foams about it in the Athenian assembly. I tell Callisthenes it's well known that Demosthenes writes all his speeches out in advance, and is incapable of putting two words together if they're not already written on a piece of paper in front of him. I tell him how he studied the gestures of actors, and how as a young man he built himself an underground room in which to practise gesturing and declaiming, and how to make himself focus he would shave half his head so he'd be too ashamed to go out in public, thus forcing himself to stay home and work. Callisthenes puts his head to the side and opens his mouth to question the ridiculousness of this, but I tell him that's not the point. The point is that the man allows these stories to be told of himself, is proud of them. I invent a word for the sake of clever conversation, the verb *to Cassandra*. He Cassandras away about Philip, I tell my nephew, like an actor hoping for a prize.

"Alexander goes to your director friend for lessons in rhetoric," Callisthenes says. He's started attending my lessons with the boys, and being younger is more in their confidence. "He has to memorize everything, though. Carolus won't let him speak with notes."

A suspicion erupts like a little bubble on the surface of my mind. "That boy of yours," I say. "Is he one of the pages?"

"Of course." Callisthenes lies on his back, gazing at the sky. "They're like a little harem, those pages. Lots of the Companions use them. His family comes from up north somewhere. He's terribly lonely. He likes the attention."

"You're over your qualms, then. Macedonian rapacity and vulgarity and so forth."

"Qualms." A blunt word for stabbing, but he tries to stab me with it. He doesn't want to be reminded.

"So Alexander goes to Carolus."

"Unofficially, of course."

Of course.

THE FIRST SNOW OF the season comes whispering late one grey afternoon, just as the light is going, and I'm walking home from my weekly obligation to attend court. I find the slaves murmuring to each other, and then the reason why: Pythias is sitting in a corner of our spare bedroom, one of the few rooms without a window, with her veil drawn over her head.

"What is it?" She lifts her arms above her head and sprinkles her fingers down to her lap.

She's been waiting all afternoon for me; won't go outside, won't let it touch her, until I've given her an explanation she can accept.

"Snow," I say.

Most of the slaves, more gifts from Hermias, haven't seen snow before either. I stand them under the colonnade so they can watch me go out in the courtyard bare-headed. I let it land on my arms and body, and tip my head back with my tongue out. It seems to fall from nowhere, bits of pure colourlessness peeled off from the sky and drifting down, thicker now. They're watching me. Pythias is first: she steps out from under the colonnade and holds out a palm to catch some of the stuff. She comes to me. The slaves slowly follow, and soon we're all standing about in the courtyard letting snow fall on our faces and wet our clothes.

"Why do they send it?" Pythias asks.

Their faces turn toward me. *Yes, why?*

"Who, love?" Though I know.

"The gods."

A conversation we've danced around a few times before; and here we are again. She prods me toward it, sometimes, I think; can't quite bring herself to confront me directly, but worries at it like a little dog with a big bone. "It" being my unusual religious beliefs (I choose this term as neither hers nor my own, but one we might skittishly agree on for the purposes of argument, if we ever were to argue, which we never do). Pythias is pious, keeps the household shrine, attends various temples, observes rites when there are rites to be observed—births and deaths and weddings. She sacrifices to thank and appease and show penitence; she is (though she tries to hide it from me) superstitious (she would say devout), and sees signs where I see only the natural beauty and familiar strangeness of the world. In fact I am not irreligious, and swoon before a smoke-plume of autumn birds just as she would, but for my own reasons.

"The gods don't send it," I say. "It's part of the machinery of the world. When the air is cold enough, rain turns to snow. It freezes. The droplets attach to each other and harden."

"But why?"

She wants to hear that once upon a time Apollo did this or that to a nymph and snow was the result. I can't offer it. Divinity for me is that very plume of birds, the patterns of stars, the recurrence of seasons. I love these things and weep for the joy of them. The reality of numbers, again, for instance: I could weep if I thought about numbers for too long, their glorious architecture. I want to weep, now, for the beauty of the sky dispensing itself across my courtyard, the cold warmth in all our cheeks, the fear-turned-to-pleasure in my slaves' eyes. Pythias sees my face and holds her hand out to me.

"For pleasure," I manage to say. "So that we may go in and warm ourselves by the fire and look out at it from time to time, and feel—"

"It's all right," she says. "Come in, now."

"—and feel—"

"It's all right," she says again, because I am weeping now, and not quite exactly for joy, though that too is part of the spice.

"Why do you think they send it?" I ask her.

She turns her face up to the sky. Flakes land in her hair and lashes. I look helplessly at the line of her cheek.

"To remind us of them," she says, and there is no arguing with that.

"Master."

I turn to the slave, take a deep breath, exhale. "Tycho."

Tycho smiles, seeing me trying to rally. We've known each other a long time. "There's a boy at the gate."

Pythias gathers her skirts up from the whitening ground and sweeps into the house. "Your lady's gone to the kitchen for some bread. Tell him he'll get something in a minute."

"He doesn't look like a beggar."

"Messenger?"

Tycho shrugs. "He asked for my lady."

In the street, people are hurrying, heads down, through the snow. No one seems to have noticed Alexander standing alone by my gate. He wears sandals and a tunic; no cloak, no hat.

"Child, where's your guard?" I ask.

"I slipped them."

Tycho opens the gate and I hustle the prince into the courtyard just as Pythias re-emerges with a crust.

"Is that for me?"

Pythias instinctively draws up her veil. "Majesty." Shock, pleasure.

"I followed you from court," the boy says to me. "I wanted to see where you live." He takes the bread from Pythias, bites, and stands there chewing, looking around.

"Tycho and I will escort you back to the palace."

"No." He swallows. "It's too dark now. Not safe. You'll have to send for my guard in the morning."

"You're staying the night?"

"Carolus said you wouldn't mind."

Pythias bows and withdraws into the house.

"I'm starving." He puts his head back, as I did, and stares up into the sky. "I love snow."

"They'll be looking for you. I'll send Tycho to the palace for your escort."

"But I want to stay here. You can't refuse me hospitality."

"Your parents will worry."

"They never worry when I spend time with Hephaestion," the boy says. "His family's very loyal."

"That's where they think you are? With Hephaestion?"

Our cock screams once; Pythias is working fast.

"Stop worrying. I'm perfectly safe here, and so are you. I

haven't brought anything bad into your house." He looks around the courtyard some more, at my pots of winter leek and onion, and the lights in the windows. "Nice," he says. "Cozy."

"You're cold." He's shivering. It's dark now, blue dark beyond the pools of torchlight. "Would you like to see my study?"

"I want to see Pythias."

I take him into the kitchen, where Pythias has every woman in the house putting together a meal. The cock lies on the chopping board, blood draining from its throat into a bowl. The fire roars high; it's hot in here. When Pythias sees we mean to stay, she has two chairs pulled up in front of the fire. In front of Alexander's chair she puts a basin of hot water.

"Take off your sandals," she says.

While he soaks his feet and the women clatter, I take Tycho aside.

"Should I be armed?" he asks when I've finished.

"Just vigilant."

He goes off to the gate to spend the night awake there, wrapped in a horse blanket.

In the kitchen, Alexander is eating a plate of cheese. It takes me a moment to realize he's wearing my best snow-white wool.

"His clothes were soaked through," Pythias murmurs behind me, touching my elbow. "I didn't know what else to give him. Supper's an hour off still, but he ate that bread so quickly."

"You did right." We stand together for a moment in the doorway, this thought between us: we would dote so on a son, worry the details of his feeding and clothing with such brow-furrowing tenderness. I brave a look at her face, but she can't, won't, look at me, and hurries back in to her women, flushing a little. It's hot in here.

"These clothes of yours," Alexander says when I take my seat across from him. "You don't seem vain, but Pythias showed me your trunk when she was finding this. You could sell some of that cloth and buy a bigger house. Are you very sensitive to the feel of things?"

"Am I what?"

"I was. When I was a baby I couldn't wear anything rough, my mother says. My skin went red and I cried all the time. Leonidas took all my nice things away. He said my baby skin needed to thicken before I could be a soldier. I like your clothes."

"Thank you. I like them too." Pythias's work, all of it fine, fine, fine; I've learned my tastes from her. She's made me a dandy, but I've lately had to hurt her feelings by buying coarser wear from the market. It's one thing to be teased for effeminacy at court but another in the street, and I don't go armed. "Would you like some more cheese? Bread? We're an hour away from the meal still, Pythias tells me."

"Wine?"

I fetch a cup for each of us: watered for him, neat for me. "You didn't have to follow me. You could have just said you wanted to visit. We could have prepared properly."

"Then I wouldn't have seen anything interesting." He looks around approvingly. "Would you have let me into your kitchen? Would I be wearing your clothes? Would I have seen your bedroom? Where will I sleep tonight?"

"Outside, in the snow."

He grins.

"So this is Carolus's doing?"

Pythias kneels beside us. "Will you have a bath tonight, Majesty?"

"Yes, please."

She rises and withdraws to arrange that.

"You're too old for her," Alexander says.

"Yes."

"She's overdressed, too."

"Yes."

"You're not going to get mad at me, are you?"

I shrug. "Do you want me to?" My darkling mood, suspended by the shock of his appearance, is threatening to reassert itself.

"Do you suppose she's happy?"

I close my eyes.

"I often wonder that about people," Alexander says. "It's a way of understanding why they do the things they do. My mother taught me that. She said not to trust happy people."

"What else did she teach you, your unhappy mother?"

He looks at Pythias, across the room.

"I assume she's unhappy, your mother," I add. "If she prizes it so."

"She says nice things about you," Alexander says.

We eat in the big room, Pythias bejewelled, our three breaths smoking in the cold. Conversation shrivels in it. The slaves come and go with plates of food. The cock, stewed too briefly, is tough and stringy; the wine is cold.

"How is Carolus?" Pythias asks into the silence.

"He coughs."

Pythias looks at me.

"I'll send him something," I say dutifully.

"Your father was a doctor," Alexander says.

"He saved your father's life when we were boys. Patched a spear wound."

Alexander touches his collarbone, *here?* I nod.

"That wouldn't kill you," Alexander says. "Everyone I know has one of those, from drills. Would you teach me some medicine, though? As part of my studies?"

"You want to deliver babies?"

He blushes. Pythias frowns.

"For the field," he says. "Wounds."

I shrug. "The little that I know, I'll teach you. Bind a bleeder, squeeze a squirter. That was something my father used to say."

Pythias pushes her plate away. Well, she shouldn't be here at all, but Alexander wanted it. Carolus's encouragement again, no doubt.

"Will you have dessert, or your bath?" she asks the prince.

"Dessert *in* the bath?"

She smiles briefly, grudgingly, at his hope-against-hoping face. I have a vision of my long-ago prostitute, amused despite herself by men's awe at the variety of pleasure in the world.

"It's not that he has *no* boundaries," I tell Pythias, later, once the boy is installed in the great bronze pot by the kitchen hearth with his plate of honey and apples, and we're in the room the slaves have prepared for him, the room where Pythias hid from the snow, checking it over. "He knows precisely what the boundaries are. It's more like he has to overstep. He has to push everyone a little bit too far, just to see what will happen. Following me here, for instance."

"I humiliated you. Supper was terrible."

"I doubt he noticed. Did you see how he ate? Like he hasn't had a square meal in days."

"I saw that." She dusts a little table with the hem of her dress. "I thought I'd leave him out a plate of fruit, in case he wakes in the night."

"Do that."

"I still think the other room is nicer, the one with the window."

"This is safer. Warmer. He's closer to us here too."

She hesitates. "How are you feeling?"

I shake my head, a shorthand she knows. Knuckles tap at the door frame, two taps: Pythias's maid.

"Lady," the girl says. "He asks for you."

"Me?" Pythias says. "Where is he?"

"Still in his bath."

"Monkey." I think evil to Carolus. Now what? "He's trying to insult me. I'll go."

That wry smile, again. "Me, surely, if anyone," Pythias says. "And he's only a boy. If it's just testing boundaries, as you say— let's at least see what he wants."

"What he thinks he wants."

She's gone a long time. I stew longer than the cock: in the guest room, first, napping the fur we've put on his bed, plumping pillows, fussing over lamps; and then in my own bigger bedroom, where I can pace.

When she returns she waves my words away unspoken and says, "He's in bed now. He wants you."

I shake my head, grimacing. "Monkey."

His room is warm and golden from the lamplight; more lamps now than the pair I trimmed. He lies under the fur, rosy and smiling, eyes round and dark as a small child's with the effort of keeping awake for me.

"All right?"

He smiles, nods.

I rest a hand briefly on his forehead. "Shall I blow out some of these lamps?"

"I will, in a minute."

I return to my room, where Pythias is sitting up in bed. "So?" I ask.

"My virtue is intact."

"Thank the gods." I get in beside her. "Let me guess. He wanted to talk?"

"He wanted to know what went into the stew. He wanted to tell his mother."

"Tell her he was here?"

"I don't think everything he tells her gets back to Philip. Actually, I don't think anything he tells her gets back to Philip."

"It's like that."

She nods.

"Hard on him."

"I think so." She lies back while I make my examination, all gooseflesh in the cold. "I think he just liked having someone to talk to while he was in his bath. Perhaps his mother used to sit with him. He oiled himself and dressed himself."

I touch my collarbone. "Did he have a scar?"

"I looked. No."

I blow out the lamp.

"He asked me if I was happy," Pythias says.

"He asked me that too, about you. What did you say?"

"He asked me if I'd like to be invited up to the palace more often, to get me out of the house. He said he could arrange it with his mother. I said no thank you."

"You didn't."

A pause. "Was that wrong?"

"Nobody likes his mother. You think he doesn't know that? You didn't have to rub his nose in it."

"I told him he could come here whenever he wants," she says.

I smack my forehead.

"Don't worry," she adds. "He said it was too difficult to get away."

"Thank the gods for that."

She lies with her back to me. I wrap a curl of her long hair around my finger, the part of her I can touch without her knowing it.

"He asked me about Atarneus. What it was like when I was a girl, the landscape and the weather and the people I knew. He asked about my mother." When I touch her breast she flinches. "He'll hear."

I roll back to my side of the bed. "Night, then."

"Night."

When she's asleep, I get up and go outside. The snow is still coming, thick and fast and silent. Tycho has a weight of it on his head and shoulders. He rears up like a bear in his great blanket when I touch his shoulder.

"Go to bed," I tell him. "I'm here now."

He goes inside briefly and comes back out with a second blanket. We sit side by side for the rest of the night, watching nothing go by.

Who am I looking for? Tycho asked, hours ago, when I first set him to watch.

I'm not sure, I said. *I guess anyone who might have seen he was alone.*

AFTER A SEASON OF sporadic sessions with the boys, interspersed with the obligations of court life and my own studies—I'm settling down, now, finally, into a routine—Antipater summons me to a private meeting. Philip is still in Thrace.

"Tell me about the prince," Antipater says.

We sit in one of the smaller rooms, with a pebble mosaic of the rape of Helen beneath our feet. I can brush dust from a pink nipple with my toe. I've developed, with the first snow, a heavy cold, and am constantly blowing great green skeins of snot from my nose. I wipe my hand now surreptitiously on my cloak, and hope Pythias won't notice the crust of it when she takes my laundry.

"He is highly intelligent and alarmingly disciplined."

Antipater laughs. "When he was small his mother would hide sweets in his bed, and Leonidas would search his room until he found them, and throw them away. He believes it's good for the boy always to be slightly hungry."

Ah. I wonder if that's why he's small.

"Leonidas used to take him on night marches to stop him wetting the bed. It worked, too. Leonidas has been good for him, no doubt about it."

I wonder if I've offended the old tutor and am about to get my reckoning.

"Leonidas tells me the prince is devoted to this Lysimachus," Antipater says. "That one who calls himself Phoenix and Alexander Achilles. Who does that make Philip, then?"

"Peleus."

"Peleus." Antipater frowns. "Well, never mind. Only I suspect his mother's in there somewhere, encouraging that shit. We don't need an aesthete, we need a soldier. We need a king." He seems distracted for a moment by the floor, and cocks his head sideways to squint at an arrangement of limbs. "All right. Philip instructs me to give you the Temple of the Nymphs at Mieza. You'll tutor Alexander there from now on, Alexander and let's say a dozen others. He'll go through his entire life with these boys; you can't cut him off entirely."

I nod.

"The mother I can control, and Lysimachus is not to attend him there. I'll tell him myself. The prince likes you. He thinks you're almost as smart as he is. Smarter than any of the rest of us, it goes without saying."

Mieza is a half-day's ride away, far enough that it will mean staying there. I know vaguely of the place; there are caves, apparently, and it's supposed to be cooler than Pella in the summertime. What else, I'm not sure. Pythias will have to manage on her own while I'm gone. Perhaps she'll enjoy it.

"Leonidas disciplined the body," Antipater says. "You'll discipline the mind."

I promise to do my best.

"Philip has great things in store for you too, don't forget. He's counting on you. You'll be his man in Athens one of these days, the Macedonian brain in Athens's skull."

I bow my head.

We spend some minutes talking about the campaign in Thrace, a campaign that's looking like it will take longer than Philip ever intended.

"Savages, the Thracians," Antipater says. "Fight like animals."

I understand this is praise.

"He'll overwinter there."

Antipater doesn't seem like he's much given to chit-chat, and I suspect a test. I like tests. "Leaving his own territory unattended for so long?" I say. "Surely war with Athens is inevitable. I'm surprised he doesn't watch his back more closely."

"Unattended?" Antipater says.

"If he were to leave someone behind, someone to give them pause. One of his better generals. Parmenion, say."

Antipater frowns. "I suppose I'm a pet rabbit?"

"A lion of Macedon. Alexander's most worthy adviser." Alexander is now old enough to serve as keeper of the royal seal, but it's clear enough who wields true power. "As such, not to be risked in open warfare if it should come to that."

"Piss off." He pats my shoulder. "Take care of our boy."

"MIEZA," PYTHIAS SAYS, without expression. I show her on a map. "Goodness."

"I'll come back to visit you."

Her face hardened a little when she saw the distance, but it's a hardening I can't read: displeasure, fear, disappointment, or a mask on some more pleasant emotion? Relief, anticipation?

"An elaborate arrangement I'm sure everyone will get tired of eventually," I say.

A few days later I pack minimally and ride out alone, for the pleasure of being alone. It's pretty, pastoral countryside, a morning of brooks and meadows and glens dotted with stone huts and sheep pens fenced with brambles.

Just outside the village of Mieza, the rambling temple complex features assorted shrines and sanctuaries and modest living quarters. The attendants give me a room, an austere little cell: bed, table, chair. I ask for many lamps. Leonidas has the room next to mine; the boys, I'm told, have a dormitory to themselves, out of earshot. The attendants are old men who accept our presence impassively; I'm reminded of Pythias. Who knows what goes on in their heads, those secret houses? They shuffle about, avoiding us, the older the shyer, shy as deer.

Once, late at night, as I'm working at my table with all my lamps, I hear a man's laughter. Once I pass an attendant carrying a tray, the remains of a meal, from a hallway I had thought uninhabited. "Penitents," he says tersely, when I ask about other guests. "They're in seclusion." Once, rounding a corner, I bump into Lysimachus, who carries on without acknowledging me. I wonder whom to inform—the attendants, Antipater, the newly recalled Parmenion (so!), Philip himself—and decide no one.

It's a charming place, though, especially by springtime, when we can take our lessons outside. Stone seats, shady walks, caves dripping stalactites I can use for my little stories for the boys, metaphors we can climb in and out of. My old master was much taken with the metaphorical value of caves. I come to enjoy the rhythm of my life here, of the commute back and forth to the city: this or that familiar rock, tree, field, face, the boys at this end, my wife at that, tossed from one to the other, always a hot meal waiting, a more or less luxurious bath. In the end I prefer to be with Pythias. Yet I don't get back to her as often as I'd planned, and sometimes months go by without us seeing each other. A ride in hard frost yields to a ride in tender spring greenery, and I'll realize how long it's been. She never reproaches me.

She weaves, she tends the garden; she reads a little, she says when I ask. Nothing, poetry.

I'm not sure how I feel about her helping herself to my library, wonder if she knows the food rule. The next time I return to Mieza, I take the cart so I can bring the most significant volumes with me. I leave her some simple, appropriate material, and make a mental note to buy her some new to make up for my possessiveness. She watches the loading of the cart as she thanks me, but I can't help it. All the way back to Mieza I fuss over the oilcloths covering the crates, and can relax only once my library is safely installed in my room, where I won't have to share it.

Private sessions are impossible here, would be impossible to keep secret, so from the start I decide to slow down and address the boys in terms they'll all easily understand. There follows, accordingly, a kind of pastoral interlude, during which I lead the boys high and low, trailed less and less often by the grimly observant Leonidas, to look at plants and animals, formations of rock, to observe the wind and the sun and the coloration of clouds. I explain the phenomenon of rainbows, a complicated process of reflection that morphs into a geometry lesson as I explain why only half a rainbow is ever visible at one time. I explain the phenomenon of earthquakes as a great wind trapped underground, and when I draw the appropriate analogy to the human bowels am rewarded with an afternoon of farting boys crying, "Earthquake!" I speak of the saltiness of the sea, and this too I relate to the body; for even as food goes into the body sweet and leaves a residue in the chamber-pot that is salty and bitter, so do sweet rain and rivers run into the ocean and disperse, leaving a similarly salty residue. I don't tell them I struck on this analogy after tasting my own warm piss. We spend a happy morning observing the flow of a river, while I tell them of the great underground reservoirs that some believe are the source of all the water in the world. Always Alexander, when I speak of geography, asks about the East, and I oblige with accounts I've read of Egypt and Persia. His eyes go shocked when I speak of the river that flows from the mountains of Parnassus, across which the outer ocean that rings the entire world can be seen.

"I'll go there," he says.

I speak of the Nile, and Alexander says he'll go there too. Once, when I'm speaking of salt and silt and the filtering of sea water, I explain that if you took an empty clay jar, sealed its mouth to prevent water getting in, and left it in the sea overnight, the water that leached into it would be sweet because the clay would have filtered the salt.

"You've tried this?" Alexander asks.

"I've read of it."

This exchange stays in my mind, though. Every time Alexander swears to visit some distant place, and Hephaestion swears he'll go there too, and the others dutifully swear that they, too, will join the company, I think of that jar bobbing in the ocean, the one I've only read of.

One hot afternoon I take the boys into the woods behind the temple and set them hunting for insects, particularly bees. I've brought along a dissecting board and knives, small clay jars for the specimens, and a book to occupy myself while I wait for them to return.

Within half an hour I realize I've made a basic mistake. The shouts and laughter of the boys have long since faded and I know I've lost them to the sweet drugged heat of the afternoon.

They're laughing at me, no doubt, wherever they are. Climbing trees, swimming in the river. No matter.

I walk on a little into the woods, calling them without conviction, and am surprised when I come upon Hephaestion and Alexander in a sun-shot grove. Alexander stands still while Hephaestion swats at him.

"They won't leave him alone," Hephaestion says, when I come close. Half a dozen bees have locked onto the smaller boy and are whizzing and darting at him, while Hephaestion tries simultaneously to knock them away and catch one in a wooden cup.

"I attract them," Alexander says. "I have been known for it since childhood. My father's astrologers tell me it is an auspicious sign."

"It's probably your smell," I say.

I spot the nest up in a tree not far from where we're standing, and point.

"I've had enough," Alexander says. I realize he's frightened and afraid to show it.

"Come." I lead him slowly away. "If you don't rush, they won't get agitated."

I take the boys back to the spot where I left my gear and tell them to wait. I go back to the nest tree and look on the ground beneath it until I find a dead bee. I scoop it up with a leaf and take it back to them.

"You should be flattered," I tell Alexander. "Bees have a powerful sense of smell, but they avoid anything rotten. They like only sweet things."

Hephaestion punches Alexander in the arm. Alexander punches him back.

"Look." I drop the dead bee onto the board. "How many parts does the body have?"

"Three," the boys say.

"The head." I touch each part as I name it with the tip of my father's smallest knife. "The middle part, which in animals is the chest. And the stomach, here. A bee will go on living if you cut off its head or stomach, but not if you remove the middle. Bees have eyes and are able to smell, but they have no other sense organs that we can discern. They have stingers."

"I know," Alexander says ruefully.

"Four wings." I delicately display them with the knife tip. "No two-winged insect has a stinger. The bee has no sheath for its wings. Do you know an insect that does?"

"Flying beetle," Hephaestion says.

I feel the sun on my head, pricking out beads of sweat. The boys' heads almost touch over the dead bee. The heat is winey on my tongue. I make an incision as delicately as I can.

"Blood?" I ask.

The boys shake their heads.

"And where does their sound come from?"

"The wings," Alexander says.

"A good guess."

"Wrong," Hephaestion says.

"Piss off," Alexander says.

I show them the pneuma and the membrane called the hypozoma, and explain how the friction of these two creates the sound of buzzing. The pneuma is like the lung of a breathing creature—though I take care to explain that insects do not really breathe—and the swelling and subsiding of the pneuma, because it's greater when the insect is flying, produces a louder sound at that time. The hypozoma, I further explain, is the membrane through which the insect cools itself, as bees and some others—

cicadas, wasps, flying beetles—are naturally hot creatures. I tell
them, too, of insects that can live in fire, for there are animals in
every other element—earth, air, water—and it follows logically
that they must exist.

"I have never seen insects in fire," Alexander says, and I tell
him that's because they're very small.

When we get back to the temple, there's a letter waiting to
inform me that Hermias of Atarneus has died. I write immediately to Pythias. I don't tell her the manner: that her guardian was
ambushed by the Persians, detained, tortured, and crucified.
Instead I tell her Hermias fell suddenly to the ground. I tell her
I'll arrange for the necessary sacrifices, and also write a com-
memorative hymn.

*Better than gold, the sun is desolate at his passing, sacred to the Daughters of
Memory,* et cetera, et cetera. Well. I killed him, I suppose, or the
treaty I carried to Philip did. It was never really a secret. Demosthenes in Athens rails against Philip's eastward scheming like a
drip-mouthed dog. The Persians tolerated Hermias while he
kept to himself, all nice and tucked in and trim about his territo-
ries, but once he started helping himself, *just this one more village, and
this tasty one too,* and once he reached out to Philip as protector
against his protectors, well. I massage my palm with my thumb
while feeling with my index finger between the bones in the back
of my hand, deluding myself about the pain (mightn't you nestle
a nail through there smoothly, somehow?). Guilt is not quite the
word. If it hadn't been me, someone else would have been the
messenger. But he was ever kind to me, wanted to learn from me,
gifted me my wife. Different if I had wanted a city, no doubt. I
can imagine the dawning, sharpening look on his face. Perhaps
he would have liked me even more. And he was such good com-

pany: he really did read in his spare time, really did like to sit and talk quietly about what he'd read, really did like to bask in the warm Atarnean evening sipping a cup of his own purple wine made by his own subjects from his own fat grapes, listening to the boom of his own waves and the lowing of his own dear beeves, see his own birds embroider the fragrant air of his own sky over his head, and talk through ideas of form and content and the mystical reality of the Good. His hair had a little curl; his nose had been broken, attractively; his voice was oddly high and strained for his big build (probably the root of the rumour about his gelding); he ignored Pythias utterly after he gave her to me. (Pythias is in all this somewhere, in my muddled, mud-coloured emotions, Pythias and Hermias's balls, or the lack of them. It's night now, and back in Pella she sleeps, here in Mieza the boys sleep, and here I sit remembering and writing in the doddering lamplight, my little bubble in the dark. Poor Pythias.) But I left him, and that's bothering me tonight. He lived a rich life and offered me the fat and the comfort of it, and I walked away. He understood ambition and would laugh at what I'm trying to understand in myself right now. He would say I'm trying to make a simple thing complicated. An ambitious man wants to go to Athens, he'd say: salt the ocean!

I reread the hymn I've just written. Tomorrow to the copyist, and then to have it circulated. Like blowing a dandelion puff, soon enough one of those pages will land in Athens and my name will fall into place with a little click. Philip will have been seen to be manoeuvring for his easternmost foothold ever, laying the sub-floor for a full-scale Persian campaign. I, in my tiny capacity (love for Hermias = love for Macedon), will have been seen to be assisting him. Assisting

Macedonian imperialism: and what state, even an Athens, is safe from that?

You see, they will say, how his Macedonian blood has frothed up in him. Oh, he is not the one we remember. He never really was one of us, now, was he? Oho!

I remember the first time I met Hermias, at a dinner in Athens while I was still a student. He brought greetings from Proxenus and the twins, and asked me about my work. We walked together afterwards, tugging the thread of our conversation on and on into the night with us, a long strand like a long line drawn on a map, from Athens to Atarneus to Mytilene to Pella to Mieza, as though if I turned around it would still be there and I might trace it back to that long-ago night when a powerful man invited me to visit him one day, and I was excited about that future.

AROUND THE TIME OF the harvest moon, I take the boys out stargazing. They're sleepy and subdued, wrapped in their blankets, while above our heads the stars wheel. I lead them up a small hill not far from the temple and make them lie on their backs in the grass. A few immediately curl up and go back to sleep; one or two grumble about the cold and the damp ground. Alexander takes his usual place at my side. I let the boys show me the constellations they know, while the moon pales their faces with a milky half-light.

"What do *you* see?" Alexander asks eventually.

I tell him of the concentric spheres that make up the universe: how the earth is in the middle, the moon in the next nearest sphere, then the planets, then, in the outermost sphere, the fixed stars.

"How many spheres are there?" Alexander asks.

"Fifty-five. The math requires it. They move; the sky is not the same in the different months. You know this yourself. This is the rotation of the spheres. Each sphere's rotation causes movement in the one adjacent to it. The outermost sphere is moved by the unmoved mover, or, if you like, by god. Each of the fifty-five lesser spheres, in addition to the impetus they gain from the spheres nearby, has its own lesser unmoved mover."

Beside me I can hear that the boy's breathing has slowed, but his eyes are open and unblinking. He gazes straight up all the time I speak.

"I can't see the spheres," he says. "Are they ever visible?"

I explain they're made of crystal.

"Lysimachus says when I go to Persia the skies will be different," Alexander says. "He says there are new stars there that no civilized man has seen, but I will see them. He says my greatest battles will be recorded in the constellations. My father's never were, and never will be."

"Perhaps Lysimachus will accompany you," I say. "To Persia."

"Inevitably. Will you?"

"Charging into battle on Tar?"

I can feel him grinning, though he still looks at the sky.

"You will write me great letters," I say. "They will last a thousand years, and forever after all the thinkers will know that you were also one of us." He likes that. But then: "What is it you expect to find there?"

"War."

I'm disappointed and tell him so. "There is more. There is so much more. You want to march all that way for the battle-thrill? To sit tall on a horse and watch your enemy go down? To—I don't even know what it is you do—swipe your sword this way and that and watch the limbs fly?"

"You don't know what it is we do," he repeats.

"I know what your father expects. Tribute, tax revenue. All those wealthy cities and satrapies up and down the coast. They're used to paying up to foreigners; they'd pay your father as soon as the next man. But what do you expect?"

"You've lived there. You tell me."

"I found family and friends. I found what I went for and what I expected to find." And I squinted my eyes to stop from seeing everything at the edges: the dirt, the disease, the people without art or math or civilized music, sitting around their fires in the evenings, muttering in their ugly language, eating their smelly foods, thinking their short-legged-animal thoughts of eating and sexing and shitting. Dirty, obsequious, uncivilized. I tell the prince as much, teach him what I know to be true about the land he so romanticizes.

"You know what I'd do?" He's up on his elbows now. "I'd sit at their fires and listen to their music and eat their food and wear their clothes. I'd go with their women."

I hear the blush in his voice though I can't see it on his face. *Go with*—a sweet pink euphemism from a hale Macedonian boy. He loves Hephaestion.

"I wouldn't go all that way just to keep my eyes closed."

"You don't know what you're talking about." And I tell him about Hermias.

"Well, but that's war," he says. "You're going to hate an entire nation because you lost one friend?"

"You're going to love an entire nation to annoy your teacher?"

"Yes."

"No. Not funny. You think you can go there, sit yourself down at their fires, make yourself at home? You'd have to conquer them first."

"That's the plan."

"You'll have to destroy their world just to get into it. What'll it be worth to you then?"

"I'm not like you. I'm not like my father. I don't want to do things the old ways. I have so many ideas. All my soldiers will be clean-shaven, you know why? So no one can get a hold of their beards in combat. My father would never think of something like that. I'll dress like they do so they'll let their guard down with me. Persia, I'm not afraid of Persia. I don't need to know what I'll find before I get there."

Inevitably, I think of my own advice to Speusippus. Youthful bravado, then? Was Speusippus as annoyed with me as I am now with my own student? Serves me right?

"Artabazus." He points at me like he's scored.

Philip's pet Persian, a renegade satrap and refugee, these past few months, in the Macedonian court, thanks to some quarrel with his own king. Canny, charming. He wrote me a letter of condolence for Hermias.

"I like him," Alexander says. "He's told me a lot about his country. You can't hate Artabazus."

"Lovely marine life."

Alexander looks at me, waiting for the punch line.

"I caught an octopus there, once. Netted it in the water, brought it slowly, slowly back to shore. I kept the net nice and loose so I wouldn't damage it. Slowly, carefully, I lifted it out of the water and laid it on the sand. It died."

"The lesson?" Alexander says.

"You make the world larger for yourself by conquering it, but you always lose something in the process. You can learn without conquering."

"*You* can," he says.

AT HOME, I PRESENT the hymn to Pythias and tell her I want to plan a dinner: some friends and colleagues and a few new faces for a meal and wine and conversation. I tell her I want it to be like the communal dinners from my student days, when everyone brought a dish and shared, but Pythias refuses. She says guests in her house will not bring food, and she'll order Tycho to turn away anyone who tries.

"Your house?" I'm delighted. "Your house!"

She will plan the menu herself, and oversee the preparation. She wants a chicken and a goat, and money for everything else: dinner party as military campaign. "My house. You just tell me which day and how many. I'll need a month, at least."

"I was thinking the day after tomorrow." I'm due back in Mieza.

She shakes her head. "A month. We have to clean. We haven't cleaned properly since we got here. Three weeks, maybe, if I had an extra girl."

"So that's what you're after."

"I'm not after anything. You suit yourself. A month, then, and not a day sooner."

I make a list: Callisthenes, of course; Carolus, the old actor; Antipater; Artabazus, because I owe him a courtesy for his condolence letter, and because my last conversation with Alexander is bothering me; Leonidas; Lysimachus; and—after some thought, as an experiment—Arrhidaeus's morose nurse, Philes.

The next day I take Callisthenes down to the market with me. We wander through the stalls, inspecting fruit and fish hooks and leather goods and knives. I've already begun mapping out the conversation, a little—a symposium on theatre appeals to me, so Carolus won't feel in over his head, and Lysimachus can show off, harmlessly, and Artabazus will see we're cultured, and Antipater can have a night off from the wars, and young Philes can just sit gobsmacked and listen. And Leonidas; who knows what old Leonidas will do. Eat, maybe. At a gem stall, watched by a bulge-bodied mercenary hired to guard the place, I buy Pythias an agate the size and coral colour of her baby fingernail, engraved with a Heracles the size of an ant. She likes tiny things, rings and perfume bottles and trinkets she can keep in a carved sandalwood box I can hold in the palm of my hand, a gift from Hermias. A reaction against Macedonian ostentation, I suspect: lately, the tinier, the better. The slave trade is new to Pella, a small business still, catering to foreigners like me, and usually there isn't much on offer. Today, though, we're in luck: a new shipment is just in from Euboea. The slaver is genial, chatty, smelling profit and taking his ease in anticipation of it. He tells us about the journey, by ship, a rough one with much sickness but no lives lost. He's got some soldiers, Thracians, prisoners of war, good for farm work but with a look in their eye that says they'd take watching. He's got three young children, brothers and sister, he says, and what hard heart would separate them? They're each eating a piece of bread (a pretty show on the slaver's part), dirty but bright-eyed, the girl maybe three, the older boy eight or nine. What hard heart, indeed, though what a soft heart would do with them is a question I'm not interested in answering today. He asks us what we're looking for. A girl for my wife, I tell him. Housework, kitchen help, nothing too rough.

"I keep the girls back here." He leads us to a tent behind the pens. "Less trouble that way. Give me a minute and I'll bring them out."

"We could just go in. Spare you the trouble."

"I'll bring them out."

"Something in there," Callisthenes says once the slaver's inside.

He brings out five. "Go ahead," he says to me, and to the women, "Show the man your teeth."

They all smile tooth-baringly, and Callisthenes and I obediently examine them. One coughs when I ask to see her tongue. The front of her tunic is blood-speckled. I send her back in. The slaver watches without comment. I have them kneel, jump, touch toes, stretch their arms high. I send a wincer back inside.

"Likes them young," the slaver says to Callisthenes.

I do indeed like the youngest, who is also the tiniest, skinny-shanked, flat-chested, with unnaturally light, curly coppery hair, light green eyes, and milky skin speckled with brown across the nose. She's not an agate, though, and I'm not sure this kind of tiny prettiness would please my wife.

"What is your name?" I ask her in Macedonian, then Greek.

She says nothing.

"Celts," the slaver says. "I got them from a man who traded them for salt. He got them from a man who got them from their own people. Some squabble with the next village over, and theirs lost. Over who had the better goatskins to dress their wives in, no doubt. They're from the far north, the islands. Have you heard about those places? Animals, of course, but proud in their own way. The men are warriors and I've heard the women are too. Don't wash, don't shave, eat dog, healthy as horses and almost as tall. That's just the women. This one's not full-grown yet. Another year or two and she'll be a monster like the others. I had some men, too, but they went fast. Like oxen, wonderful for field work. Hair down to here." The slaver slaps his own ass. "The men, I mean. All reds, like that." He points at my tiny girl. "You know that's real, by the way? Pull it out and check it from the root if you don't believe me. A conversation piece for your neighbours, just for starters. Twelve, thirteen years, I put her at. Hard to say exactly with these people. You'd be her first owner. You can train her up just the way you want her."

Callisthenes nods at her foot, which is heavily bandaged.

"May I see?" I bend down. She glances at the slaver, but I don't need to unwrap it: the smell is of gangrene. How she jumped up and down on it is amazing. I send her back.

"Can't say I mind," the slaver says. "I might keep her myself. Doesn't speak a word other than gibberish. Bites. I adore her."

"You want that foot seen to. It might have to come off." My father would have offered to do the job himself. I still have his saws somewhere. Me, I don't even ask what happened. Am I the more worldly or was he? Two left: a tall one from the same village as the tiny girl, I'd guess, with the same rusty colouring and a more general, less attractive speckling of the skin—a rash, on closer inspection, peeling and bloody by the hairline—and an older one with a sullen face who looks me in the eye like that's her way of spitting.

"Can you cook?" I ask her.

"Hey fuck you." Her Greek is heavily accented but clear

enough. She's dark, not red, but I noticed her earlier muttering to one of the others. Either they share a language or she's out of her mind.

"What can you cook?"

"I cook poison for you. Your wife, your children. All dead by morning."

Her teeth are good; I sniff her breath while she's talking and there's no rot there. She's solid, solidly hipped, with a good colour in her skin. She stands with her feet braced, hands in loose fists. She looks me in the eye. I like her.

"You like everyone," Callisthenes says.

Her hair is shot through with grey and she's deeply tanned; I see the paler lines in the crinkles around her eyes. Happier days, once, maybe. "What's the story with this one?"

"I don't know why you bother asking," Callisthenes says afterwards, as we're walking home. "They only ever tell you what they think you want to hear. Did you see how happy he was to get rid of her?"

"You think I fell for it?"

The woman walks a few paces behind us. The slaver offered to rope her wrists for me to lead her like a horse, but I declined. If she runs, Callisthenes will catch her and then we'll all know where we stand.

"Maybe just a little bit," Callisthenes says.

"Hey fuck you," the woman says. "He got deal. I'm cook like how you say."

"She's cook like how you say." Callisthenes turns to the woman. "What was in the tent?"

She shrugs, makes a loose fist with one hand, and plugs a finger in and out of the hole with the other. "Customer."

"And where are you from?"

She says a name, a guttural I can't get my mouth around. She laughs when I try.

"Forest country?"

"Sea. Real sea. Cold, not like here."

"Somewhere up north," Callisthenes says helpfully.

"Far." She ignores him, looks at me, seeing I want to know. "You no go farther. You fall off edge."

"Of the land, or the sea?"

"Sea pour off edge to hell," she clarifies.

It's fun to watch Athea—that's her name—and Pythias take each other's measure.

"Thank you." Pythias's face lights with surprise.

"Hey fuck you," Athea says.

Sometimes I mistake Pythias for being frailer than she is.

"Don't speak to me so rudely," Pythias says. "We are kind to each other in this house. If you speak to me unkindly, your new master here will have to take you back to the market and I promise wherever you end up next won't be as congenial. Shall I show you the house and the kitchen, and where you will sleep? Are those your belongings?" She means a clinking lump of things Athea brought with her from the slaver's tent, tied up in a cloth that she dangles by the ears.

"Ah, ah, ah," Athea says. "Everyone so nice. All right. Maybe we are best friends by tonight, yes? Maybe everyone wake up tomorrow after all?" She winks at me.

"It will be better here," I say awkwardly, meaning better than wherever she was before, but she just waves a hand at me, dismissing me and my reassurances, and follows Pythias from the room.

Callisthenes makes his fingers into horns and pretends to clash them together.

"She's awful," Pythias says that evening, after supper.

We're sitting in the courtyard while the slaves tidy up around us and dusk falls. One of our last out-of-doors meals; it's fall now, cooling fast, the sunlight a thinner gold. Paler colours everywhere, paler pink at sunrise, green slowly leaching from the trees, in this last serving of hospitable days. The rains are on their way. The smell of smoke and burning everywhere now. We're alone now, but can hear them in the kitchen, the clatter of their work and their voices, talking and occasionally laughing. Pythias seems content. Her cheeks are rosy, perhaps from the wine.

"She made one of the girls cry just by staring at her. She told me my house was filthy and Macedonians are animals. I told her we weren't Macedonian."

"And she said?"

Pythias has drunk more than usual, actually, or she would never say what she says next: "She said she could cure our problem."

She's blushing, and I assume none of this is very serious. "What problem is that?"

"She showed me what she had in that bag. Some stones, some bones, some dried herbs. She's a kind of witch, or thinks she is. She says she's helped people like us before."

"That's what we got her for." I'm assuming she'll come out with it eventually, our problem as diagnosed by Athea the snarly witch.

"Tomorrow I'm going to have her start on the big room. You'll have the dinner there, I'm assuming. We still have barrels and crates and things in there from when we moved. We'll have to find somewhere else for all that. The floor will need scouring, and the walls, and the ceiling. Have you ever really looked at the ceilings in here? Black, all black from the lamps. I don't think they've been cleaned ever."

"Stones and bones and herbs?"

"You bought a witch," she says, and giggles.

"The slaver told me she was a Scythian healer. He said her village exiled her when a child she had been caring for died. She was walking to the next village, hoping to go to some family there, when she was picked up by an army. She didn't know which, didn't speak their language. When they were defeated, she was sold off with the other prisoners of war. He said she was next employed in the house of a wealthy man in Byzantium as a cook, but she tried to run away and so he sold her to the slaver. He said he'd refused a couple of times already to sell her because the buyers wanted her to work in the fields, and he knew she had more skills than that."

A failed healer: Callisthenes saw it right away. Pythias may or may not, I can't tell. Sometimes I think she knows all of my weak spots, sometimes none.

"That starts out right," Pythias says. "The child was brought to her too late, she says. There was nothing she could do, but they blamed her anyway. They made her leave her family behind, her own children. She doesn't know who got them. She scavenged for the army until they were wiped out, and spent a month in the slave market before she was bought. The wealthy man was a miser who bought old meat for the household because it was cheap, and when they all got sick after she cooked a meal for them she got a reputation as a poisoner. They took her back to the market and sold her to the man you bought her from. She said he made his living travelling, selling cheap goods cheap. He never refused anyone. He'd be gone before the buyer could realize they'd bought dregs. I doubt he kept her for soft work. She said he told her if he didn't sell her in Pella, he'd kill her rather than have to feed her another day. She said she was getting ready to die when you showed up."

"The family got sick, or died?" I ask.

"She says her training was as a midwife. They never should have brought the child to her in the first place, it needed a doctor, but there was no doctor. She had no idea what to do for it. She says she told the rich man's wife the meat was no good and the woman beat her. She says I should eat more fruit, and you shouldn't take any hot baths, and we should pay attention to the cycles of the moon."

"She told you a lot for the first day. Do you want to eat more fruit?"

Night now, and I waved the lamps away some time ago. We're sitting in darkness while the slaves wait for us to finish so they can clean up after us and get to bed themselves.

"I like fruit," she says.

I can't see her face.

I send her to bed and sit a while longer on my own. It's Athea herself who comes over to clear our last dishes and wine cups. I wonder if she's been listening, though we've kept our voices low. A witch, so.

"All right?" I ask.

"Go to bed."

I tell her to take a lamp to my library. I want to sit up and work for a while.

"Go to bed, you."

I tell her to take a lamp to my library.

"What you work on?"

"Tragedy," I say.

"Hey fuck you. You don't want tell me, I'm nothing, don't tell me. Your wife tell me other day, maybe. She like to talk."

My wife likes to talk? "Goodness. The good life. What it means to live a good life, and the ways in which that goodness can be lost."

I wait for her to laugh, or say something sarcastic, or tell me to fuck myself again, but she is only silent. Then she says, "I give garlic your wife, okay?"

"I don't know. Is it okay? What does she need garlic for?"

"You are not doctor?" She looks proud of herself, like she's trumped me with this piece of information she thinks she's ferreted out from somewhere. "You know what for. I am surprise you not try this yourself. Shy, maybe. Is okay. I explain to her."

"Explain it to me."

She studies me, assessing whether I'm being disingenuous or genuinely don't know what she's talking about. Apparently I pass. "Some doctor," she says, not displeased. "Your wife she stick the garlic up. In the morning, smell her breath."

This is what I thought. "Up where?"

"Up." She shoves a hand at her crotch. "Where you fuck. Put the garlic there. One clove only, is enough. If her breath smell, passages are open. If not, no baby for you."

"I've heard of this. With onion, though."

She waves this away. "No, no, no. Garlic. Stronger. Fit better also."

"And if the passages are closed?" I feel like my father. "I suppose you have a charm to open them?"

"I don't know charm. We try this first, then we see."

"Athea," I say. "Listen to me. My wife is right: we are kind to one another in this house. But you have only been here one day. There is no 'we.' We have not retained your services. We do not have any kind of problem that concerns you. You will not mention this or anything like this to my wife. No garlic. No charms. If you speak of this again, I will take you back to the market. My wife was right about that also."

"Is stupid." She shrugs.

"Probably. Now go and do what you're told."

She does indeed cook like how you say. Supper this night was a bean soup, bread, cheese, olives, fish, a spread of colourful little saucers we emptied and stacked in a teetering pile, licking our fingers as we went.

"These are ours?" I asked Pythias, of the saucers.

"Athea found them in one of the crates. She asked if she could use them."

The soup was thick with greenery, herbs and some kind of tender, deep green leaf that withered in the liquid but kept its jewelled colour. She'd found a marrow bone for it too. The bread was gritless and still warm, the round white cheese pressed with walnuts in a flower pattern, the sardines intact but magically boneless. The witch has knife skills worthy of my surgeon father.

"I've read this already," Alexander says.

We're in Mieza, in the kitchen, seated beside each other in front of the hearth. Not where I'd prefer to be sharing books, but he's lately pulled something in his leg in games and has been told to sweat the muscle until he can run on it again. He sits with his heel propped on the bar where the pots hang, my Homer in his lap. I'm anxious for the book—embers, smuts—but so far he's shielding it nicely, taking care. It's sweet to see.

"I know you have," I say. "You are Achilles, your father is Peleus. Hephaestion would be your Patroclus, yes? Who's your Odysseus?"

"Ptolemy. He's clever."

He glances automatically toward the door at the sound of bark-shouts from outside. I have him alone today; his companions are out doing drills as the leaves crisp and drift from the trees in the high fall air. He's annoyed not to be with them. Hell, he's annoyed not to be in Thrace with his father, deposing kings, founding cities.

"Do I have to go through it again?" he says.

"You've read it with Lysimachus. You haven't read it with me."

He starts to say something, then stops. I wonder if Lysimachus has got his ear pressed to the door even now. "Let's talk about book one, the argument," I say. "Can you summarize it for me?" We'll see if the prince considers this an exercise of memory or attention.

"Nine years into the Trojan War." He's still staring at the window. "Agamemnon has been allotted a girl, Chryseis, as a battle-prize. Her father, a priest of Apollo, offers a generous ransom for her return, which Agamemnon refuses. Apollo comes down like the nightfall—" Here he hesitates, leaving a little space for me to admire him; exercise of memory, then; I say nothing. "And besieges the troops until Agamemnon is forced to relent. But since he must give up his own prize, he requires Achilles to hand over *his* girl Briseis. Achilles, feeling the injustice of this, refuses to fight until she is returned to him."

"Very good. And the squabbling ensues for the next twenty-three books."

Now he looks at me.

" 'Briseis of the lovely cheeks.' Do you suppose Achilles is in love with her? Or is his honour slighted? Or is he petty and pompous and rather full of himself?" I ask.

"Why not all of the above?" He shifts his leg on the bar, winces. "I've noticed something about you, Priam. You don't mind if I call you Priam? You remind me of him, the sad old king who doesn't fight and has to beg for his own son's shreds so he can give him a proper burial after he's been defeated. I've noticed you like to say, On the one hand"—he holds out an open hand—"on the other hand"—he holds out the other hand—"and then what we're look-ing for is some conflation of the two." He brings his hands together. "Don't you ever worry about being too tidy?"

"I don't *worry* about it. Isn't tidiness a virtue?"

"A woman's virtue."

"A soldier's, too. Tidiness is another name for discipline. Let me put it this way. Do you think the story is a comedy or a tragedy?"

He holds out both hands again, juggling them up and down.

"Well, it has to be one or the other, doesn't it?" I say.

He shrugs.

"You didn't enjoy it at all?"

"Finally," he says. "Finally, a question where you haven't already planned the answer. I liked some of it. I liked the battles. I like Achilles. I wish I were taller."

"Men regress. It's a rule of nature. In Achilles's time, men were taller and stronger. Every generation shrinks back a little from greatness. We're just shadows of our ancestors."

He nods.

"You could read it as a comedy: the squabbling gods, the squabbling kings. The warriors running around whapping each other upside the head for nine years. Nine years! The farcical showdown between Paris and Menelaus. The trope of mistaken identity when Patroclus masquerades as Achilles. These are the elements of comedy, aren't they?"

"I laughed all the way through," he says.

"I know you have a sense of humour." I'm going to allude to Carolus's production of Euripides, to the head, but he's looking at me so brightly and expectantly, now, waiting for praise, that I falter. Such a needy little monster cub. Shall I continue to pose him riddles to make him a brighter monster, or shall I make him human?

"I've been working on a little treatise on literature, the literary arts. Tragedy, comedy, epic. Because I've been wondering, what's the point? What is the point of it all? Why not simply relate such history as has come down to us in a sober manner, not pretending to fill in the gaps?"

He hikes his leg down from the bar and massages the muscle for a moment. "I've been reading something. I brought it from the palace library. Wait."

He limps off, to his room I guess. Except he doesn't limp, though he must want to. He takes care to disguise the injury and walk evenly. A leader must never reveal weakness in battle, in case he demoralize his troops and encourage the enemy. Something he figured out for himself, or had to be taught? Something a king would teach a king; I hope it comes from Philip.

He's back, breathless. He ran on it once he was out of the room. The book he wants to show me is one I know well, one of my old master's, where he rails against the depraved influence of the arts on decent society.

"Only, you know, he can't mean what he says." Alexander sits again. "Because he uses theatre to convey his arguments, doesn't he? A pretend dialogue between pretend people, with a setting and so on. He needs the artifice for something, doesn't he?"

"Exactly. That's exactly right."

"To get the reader's attention. It's more fun to read than a dry treatise."

"It is that." I think of my own early attempts at the dialogue form. I had no gift for it, and gave it up. "Then, too, I think, you feel more when it's set up that way. You care more about the characters, about the outcomes of things. That's the point of the literary arts, surely. You can convey ideas in an accessible way, and in a way that makes the reader or the viewer feel what is being told rather than just hear it."

"Agreed." He's mocking me, but nicely.

"I too have been reading a book, wondering if it might interest you."

"It interests me."

I hand it to him.

"Small," he says.

"An afternoon's read at most. I hope it will amuse you. It's by the same author. The setting is a dinner party."

"Majesty, Master." An attendant in the doorway looks stricken. "A visitor."

"Go away," Alexander says.

"Don't tell me to go away, you miserable little brat."

Olympias brushes past the attendant, who jumps away from her as though scalded. "Kiss your mother." Olympias herself, all in white furs, silver stars in her hair, bringing in a fragrant cold breath of the outside.

Alexander looks at her but doesn't get up. She bends to him and presses her cheek to his.

"Lovely warm boy. I wrote you I was coming. Don't you read my letters? Don't lie to me. I know perfectly well no one was expecting me. That attendant looked like he'd seen a ghost. Hello, sir," she adds, to me. "What's the lesson?"

"Majesty, Homer. What an unexpected—"

"Not to me," Alexander says. "I've been waiting and waiting."

"Sweet." She helps herself to a chair and pulls it up to the hearth to make a threesome. "Well, sit down," she says to me. "Go on. I won't interrupt."

"Yes, you will," Alexander says.

"May I ask to what we owe this—"

"You owe it to her majesty being bored out of her mind in Pella and missing her baby boy. I see little enough of him, and then that animal of a husband of mine sends him out here. Dionysus himself blew on my little pony's heels to speed my way. No, actually I left all the servants outside. There's rather a lot of us, and then quite a bit of luggage." Her eyes drift up to the ceiling, perhaps the original of her son's mannerism. "I brought food," she murmurs.

"I love you," Alexander says.

"You had better. No one else does. Do you hear from your father?"

"You're not allowed to ask me that, remember?"

She rolls her eyes. He rolls his, mocking her. The whole performance is shocking: the anger, the meanness, the grotesque intimacy, their willingness to do it for an audience, me.

"Run away, now," mother says to son, as though reading my mind. "I want a private moment with your tutor. Go get them to fix me a room for the night."

He goes, taking all three books with him.

"We really did bring food. Rabbits and cakes and things. I'll be terribly popular with the boys for an hour and a half. What a horrible place."

"Yes," I say.

"How's he doing?"

"I think he's bored."

"Yes." She glances at the ceiling again. "Aren't we all. You will develop the existing faculties, though, I suppose?"

"Of course."

"*Of course.*" She makes an ugly mouth, imitating me. "Does everyone hate me? We're not talking about Arrhidaeus. We're talking about my son. *My* son. The hell I will have to pay, when I get back, for coming out here without permission, just for a glimpse of my baby. Into the dispatches it will go: Olympias rode a horse. Lock her up! You know they'll do that. They'll lock me in my rooms. They've done it before. Last time it was for a month, because I went down to the parade ground to watch him drill. I just wanted to look at him, up on that great beast of his. I wore a veil but they knew it was me. They always know. Can't think how."

"Why did you come, Majesty?"

"I needed to see him. That animal thinks he can keep me in a box. He—"

"Mother." Alexander's in the doorway. "Why don't I give you my room? I can share with Hephaestion."

Olympias takes a swipe at her eyes with the hem of her cloak. "I would love that. Did I tell you I brought food? Rabbits and cakes and things?" She starts to cry. "Do you think they'll let me stay this time? Just for one night?"

"This time?"

"She tried last month," Alexander says. "Antipater caught up to her an hour out of Mieza. Why don't you go lie down now, Mother? In case you have to ride again tonight."

"You'll sit with me, though?" she says.

Noises from outside: a warning bell, men shouting. Olympias begins to rock back and forth, hugging herself and weeping.

"Go," I say. "I'll delay Antipater. An hour, anyway. Both of you, go."

Alexander leads the way, allowing himself to limp heavily now.

"You're hurt," Olympias says. "Oh, lean on me."

He takes her arm and they hobble out. Exit royalty.

THE TABLES HAVE BEEN CLEARED and the door propped open for a bit of air. The first pretty days of fall are long gone now, and raindrops bluster in on sweeps of wind to darken the stoop. The rain is socked in, and each day is colder than the one before. Fall is blurring, smudging into winter. The musicians, a couple of flautists, are finished for the evening, and are being fed their pay in the kitchen. Pythias stood at the door with me in her new dress, welcoming each guest as he arrived, and then disappeared. Only I am still aware of her presence, in the polish on the floor, the trim of the lamps, the twining flowers on the lintels, the plump new cushions on the couches, the delicacy and thought in the succession of dishes. She's spent a lot of my money tonight, in her quiet way. I've put Carolus next to me and the others in careful order after him, with Callisthenes last; I've had a word with him, and he understands it's not a slight. After a bit of a shaky start, it seems to be working, though Carolus has contributed only monosyllables so far and coughs repeatedly into his sleeve. At first I thought he was embarrassed, but I wonder now if he's unwell. He drinks without eating and follows the conversation doggedly but with dead eyes. Antipater and Artabazus have already clashed swords over the king's foreign policy and his plans for Persia; Philes and Callisthenes whispered for a while between themselves like schoolboys at their first grown-up table. Leonidas jumped in to spar with Artabazus, though, and soon everyone was laughing. Not a talent I would have attributed to Leonidas; I'm enjoying myself, learning things, already. Lysimachus has simply failed to appear.

Here come the slaves with cups of wine and bowls of water. The formal part of the evening, my favourite part, starts now.

"No jugglers?" Antipater says drily. "No girls?"

Not tonight. The slaves bring each guest a cup and we sip the wine unmixed in the ritual gesture to honour the good demon. A hymn to Dionysus and then I order the wine to be mixed with the water. "Two to five?" I ask, for form's sake. The standard ratio; I don't wait for my guests' assent. Three large bowls are mixed and I hold up a cup of moderate size, again for ritual approval. At the Academy there would be nods all around; here my guests just stare at me. The cups (new, Pythias again) are distributed and the wine is poured, the slaves proceeding around the room in a circle, beginning with Carolus, ending with Callisthenes, who sits on the other side of the doorway from me.

Dessert is brought in on more trays: cheeses, cakes, dried figs and dates, melons and almonds, as well as tiny dishes of spiced salt are placed within everyone's reach. It's all been mounded into neat pyramids, even the salt, and I can't help but look for the shape of my wife's fingers in the slopes of these dainties. I hate to bring down such painstaking architecture with the yen for a spicy nut. I'm reaching for the more stable brickwork of a pile of dates instead, preparing my opening words, when Callisthenes calls, "Uncle?"

"Nephew?" I say.

"Do you love me, Uncle?"

"Why, what have you done?"

Laughter. "Only you have to excuse me, tonight," he says. "Everyone has to excuse me. I just can't do it."

"Do what?" Antipater asks.

"The talk," Callisthenes says. "The talk, the speech. I've drunk too much and I just don't think I can put the words together. Forgive me? I'll just retreat, maybe—" He waves a vague hand toward the door.

He's performed his little part very well. This way, anyone else who doesn't want to speak—Leonidas I was thinking of, primarily—can opt out with Callisthenes, save face, and eat sweets in the next room. I've thought of everything.

"Speeches?" Antipater says. "I thought that was a joke."

"I didn't understand that part at all," Artabazus says. "I thought it was because I'm an ignorant foreigner."

"But it was in the invitations." Antipater, Artabazus, and

Leonidas are already on their feet, going after Callisthenes. " 'Tragedy,' " I say, raising my voice over the noise of their leaving, repeating the words in the invitation. " 'The good life. What it means to live a good life, and the ways in which that goodness can be lost.' "

"Shut up," Carolus says. Only he and Philes are left. "They don't know how to do that here. You're embarrassing them."

I look at Philes, who looks desperately at Carolus.

"The boy's going to pee himself if you try to make him talk," Carolus says. "You have to let it go."

It occurs to me that the only person I can think of who would have enjoyed the evening just as I planned it, who genuinely would have tried to do his part, is Alexander.

"How's the book coming?" Carolus says. "Your tragedy for beginners."

"Comedy too. I've decided I need to treat both."

There's noise from an outer room, a raised voice, laughter, and then Tycho murmuring in my ear: "Lysimachus, Master—"

"Lysimachus," I say, because never mind announcements, he's in the doorway, showing himself in.

My other guests trail back in behind him, retake their places, assuming—correctly—that the formal part of the dinner is well and truly buried. Well, I was the one who wanted a student dinner. Who am I to stand on ceremony?

"Here you are," he says. "Who lives next door? I sort of went there first. Scared the women, I think. They said you were all over here. Got the houses mixed up. Sorry, sorry. Flowers for the women. I'll send them in the morning. Like flowers, yes? Any special colour? Oh, that's kind." Callisthenes has slid over on his couch, making room. Lysimachus sits heavily and looks around. "Very nice, very nice." He's laughing at me again; he's drunk.

"Will you eat? I'll have them get you a plate from the kitchen."

"I'll drink, if you're offering. Got to keep the levels constant. A sudden dip in the levels and then who knows. Already scared the women. No women here."

"No," I say.

"That's what I thought. Boys? He likes boys."

Everyone looks at me.

"One boy especially," Lysimachus says. "Well, nothing wrong with that. We've all been there. Excellent taste in all things, always. A bit hopeless in this case, though."

I tell Tycho to bring him a plate of food.

"Dotes on him," Lysimachus continues. "Poor bastard. You should have seen them at Mieza, when he thought they were alone. I know, I know, I wasn't supposed to be there. But if the prince wishes it—"

"I thought I'd seen you, once or twice," I say. "You didn't have to hide from me."

"Besotted with him," Lysimachus says. "Oh, gods, that gives him a thrill. Look at him. Just an animal like the rest of us, after all. Don't worry, I haven't told anyone who'd care."

"Don't threaten me," I say. "Eat your food."

He takes the plate from Tycho. "Goat!" He laughs and starts to eat.

I'm aware of my guests watching me.

"I'd fuck him," Lysimachus says, mouth full. "He smells so nice. Been there yet?"

It's Antipater I'm most aware of. "That's enough," I say.

"All creamy and tight and miserably confused," Lysimachus says. "I'd fuck him senseless."

"We're not talking about anyone I know," Antipater says.

Then everyone is leaving. I walk them into the street.

"I'm drunk," Lysimachus says loudly to Antipater, to me. "I didn't mean anything by it. Anyway, you're old enough to be his father."

"I am," I say.

We look at each other.

"You're not his father, though," he says, more quietly.

"I know that."

"I love him," he says, so only I will hear.

I nod.

"Maybe you could—" he begins, but Artabazus is at his elbow, smiling and bowing his thanks to me, leading him gently away.

"I know where he lives, not far from me," Artabazus says. "We will go together, and so. I thank you many thousands of times."

"And I you," I say, meaning Lysimachus.

He nods, knows.

Antipater is waiting by the door, shaking his head.

"I guess you heard all that," I say.

"Not a fucking thing. I only hear what I can put in dispatches."

"What about Olympias?"

Antipater shakes his head again. He gave me the hour I asked for in Mieza, two weeks ago, but made it clear he was giving it to me, not to her. "Devoted tutors are one thing, meddling queens are another. She's in seclusion for a while."

Back inside, after those brief breaths of sharp street air, the atmosphere is close, still thick with food and wine. I pour myself a last cup and take it in to see Pythias in our room. She's waiting up for me, dozing over her needlework by a table full of candles to give her enough light. She starts awake when she senses me standing near. "Scared me."

"What are you making?"

She holds it up to show me: a bit of elaborate embroidery, a landscape crawling with tiny figures all in pink and red. It's pretty.

I sit on the bed while she puts her work aside and blows out most of the candles. I tell her about the evening, about how everyone praised the food and how Lysimachus was more or less the pest I'd thought he might be, and how Antipater gave his best to her specially, and how lovely the house looked and how it had been like having her in the room with me, looking every way and seeing her work there.

"And what did you talk about?" She knows that's the main thing.

I close my eyes to imagine each of them going home. Antipater, stumbling by the end—bored, I suppose, and so drinking more than usual, or maybe that is usual for him—I don't know him very well—has the palace to go to, to a wife Pythias is cordial with and has sewn with once or twice (older than us, she has told me, a bit stern and formal, which Pythias can manage very well; she'll end up that way herself, probably. Rude to the servants, which Pythias doesn't like, but modest in her clothing and her gossip, as suits a woman of her position, of which Pythias approves). I wonder if she warms the bed for him, or if they use separate rooms. Artabazus the bachelor won't sleep alone. I don't quite know how I know this, but I'd bet on it. He lives in a grand house near the courts, the kind Pythias and Callisthenes find so painful, too big for one man and sumptuously decorated. He might as well swag money around it, Callisthenes has said. I indulge in a little fantasy of him stopping off for a boy and a girl to warm his bed, and that after a night of debauchery he'll wake in the morning fresh as a lamb, pink-faced and bright-eyed, eager for his breakfast and the subtle business of the day. Lysimachus, too, will return to his house, though no doubt he'll bid Artabazus a cheerful but firm good night and choose to walk by himself. Leonidas will walk with Antipater to the palace. Carolus I sent home on the arm of a slave; I've never seen where he lives but understand it's in a poorer district, probably a hut like Illaeus's. Cozy, I hope. Callisthenes took Philes by the arm and has probably led him off to find someplace to drink and keep talking. They'll solve everything I've spent my life on in the next hour or so, I'm fully confident.

"Love," I say. "We talked about love."

Pythias takes the wine cup from me so I won't spill it. "Lie down."

She starts rubbing my feet. She works her thumb up from the heel to the tender arch and kneads a long time under the balls of my toes. After a while she gets up and I wonder if she's left me; I'm too lazy, my head too full of fumes, to open my eyes and see. But then I feel her weight on the bed again beside my knees and hear the click of clay on clay, a vessel on a plate. She rubs her hands together to warm whatever it is and then she's rubbing my feet again with something slick, some oil. Something of hers: the scent is pretty, not any oil from the kitchen. I roll onto my front so she can work her way up my legs. I'll smell pretty too in the morning, and will need a bath to get rid of it. I widen my legs a little when she reaches my thighs. Maybe she'll let me return the favour, though I doubt it. This is a pure gift. When I feel her little nails on my buttocks I have to turn over, but she continues just as slowly and methodically, hips, chest, shoulders, arms, hands, even palms and fingers, each anointed to its end. Some ritual she needs, maybe. I want to tell her she's making a meal out of a cracker and we could be finished in a minute if she put her mind to it, but she can surely see that. I let her do it her way this once. She drapes her dress over my face. A flicker of this, a flicker of that through the gauzy cloth: a few bright points of candles, the misty moving shape of her above me, and something coming she doesn't want me to see. I reach out but she puts my hands back on the bed and holds them there while she rubs her breasts up and down my chest. My face briefly smothered. A poised moment between offerings, and then she sets her weight on me, hips on mine, easing down. It's not an easy penetration, involving much flexing and adjusting on her part, fingers spreading her dry pink self open, trying to complete the fit, and then she moves too slowly, rocking a little, not knowing what to do. I take her hips and try to move her the way I want but she sucks her breath in, a sharp hiss of disapproval, or perhaps pain. A moment of stillness and then she tries again, the frustrating, tentative rocking that chafes not nearly enough. I take the cloth off my face so I can at least look at her, and she stops again.

"This isn't working," she says.

"It's fine." The candlelight is flattering and she's as pretty as she'll ever be, with her hair hanging down over her shoulders and tendrils licking at her breasts. I reach for them, small, almond-tipped, and she lets me. She looks determined, just short of grim. I decide not to look at her face.

"Harder," I tell her. "Like grinding meal."

It comes out more sternly than I mean, but I decide it's a game I could like. "Fuck me, for once." Saying the words aloud instead of thinking them becomes entwined with the pleasure coming, but incredibly she stops a third time and gets off me. "What?"

"We have to finish normally, for it to take."

Normally. She wants to lie on her back, but I don't let her. We finish with her face down, taking it hard, her two hands pinned by my one. I come like a monster. When I get off her, she rolls onto her back and pulls her knees up neatly and stays like that for a long time. She might be crying. My wife's taken lessons from a witch.

This is the best sex we will ever have.

My father explained to me once that human male sperm was a potent distillation of all the fluids in the body, and that when those fluids became warm and agitated they produced foam, just as in cooking or sea water. The fluid or foam passes from the brain into the spine, and from there through the veins along the kidneys, then via the testicles into the penis. In the womb, the secretion of the man and the secretion of the woman are mixed together, though the man experiences pleasure in the process and the woman does not. Even so, it is healthy for a woman to have regular intercourse, to keep the womb moist, and to warm the blood.

I FALL SICK, my old usual. It encroaches slowly, as it always does, slowly enough that I can persuade myself it's nothing this time, only fatigue, only tension from the palace preventing my sleep, hurting my head, nibbling at my memory, sucking colour from the sky and warmth from the world. I grow short-tempered, snapping at the slaves, who remain impassive. I suppose they've seen it before, and anyway it's nothing this time, just fatigue, just tension.

"It's this miserable climate," Pythias says. "Always raining, always dark. I feel it myself, sometimes."

"What is it you feel?" The impatience that makes me bark at the slaves makes me over-formal, over-polite, and wilfully obtuse with her. I don't need to be told I have a woman's problem, and I above all don't need Athea sniffing round me after a few dropped words from her lady, lecturing, prescribing, curing for all I know, and gaining strength from my weakness thereby.

"Tired," Pythias says. "Sad. Soft, sort of, in my thinking. I forget things, can't summon the energy to do all the things I would normally do in a day."

"I feel better already. To have a partner in suffering. My books go unwritten, your sewing goes undone. What a consolation to me, to know I am not alone."

"Don't be nasty," she says.

"Love." I repent immediately, but she's already out of the room. Still, I can't accept that what afflicts me is not somehow unique, a disorder with no previous name. Long ago my father diagnosed in me an excess of black bile, which is true enough some of the time, but does not account for the other times, when I simply don't need sleep, and the books seem to write themselves, and the world seems painted into every last corner with colour and sweetness, a kind of glowing, divine infusion. Nor, again, does it account for the whiplashing from the one condition to the next, from black melancholy to golden joy. Though melancholy has always been the more predominant of the two states, and has become increasingly so as I've grown older. Perhaps one day I'll cease to have moods, as my mother long ago called them, altogether, and will simply settle into a constant state of bitterness and misery, a pain not physical but no less a burden for that.

Philip is home from Thrace after an absence of some eighteen months; not the happiest homecoming, and he'll be heading back again in a week or two with his replacement troops, leaving behind some of his longest-serving units for a well-earned winter at home. At court we hear the details. The cities of Perinthus and Byzantium, probably goaded on by Athens, refused to assist Philip's efforts in Eastern Thrace. While the Athenians sharked their navy up and down the coast, Philip went after Perinthus. Built on a long, narrow headland, the city was difficult to attack by land, and Philip's navy was weak. Siege, then, and a chance to try out the shiny new Macedonian torsion and arrow-shooting catapults. The catapult attacks were conducted in relay, day and night. They used battering-rams; they had sappers to tunnel under the city walls and scaling ladders to get over them; they built towers the height of fifteen men to let them shoot down on the enemy, over the walls. When the wall was finally breached, Philip's troops poured in, only to discover a second wall the Perintheans had been building while the Macedonians pecked and poked and wormed and beetled away at the first.

The siege began again on the second wall. Behind it were tiers of houses accessible only by narrow, steep streets, easy to plug. The Perintheans throughout the siege received money, arms, and corn from Byzantium and several Persian satrapies. The Athenian navy hung back and watched. Philip, foreseeing a nasty fight, suddenly withdrew half his forces and rushed to Byzantium, short-handed now because of its support of Perinthus. But somehow that city, too, escaped a quick defeat.

Philip, in a second surprise attack, took the Athenian corn fleet, then on its way back from the Black Sea, heading through the Bosporus. A success to enrich the Macedonian treasury and boost the army's morale; open war now, incidentally, with Athens, though hostilities did not erupt immediately. Now the siege of Byzantium began in earnest, and lasted most of the fall and winter and into the following spring. Again the siege-train came out; again the city, backed by its allies in the region and Athens openly now, resisted. Then the Macedonian navy took its first hard hit from the Athenian navy, and finally Philip had to cut his losses and withdraw.

"Am I boring you?" Philip says.

I snap to. When I woke this morning I wept to realize I was awake and had a whole day to get through. Pythias woke too but pretended not to while I wiped my eyes. My tears must bore her, at least sometimes.

"No. I was considering the problem."

Thrace something, Alexander something, I could weep again for the stupidity of all of it. Should he take Alexander to Thrace? Was that the problem? Truly, I have no idea what he was asking.

"May I offer a suggestion?" Lysimachus jumps in.

I'm grateful, and give him a look that says so. He's a scholar, after all; maybe he suffers something similar. Maybe he recognizes it and is helping me. A kindness returned, for the invitation to dinner.

"May you fucking the fuck get on with it?" Philip says. "Can't any of you just get a sentence out?"

"Leave him here," Lysimachus says. "He's in the best of hands, and at a delicate age too, when the metal is just hardening, if you see what I mean. Don't want to muck with the tempering."

"Eh?" Philip says.

"My esteemed colleague here has been a wonderful influence." Lysimachus bows to me. "A wonderful influence. I've never seen such an influence on a boy. I've never seen a teacher have such an impact on a student. I look at them together sometimes, their heads bent together over something, and it's hard to believe they're not father and son. Modelled so finely after the great one's mind, if you see what I mean. I'm not sure anyone apart from me has quite realized how close they've become. Rip him away now and he'll bear the wound for the rest of his life. The mind is just ripening. What's more important than the mind?"

Philip looks at me. I look at Antipater. Antipater shakes his head, minimally.

"He very much wants to see the world," I say.

Philip looks at me.

"He's the brightest student I've ever had."

Philip looks at me.

"I'm unwell. Will you excuse me?"

I leave the court with Lysimachus's dagger sticking from the small of my back.

TEN DAYS LATER, I'm told by an attendant to gather my things: Mieza is done. Alexander is required back at court; his military training has been neglected; we are at war with Athens; he is enough of a philosopher for now. Lysimachus's dagger, in to the hilt, though Philip has returned to Thrace without his son after all. The prince will be disappointed. Abruptly the boys are gone and we old men, their retinue, linger in the slow business of packing, myself especially, two years' worth of books and specimens and manuscripts, while the temple attendants watch impassively as ever. We are a storm that has finally passed from their lives. I am told I will continue to attend the prince in Pella, but less intensively, less often, as other duties encroach on their studies.

Pythias welcomes me with an expensive meal and later a shy fuck in my own bed, an echo of our last coupling, an unexpected pleasure I feel even in the soles of my feet. I am home.

I ATTEND THE TEMPLE of Dionysus at Pythias's request, to thank the god for her pregnancy. I give the attendant money for a pure white lamb.

"The god is pleased," the attendant says.

It's an expensive choice—these things get around—and I decide to enjoy it a little, the luxury of it. A slice across the throat, blood caught darkly in bronze bowls, and then a bit of amateur butchering to release some thigh meat from the animal's sinews to throw on the fire. An attendant makes off with the rest of the carcass. Lucky attendants today, lucky tummies.

I'm washing up when I see Philes kneeling before a slightly larger than life-size statue of the god. It's a lovely piece in white marble. The god's long curls are twined with ivy. The torso is muscular but sleek, the hips narrow, the legs strong, the feet bare. The face shows restrained amusement, not what you might first associate with the god, and always suiting my mood when I have to come here. The nurse is praying fiercely, eyes closed, rocking a little, tears running down his cheeks.

"Hello," Arrhidaeus says.

"What are you doing?" He holds up his tablet for me to see. "No, tell me," I say. "Use your words."

"Drawing."

I have more time for him now that his younger brother is occupied elsewhere. I look at what he wants to show me, something like a face: a circle, anyway, with eyes and a line for a nose, a swirl of hair, and another line for a mouth.

"He needs ears."

Arrhidaeus dutifully frowns over the task, and soon the circle has smaller circles appended to its sides.

"Does he have a name?"

The prince laughs and won't tell me.

"Can you write it?"

"No," he says confidently.

I take him through the alpha-beta-gamma, which he recites fluently now. "What letter does it start with?"

"Horse," he says. So we talk about the ways to draw a horse, the parts a person would need: body, muzzle, legs, mane, tail.

"I would draw an oval for the body, rather than a circle." I look over his shoulder. "Like an egg. Where is your nurse today?"

"Take a bath."

Philes has been friendlier since the invitation to supper. He could hardly be otherwise, but I feel myself changing toward him too, softening. I have a little plan for him, a little idea I want to test. Not today or tomorrow but soon, I anticipate.

I tell Arrhidaeus to fetch his lyre and he frowns harder in

concentration over his drawing, pretending not to have heard. His body is cleaner and stronger; his language is improving and so is his dexterity—hence the drawing, which I've long encouraged him toward—but he seems, distressingly, to hate music. Who hates music? He's clumsy, of course, and can't fit his thick fingers to the simplest positions on the instrument from one week to the next, which is forgivable, but my persistence seems to infect his reaction to all music, and he flinches away if I strum the lyre myself or even if he should hear someone singing in passing. Hates what he cannot master: there's a lesson there, I suppose, though I wish a sweet melody would make him smile and relax and that could be the end of it.

"Is it necessary?" Philes asked at a previous session, with Arrhidaeus cowering in a corner in snotty tears, the instrument flung down and cracked on the stone floor. "He can't even clap a steady beat, and he sings like a cow calving."

"So do I," I said, but I liked something the nurse had said. "Come for a walk with me, both of you."

Their preparations were painfully slow, as always, but when we were finally outside I asked the nurse to clap his hands in rhythm with his steps. I did the same. Arrhidaeus ignored us. He'd become a canny animal, knowing when a lesson was coming, and this was how he resisted. I took his hand and beat it against my own in time with our steps. He allowed this.

"Begin there," I told the nurse. "We'll come back to the instrument later, as you suggest." I'd found by then that treating the nurse as a peer, pretending my ideas came from him, warmed him until he became buttery and would do whatever I asked. Soon he had Arrhidaeus clapping well, something we practised on horseback also, but our music lessons had stalled there. Nevertheless.

"That is enough drawing, Arrhidaeus," I tell him today. "We play music now."

"No."

I try to take the tablet from his hands but he fights me. He stands up and shoves me, and I lose my balance and fall on my ass, at which point of course Philes returns. He stands in the doorway, his hair still oily-damp from the baths, surveying our wretched little scene.

"Help me up, please, Arrhidaeus," I say. "I think that was an accident, wasn't it?"

He gives me his hand, pleased, and yanks on my arm about as forcefully as he pushed me down. Warrior stock, I remind myself, and it was I myself who suggested he be trained at the gymnasium.

"What happened?" Philes is all womanish concern, advancing into the room. "You're not hurt?" He hovers close, plays at straightening my clothes and brushing me off, while I shrug away, fluttering my hands like a man beset by bugs.

Arrhidaeus picks up the lyre as studiously as he bent over his tablet a few moments ago, ignoring our clown show, and strums a passable chord, stopping us both.

"Again," I say.

He refits his fingers and manages the same chord again. He's remembered something.

"Shall we sing?" I say.

And we make a ridiculous joyous noise, the three of us, clapping our hands, snapping our fingers, the prince strumming his one wavering chord, Philes and I singing like cows (he's no better than me), *the boat, the boat, the boat and the silver sea,* until a palace guard sticks his head in the door to see who's in so much pain and smiles despite himself when he sees the morose nurse, the idiot prince, and the great philosopher conducting themselves like people who are simply happy.

ONE MORNING AT THE BATHS I find Callisthenes scrubbing himself vigorously with pumice.

"You haven't heard?" he says. "Alexander rode out this morning. A revolt at Maedi. A courier came in the night."

The young man seems invigorated, by either his scrubbing or the potent news.

"He is a child," I say.

"Well, he's not, though." My nephew turns the stone over in his hand thoughtfully. He's right, of course: Alexander is sixteen. "I hear Olympias isn't too pleased," he says.

"Respect."

"The queen would have preferred him to leave the Maedians to the generals. You should have seen him ride out, in full armour, on Ox-Head. He looked like a king already."

"I should have been told."

Again, my nephew seems perplexed and thoughtful and amused and sweetly reasonable all at once. "Why? He can't get permission from his own mother and he's going to ask it of a philosopher?"

I feel a hot sweet splash of guilt in my chest and wonder if guilt, too, is a humour, and, if so, where is its gland.

"We got up before the cocks to see them ride out."

"Did you wish you had been one of them?"

"You should have seen them," my nephew repeats, frowning, avoiding the question, answering it, and chiding the questioner all in the same breath. He, too, is young.

Alexander's troops retake Maedi and, for good measure, establish a colony named Alexandropolis. A bit of arrogance with Philip still alive, but there were already a Philippi and a Philippopolis in Thrace, and the man was probably more than happy to indulge his son's first successful command. I attend the formal greeting of the victors at court a few weeks after my conversation with Callisthenes, where Alexander is subdued and leaves almost immediately after the ritual offerings. I can't get close enough to see if he's picked something up on his travels, some bit of sickness, or if he's just tired from all the excitement.

When I return home, I find Pythias has ordered a lamb sacrificed in the boy's honour.

"You do love him," I say.

Pythias, by now, is fat with child, and her lassitude has given way to dogged industry as she prepares for its arrival. She strokes her belly placidly while we speak. Athea no longer speaks to me, won't look me in the eye. If she had anything to do with it, I don't want to know.

"They say he is not Philip's child at all," she tells me.

"Women's gossip."

"Men's, too."

"All right, then. Who does slander make the father?"

Pythias wrinkles her brow earnestly. "Zeus, or else Dionysus. Olympias herself says so."

I laugh. "Spoken like a true Macedonian."

Late that night comes a tapping at my gate. Tycho gets me from my study, where I'm just finishing up. The rest of the household is already in bed. A messenger in palace livery informs me I am required by Antipater.

"Now?"

"A medical matter."

The palace has doctors, the army has medics. The messenger has a horse for me, for speed and discretion, so I won't raise the household saddling Tar. Antipater himself, then, or the prince, and it's something shameful. I scour my memory for what my father taught me about diseases of the cock, and annoy the messenger by making him wait while I run back to my study for one of my father's old books.

"Finally," Antipater says. "Though I think the danger has passed. He looked worse an hour ago, when I sent for you."

I ask if there's blood in the urine or a burning sensation.

"What?" Antipater says. "I'm not worried about his piss, I'm worried about his arm. Alexander slashed him with a meat knife. Thought he was back in Maedi."

He leads me to a room where Hephaestion is sitting with a cloth held tight to his arm.

"Bind a bleeder," he says, seeing me, grinning weakly. He starts to cry.

"All right, child. Let me look."

Antipater, that good soldier, has already washed him; there's not much more I can do. The bleeding's down to a trickle. It's a long, vicious slash, deep enough. I advise him to keep it bound and prescribe poppy seed for the pain.

"Stop crying," Antipater tells him.

"I don't need poppy seed," Hephaestion says. "Will he be all right?"

"Where is he?" I put bandages and scissors back in my father's old bag. "I'd better see him, too."

We walk Hephaestion back to his room, next door to the prince's. Antipater rests his hand briefly on the pretty boy's head.

"Go, sleep. And for fuck's sake, stop crying. The prince will be fine."

"Thank you, sir," Hephaestion says.

"What happened?" I ask once Antipater has dismissed the sentry.

"Soldier's heart, we call it." He shakes his head. "They think they're back in battle. I wondered if it was coming. He's been odd, since they got back. Flinching at sounds, anything metallic. Dead-eyed, drinking too much."

"I'm surprised you let him go alone."

Antipater gives me a look. "Alexander didn't ask me. I wanted to give him hell, but Philip's letters couldn't have been prouder. What can I do? I'm not his father."

"So you've seen this before."

"Usually on long campaigns, when we're losing. It shouldn't have happened this time. Maedi was an easy victory. His first real battle, sure, but he's Philip's son. He's trained for this."

"Do you think something happened there, something unusual? Something he hasn't told you?"

"I can hear everything you're saying, you know," Alexander says through the door.

We go in. The room is neat, bed made, books tidy. The remains of a meal are on the table, with two chairs pulled up: a late supper for two. Poor, sweet, loyal Hephaestion. The cutlery is gone.

"Is he all right?" Alexander is pale but seems composed.

"Are you?"

He makes a noise, tick of the tongue, annoyance. "I'm tired. I suppose I'm allowed to be tired. I got confused for a minute. It was just a scratch, wasn't it? He knows I wouldn't hurt him for real. What's the book?"

I've put my father's book down on the table with my bag, next to his supper. I show him.

"That's what you thought this was about?" Antipater says.

"Drag me out in the middle of the night, what do I know?"

"That's disgusting." Alexander scrolls on. "That too."

"Any bumps on the head while you were away?"

"No." He lets me examine him briefly. A few bruises and scratches, and pressure on one knee makes him wince. "This doesn't have to go in dispatches, does it?" he asks Antipater.

"That Hephaestion took a wound in battle?"

They look at each other a moment. Alexander nods slightly, *Thank you.*

Back in the hall, I say, "Does it?"

Antipater beckons me away from the door. "Every account I got, from every soldier I asked, said he was brilliant. Everything textbook. Said he threw his spear like he was at games, just beautiful. Effortless. He could have hung back and let his men do it, but he led. He went first on every charge. That's what his father needs to know, and that's what I told him. This other, we'll put it down to first-time nerves. Find your own way out?"

"Soldier's heart," I say. "Did you ever have it?"

Antipater stalks off down the hall. "Never," he calls back, without turning around.

Hephaestion is still awake, as I'd hoped. "He didn't tell you? Maybe he didn't want to say anything in front of Antipater. He killed a boy who was trying to surrender. He'd thrown his weapons away and got down on his knees, crying for his mother. He can't stop thinking about it. Do you have any of that poppy seed after all?"

I look through my bag. "Not too much, though. It'll make you sleepy."

"Not for me, for Alexander. He gets headaches."

I show him how to grind it down, what dosage, and screw a sample portion in a twist of cloth. "He feels guilty for killing the boy, then."

"No, he enjoyed it. He said it was his favourite kill of the battle."

"He ranks them?"

"Oh, we all do that." Hephaestion moves his arm gingerly. "I think he went back after, though, and did something to the body."

"Do you know what?"

"No. He made me stay behind."

I believe him.

"But that's when it started. Whatever he did to the boy, after he was already dead."

THREE YEARS AFTER IT BEGAN, Philip's Thracian campaign is over. Callisthenes and I go into the city with thousands of others to greet the returning army and watch Alexander walk to his father, holding out a bowlful of wine, which Philip accepts as the traditional libation of a king returning to his city. They embrace and the people cheer. They turn and continue the walk to the palace together, Philip's arm around Alexander's shoulders. I've heard no gossip about Alexander since my late-night visit to the palace—nothing, that is, beyond the usual do-they-or-don't-they speculations about him and Hephaestion—nor have I been summoned for a lesson. The former I attribute to Antipater's white-knuckle discretion, the latter to my student's. I've seen him naked now, the soft white places; soft, or rotten. We both need time to forget.

We stay a long time to watch the procession that follows them. The news of Philip's long withdrawal from Thrace, after the disappointments of Perinthus and Byzantium, precedes him.

A campaign in Scythia netted some twenty thousand captives, women and children, as well as another twenty thousand breeding mares, flocks, and herds. Philip's army battled the Triballians on the way home, encumbered by all this living baggage, and were forced to leave a good deal of it behind. It was a vicious battle. Philip took a spear to the thigh and lay for a time pinned beneath his own dead horse. He was briefly taken for dead, and he limps distinctly now. A representative sampling of Thracian women and children and geese and ducks and pregnant horses and Triballian prisoners are paraded past. Along the way, too, Philip has picked up a sixth wife, a Getic princess named Meda, and here she is in a blue dress and sandals, walking in the middle of this great mess of prisoners and soldiers and horses, a blonde for his collection. I remember my long-ago description to Pythias of Thracian women, but she has no tattoos that I can see. Pythias will have to sew with her soon enough, no doubt, and will be able to inform me definitively.

But the invitation never comes. Pythias points this out to me one evening as we're getting ready for bed. "I haven't been asked up to the palace in ages," she says. "By Olympias or anyone. Also

I sent a note to Antipater's wife asking her to visit and she never replied. Have I done something wrong?"

I press the heel of my hand to my forehead, trying to hold back a headache. "They perceive us as Athenian."

She laughs. "What? I've never even been there."

"Me, then, and you as an extension of me. We're at war. I was afraid of this."

"You're joking." She sees my face. "You *are* joking. The king trusts you to tutor his heir. If Philip doesn't doubt your loyalty, why should anyone else?"

"You expect reason to govern passion. You've been around me too long."

She grabs my hand and clasps it to my belly; the baby's kicking. Her face is a joyful question.

"Yes," I say. "There."

"Not long now."

"You think?"

She wrinkles her nose. "How much heavier can I get?"

"All the more reason not to go trekking up to the palace, then. Maybe they're just mindful of your condition— Baby," I add sternly, "stop pummelling your mother."

"No, it's nice." She shifts a little in the bed, trying to get comfortable. "It's different this time, isn't it? War with Athens will be different from all the other wars. If Philip loses—"

I clap my hands over my ears.

"If Philip wins—"

"When."

"When Philip wins—"

"That's it."

"He'll rule the world?"

I lean down to kiss her belly.

"Won't he?"

"This isn't a battle with the Triballians. Philip stands to lose more than a few thousand geese. It's an endgame this time. Endgame—"

"I understand."

"It's a bad time to be associated with Athens, however distantly. We should plant crocuses."

Pythias raises her eyebrows.

"Philip won a battle against the Thessalians in a crocus field. It's considered patriotic."

"Crocuses," Pythias says.

"By the front gate, where people will see."

"And that will take care of it?" Pythias says.

By early autumn, she's confined and my presence at home is unwelcome. I tell Athea I've attended any number of births, assisting my father, but she waves me away. "You faint."

"I will not."

"You see wife, all bloody, open between like meat. You never fuck her no more."

"Even if that were to be the case, I can't see how it would be your business."

She laughs. "Trust me little bit, okay? I know how. If problem, I send for you. Better for you, better for her. She no scream, cry, push in front of you. You know."

I do know. That sounds about right, astute, even. My father believed slaves should treat slaves and free should treat free, but he never had a witch, and especially not one his wife liked and trusted. "You will send for me immediately if there are any problems."

"Yes, yes, yes." She pushes me away, actually puts her hands on my arm and pushes me.

She's happy, I realize. This is her job, what she knows how to do, what she wants to do and hasn't been allowed to. She won't make a mistake.

I'm just walking into the street, thinking to drop in on my nephew, when a courier approaches to say the prince requires my presence for a lesson.

"Wait," I tell the courier, and run to the back of the house for supplies.

At the palace, in our usual courtyard, the prince and Hephaestion are wrestling. They go at each other in silence, ferociously. I clear my throat softly, but only one or two of the younger pages looks at me, then away. I slowly pace the perimeter of the courtyard, under the colonnade, where the pages have encircled the fight. Through the forest of them I glimpse the sexual grappling of their leaders: a foot hooking an ankle, sudden collapse, a turtling stasis as Haephestion presses his chest to Alexander's back and tries to yank him off his fours and onto the floor, tiled with the sixteen-point starburst of the Macedonian royal house.

"A power struggle," I murmur to Ptolemy, who stands as is his habit a little apart from the younger boys. Alexander's cousin does not reply. I've tried before to engage with him on a different level from the other pages, a level more suited to his maturity, with quiet asides and small ironies, but Ptolemy is loyal to the prince and cannot be cut away from him. He tolerates my dry little droppings of wit with the barest of grace and moves subtly away from me, as now, without apology. Yet I know him to be intelligent, and wonder why our minds don't resonate in greater concord, like strings on a common instrument. I know from Leonidas that Ptolemy has a passion for the logistics of battle and will one day make a fine tactician. Perhaps the young man smells my eagerness to encourage any passion of the mind and my desire to contribute to it, though my own knowledge might be weak in that particular area. He finds me arrogant, I think with sudden insight, or possessive. I confess I want to touch all their passions, smooth and straighten and freshen them, like a slave at laundry, and thus leave my mark.

"Ahem," I say, more loudly this time. "Shall we begin?"

"Greek," a voice says, all insolence, and the insult is taken up in a chorus of hoots and jeers: "Greek! Greek!"

"My mother told me otherwise," I say. The boys snicker.

"It's true." Hephaestion seems not even to have to raise his voice, though his chest heaves. He and Alexander have broken apart and are circling each other again; I guess he spoke only to taunt his opponent with his casualness. "He's a Macedonian. A Stageirite."

"He's an Athenian," another voice cries, and the hooting starts again. Oh, for the repressive presence of Leonidas.

"What's in the jar, Stageirite?" Ptolemy asks from his corner.

"My father wiped Stageira off the map." Alexander abruptly stands from the wary crouch in which he's readying to meet Hephaestion's tense embrace. "Like shit from his shoes."

The pages part to let him through.

"What's in the jar?" he asks.

I upend the jar into a large, shallow dish I've brought from home for this purpose. Pythias and I and the servants have lately eaten a stew from it. The tiny creatures scramble blackly over each other, half-scaling and then tumbling back down the shallow sides.

I give the jar's bottom a spank to disgorge the last of them and the chunks of earth I've provided as a temporary home.

"Ants," Alexander says. His interest is no longer a boy's interest in their dirtiness and squirming, but a man's interest in the metaphor to come.

"Tell me about ants," I say.

As Alexander speaks, I'm aware of Hephaestion, who is lingering in the colonnade, towelling the golden sweat off himself and laughing with two older pages who likewise have hung back from the lesson. Extraordinary behaviour, since lovely Hephaestion does not noticeably have a mind of his own. When he sees me looking at him, something in his face falters. He's a sweet boy, essentially, and it goes against his nature to be malicious or manipulative, as he's attempting to be now. I wonder what the quarrel was.

"Indeed," I say to Alexander, who has concluded his little peroration on the inferiority, the absolute inconsequence, of ants, and is looking calmer. If it rouses him to use his body, it settles him to use his mind. "Yet they are like men, also, if we care to see it."

Man and young men and boys stare into the bowl, into the writhing mass there.

"You have a way, Athenian," Alexander says in his dreamiest voice, "of beginning all your teachings by putting me wrong."

"Ants were the easiest to collect for my purpose. I could equally have brought you wasps. Or cranes. Willingly would I have brought you a flock of cranes, had I the traps."

Alexander says nothing, waiting.

I explain that these animals share with men a need to live communally, with a single purpose or goal common to them all:

they build dwellings, share food, and work to perpetuate their kind.

"We live in an anthill?" Alexander says. "Or some shit-splashed crane's nest? Athens must have been grand."

"But the difference, the difference is that man distinguishes good from bad, just from unjust. No other animal does that. That is the basis of a state just as it is the basis of a household."

"Laws." Ptolemy looks interested.

"Athens has the grandest of laws, too, doesn't it?" Alexander persists. "The most just? I think it must have the very best of everything. How you must long for it."

"Indeed, at times, when my students are tiresome. It is the ideal state."

The sound of twenty pages who have momentarily forgotten how to exhale.

"Macedon is the ideal state," Alexander says.

"Macedon is an empire, not a state. In the ideal state, every citizen participates in the life of the polis, in the judiciary, in the promotion of the good and the just. Different states have different constitutions, of course, governing the amount and kind of power each citizen may possess. I might speak to you of Sparta, of Thebes, of their different constitutions. I might speak to you of polity, where the middle class holds the balance of power. Although each individual may not be utterly good, or utterly fit to lead, the ability of the collective of individuals always exceeds the sum of its parts. Think of a communal dinner, so much more enjoyable than a dinner provided at one individual's expense. I might in this regard speak of Athens."

"We are at war with Athens." Ptolemy comes closer. "You might rather speak of Macedon."

"I might, equally, speak to you of monarchy." I skate over the interruption and the warning it implies, of thin ice below. "Where one family exceeds all others in excellence, is it not right that that family should govern?"

"Is that a question?" Alexander says.

"What are the goals of the state? I propose two: self-sufficiency and liberty."

Ptolemy, at my elbow now, leans over and upends the bowl of ants. The boys cry out in shivery pleasure as the ants spill over their hands and feet and clothes and onto the floor.

"Liberty." Ptolemy shrugs, brushing dirt from his hands. "Chaos."

"You said best of seven," Hephaestion calls suddenly, with the precisely ridiculous timing of a very bad but determined actor. "We're only at three and two. Caught your breath or do you need more time?"

Their collision, the sound of it, reminds me that men, too, are meat. The cheers of the boys drown out the sounds of the fight, and I quickly recover my bowl before it gets broken. They have no respect for me today; there will be no further lesson. As I prepare to withdraw, I meet Ptolemy's look.

"Pretty place, was it, Stageira?" Ptolemy asks, not unkindly.

I thank him for his interest.

"In fact, I know it was pretty." The boys scream and roil about us and Alexander and Hephaestion abandon wrestling for fists, messier and more true. "I was there when they—"

"Yes. I wondered."

"Only you should be more careful." Ptolemy glances at the pages, then meets my eyes again with his straight, cool, frank look, sympathetic, though with no purchase for friendship in it.

"No one wants to hear about the glories of Athens right now. We are at war."

"Am I to fear boys, then?"

"Boys," Ptolemy says. "Boys, their fathers."

"What do you hear from the army?" Philip is on campaign again. Thermopylae was supposed to hold him back, as it had so many invaders in the past, but the Athenians and the Thebans between them forgot to reinforce the back roads, and Philip simply took the long way round. He has recently taken the city of Elateia, two or three days' march from Attica and Athens.

"Diplomatic overtures to Thebes," Ptolemy says. "Join us against Athens, or at least stay neutral and let us pass through your territory without trouble. Though I hear Demosthenes himself is in Thebes, waiting to deliver the Athenian pitch."

"You hear a lot."

"I do."

"I'm surprised you're not with them."

"Antipater asked me to stay here."

We watch the fight.

"He's feeling much better," Ptolemy says.

I thank him for the information.

At home I'm met by Tycho, who tells me Pythias has given birth to a daughter. I find her asleep in clean sheets with her hair dressed, and the baby already bathed and swaddled, sleeping in a basket beside her. Athea is in the kitchen kneading bread, thank you, as though this were the day's real work that she's had to interrupt to deliver a baby.

"Easy," she says before I can speak. "Long time but no problems. Always first is long time. Next is easier. My lady—"

She struggles for the words. I wonder when Pythias became her lady instead of my wife, when that affection set in.

"Resting?" I suggest.

She raps a knuckle on a cooking pot. "Iron." Satisfied, she turns back to her doughs.

"Thank you."

"Next time easier." She doesn't bother to look over her shoulder at me. "Maybe I even let you watch."

A week after the birth, I carry the baby around the altar Pythias has lit, purifying her. We've hung wool from the doors to show the world it's a girl, and prepared a feast, overseen by Athea, to celebrate her life so far. Athea is fiercely possessive of the creature, to the point where I've seen her take the baby from Pythias's arms and make Pythias cry, but I don't intervene. After ten days we prepare another feast, inviting some friends this time, for the name-day. Callisthenes brings rattles for my daughter and pretty painted vases for Pythias, as is the tradition, while Athea watches us all blackly, muttering to herself, her face softening only when she looks at the baby.

Little Pythias has a boxer's crease across the bridge of her nose and looks at me with a gaze the slaves say is preternaturally calm and steady, and foretells great wisdom. Other auguries: a white bee in the rosemary, a flight of swallows across the moon at dusk, unseasonable warmth and a sweet-smelling breeze at midnight, a pepper of sparks from a kitchen fire that had supposedly been extinguished. The household collects these happenings and trades them like rare coins. These and other wondrous events continue for weeks, reaching a fever pitch when we all are at our most sleep-deprived. I understand that every household with a new baby goes as foolish fond, and I collect more quietly, and keep to myself, my own talismans: the spider's thread of milk from wife's breast to daughter's lip when they draw apart after a feeding; the abrupt drop of the baby's brows when something amuses her; the way, at times of greatest distress, she buries her entire face in her mother's breast, as though seeking oblivion there. Liberty and self-sufficiency: the house is like a ship, Pythias and I and the servants like mariners, united by the determination to protect our tiny, mewling freight. Tycho lines a handcart with pillows and clean woollens and clatters the baby up and down the courtyard while the servants clap their hands in time and cry, bump, bump! for her greater amusement. She smiles pacifically, with an infant's mild aristocracy. Everything, everyone, it all belongs to her. When she mouths her first bites of honey pap, the slaves meet my eye, smile, and congratulate me. I realize they don't often look me in the eye.

Pythias I had worried for, not knowing if she would rise to motherhood or be sunk by it; her cold elegance and alien distance didn't bode well. But her breasts went plump with milk, and she sat on the floor, even in her linens, to fuss and coo at the baby. She weeps with exhaustion, from time to time, and both she and the baby fret when anyone—from myself to Tycho—leaves the house for too long. Liberty we have none, but there is self-sufficiency in our pleasure in the child and each other. Everyone, myself included, seems to touch more, as though the urge to touch the baby, to finger the downy depth of her scalp or the delectable fat toes, has transferred to one another. I myself, though she's only a girl, undertake to supervise her education, which must begin, I tell anyone who will listen, as early as possible. In the ideal state, the education of children will be the highest business of government.

"Oh, the ideal state," Pythias says. "I suppose she will need to know how to read, in the ideal state?" For she has caught me reciting the alpha-beta-gamma to the baby, who watches me wide-eyed from her bassinet of woven reeds, working her fists open and closed.

"I work with the materials I'm given."

"I suppose, in your ideal state, she will be a citizen?"

I explain why that is ridiculous. The hierarchy of the state mimics that of the household, where men lead and women and slaves obey, as nature has fitted them to do.

THEBES VOTED TO GO WITH ATHENS, initiating a rare winter campaign. Philip, in an unusual tactical error, didn't rush south to take the pass, but hung back thinking he might still politic a resolution. The Athenians raced north to seize the pass and for some months the opposing armies are locked in position, making small feints at each other with no real engagement. When spring comes, Philip falls back on the oldest trick in the book: he allows a false letter to fall into Athenian hands suggesting he's giving up and going home. He even backs his army up a little, only to turn in the night and ram the pass, where the Athenians have let their defences down. Philip takes the pass and the city, and the stalemate is ended.

Pythias has been distracted lately, frowning, and asks me to write a brief life of Hermias for a keepsake, which I do one morning in the courtyard while my fat daughter sits on the sunwarmed stones, babbling and staring at her fingers. I haven't permitted her to be swaddled, believing it inhibits the development of the muscles. And here she is, a healthy baby, pink and blooming; Hermias's own blood, perhaps, babbling prettily in the sun. I think the old fox would have been moved despite himself.

"It's lovely," Pythias says.

"I was thinking of our Little Pythias as I wrote it."

She thanks me again, then frowns and puts a hand to her side. A moment later I'm calling for the slaves, supporting her in my arms. She has to be carried to her bed, where she lies in great pain for several days.

"What is?" Athea asks me. She's stopped me in the hall outside our bedroom. Asks; demands, truly. She doesn't look happy.

"I don't know."

"I look. Is no baby again."

"She is not pregnant, no."

"I'm tell you," she says, annoyed. "Is sickness."

"She is a little warm. Apart from the pain in the belly, there is some paleness, a bit of sweating. Cool cloths, I think, and a light diet. Clear liquids. We will wait a few days and watch how it progresses." I have begun a case study, as my father would have; my first since boyhood. I'm not happy, either.

"I tell women," Athea says.

I'm not sure I understand; I wonder if it is the chasm between our languages, if something is getting lost there. "*You* are her woman," I say, slowly, loudly. "I am instructing you in her care. You are skilled in these things, more than the others; you will follow my instructions and report to me if there is any change."

"No," Athea says. "I tell women. I no do with sick."

For a moment I have no words. Then: "What are you talking about?"

"I no do with sick." She crosses her arms across her breast for emphasis, a bit of business that makes me think briefly of Carolus.

I could hit her, whip her, maim her, slit her thick throat for impudence. Could.

"I tell women for you," she says. "Cool cloth, light food. I tell."

"Will you not do what you're told?"

She shrugs.

It comes out of me before I can stop it: "Please."

She flinches. I might as well have hit her, because I can't keep her now.

"You stupid woman," I say.

The talk at court is of war and war and war, now, but Philip is playing a deeper game, and once again his army seems to stall. He takes the port city of Naupactus but then sends embassies to Thebes and Athens. Word comes, too, that Speusippus has died at Athens. With Philip in a diplomatic mood, I write immediately to put my name up for election as leader of the Academy, and write to let Philip know. At night, by lamplight, I sit with Pythias and tell her about Athens, try to conjure it for her in the shadows. She's a flower, I tell her, in Macedonian mud; her refinement is better suited to a Southern life. The weather is milder there, I tell her, none of these endless winter rains. The houses, it's true, are smaller, but more tasteful and elegant. The temples are more diverse, the food more tempting, the theatre more sophisticated. The greatest actors, the greatest music in the world! And the Academy (is she asleep? no, the room is too silent; she's listening), the Academy, where the greatest minds apply themselves to the greatest problems, where one glimpses order behind the chaos. On and on I speak, sketching the beauty of the life I'll arrange there, the tranquillity, and eventually, toward morning, she sleeps.

The next day, as she lies drenched and feverish, I palpate her swollen belly and she screams.

"How is lady?" Athea stops me again in the hall, Little Pythias on her hip.

I will have to find a nursemaid. Pythias is too weak to care for the child, and Athea—Athea, Athea. I won't sand my baby girl down with such rough Northern paper.

"Go see for yourself."

Little Pythias holds out her arms, and shouts at me when I don't take her.

Ten days later I receive a response to my letter: the Academy thanks me for my interest, and informs me it has selected an Athenian, Xenocrates, to lead the school. He is a senior Academician, and known to all as a scholar, an able administrator, and a patriot.

At court, Alexander sits in a lesser chair beside the empty throne, Antipater beside him. They look over the Academy's letter together. Alexander reads faster but pretends not to. I see his eyes fall from the paper to his lap when he's done, even though his head never moves.

"I'll put it in dispatches," Antipater says. "Other business?"

I clear my throat. "I thought we might discuss other tactics. If there's some leverage that might be used, some political pressure, some way of making them reverse the decision—"

"This is not a pressing issue," Antipater says.

I look for something yielding in him. Grim mouth, unblinking eyes. His wife won't sew with my wife. "I'm not Athenian," I say.

He gestures at the letter as though to say, *You want to be.*

"We could have Xenocrates assassinated," Alexander says.

"Other business," Antipater says.

Smirks, sniggers. The other men in attendance are too old or too young to fight. I, of course, am neither.

"See to it yourself, my buck," one of the old ones says, for me to overhear. "If you want it so badly."

"He wants it," another says. "Look at him. He's crying." Hisses from around the room.

"Shut up, all of you," Alexander says. "My head hurts."

Antipater looks up at me.

"I'll do it myself," Alexander says. "Why not? It's a valuable position. We could use him there."

"We will discuss this privately," Antipater says. "Other business?"

"Fuck you," Alexander says. "You're not my father."

"Let's discuss it now, then," Antipater says. "No. You are not going alone to Athens to snuff some hundred-year-old egghead with a protractor for a dick. You're a prince of Macedon. That particular piece of nonsense is not for you."

Antipater catches my eye.

"Xenocrates was a friend of mine, long ago," I say. "We studied together." I bow deeply to Alexander. "Forgive my emotion. My disappointment makes me irrational. Shall we discuss the embassies, instead? I had an idea—"

"Dismiss," Antipater says.

A bark of laughter all around at the half-second it takes me to realize he's talking to me. Alexander flinches at the sound.

"They abuse you," the prince says that afternoon.

We're alone. Hephaestion doesn't show and Alexander has

dismissed his remaining companions with a rare pissiness. "You, too," he told Ptolemy, who hesitated at the door. "I'm sick of you. You like being a nursemaid?"

"Understandably," I say now. "They've chosen me to represent what they hate. Whether that's a fair choice is beside the point. How's your head?"

"I should have thought it was the entire point. You were a friend to my father and to Antipater, and they treat you this way."

I look at the range of possible responses to this and decide to lay down two or three at once.

"One, I would not so glorify myself as to call myself a friend to your father. I am his subject, his sometime adviser, and his son's tutor. One does not easily befriend a king. Two, if your father loses to Athens, he loses everything. That is an enormous strain to be under; understandably, he and Antipater will be hostile to anyone even remotely connected with the enemy. Three, you yourself know friendship is a most complicated relationship, more complicated at times than the affection between man and wife. It is also the more valuable."

He shrugs.

"No," I say. "A king is at all times articulate."

"Talk, talk, talk. I'm tired of it. I'm tired of lessons and diplomacy and staying home to charm visitors to my father's court. Do you know what Carolus taught me? He said there is never truth in words, but only in the body. He said whenever a character speaks, it's to hide his true meaning. Words are the surface you have to look beneath. He said the best actors speak with their bodies, and their gestures are more memorable than their words."

"I assume he was speaking of the stage." I assume he was try-ing to get the boy on all fours.

"He was speaking of life. We are all truer in the body than we ever can be in speech."

"I would love to see Carolus express a Pythagorean theorem without speech."

"I want to fight." Alexander looks at me bleakly. "Means and ends, you always talk about means and ends, and what a thing is fitted for. That's your genius, isn't it, applying a few little con-cepts across such a wide range of subjects? That's what Lysi-machus says. Such a very few ideas that you apply so very, very broadly."

"Lysimachus."

"Why won't my father go to war? Why won't he summon me? I'm fitted to fight. War is the greatest means to the greatest end, the glory of Macedon. Why won't he just fight?"

"Your father is engaged in diplomatic overtures—"

Alexander spits.

"—as the smartest means to the end you both so value, the glory of Macedon. Your father wants Persia. He doesn't want to cripple the Greeks, to rub their noses in it. He's going to need them. They're not an expendable enemy, they're irreplace-able allies. He needs their resources— You're having headaches again?"

I don't know if he hears me or not. "I'm sick of staying home. Look what I did at Maedi, and you know what he said to me?" A moment, a ripple across the clear surface of things. It's the first time either of us has mentioned Maedi. "He told me if I ever went out on my own again while he was alive he'd sever my hamstring and tell everyone I tripped on my own sword. Then I'd have to stay home for the rest of my life."

"Your father suffers from what in an ordinary man we would call an excess of the virtue of pride. I'm not sure if such a thing is possible in a king. We are wasting time." I'm angry suddenly and don't care if he knows. I'm Macedonian to the Athenians and Athenian to the Macedonians. Maedi was a triumph; the Academy is not a pressing issue. "We are wasting each other's time. You would like to be with the army and I would like to be in Athens writing books. Alas, we are left to each other's company. Shall we make the best of an unpleasant situation and get this lesson over with as quickly as possible so we can each return to our own solitary pursuits? Show me your notes from last time."

I've only ever lashed out at him like this once before, in the stables years ago. His response takes me right back there. His eyes widen, and he immediately hands over his notes to placate me, to get me to lower my voice. I've found his Achilles' heel, the one thing he fears: someone abusing him who won't lower his voice. Her voice?

We review the work we began on ethics and the virtues. That ethics is indeed a science, though it wants the precision of a science like geometry; that, as we learned from our study of metaphysics, everything aims at some end or good; that such ends exist in a hierarchy leading to the ultimate human end, happiness. And what is happiness? Pleasure is superficial, virtue is compatible with unhappiness, great wealth is merely a means to a further end rather than an end in itself, "goodness" is an abstraction, an empty concept. Happiness is an activity of the soul in accordance with virtue, where a virtuous act requires both act and motive. "Name me a virtue."

"Courage."

"Yes. What do we call a want of courage?"

"Cowardice."

"Yes. And an excess?"

"An excess of courage?"

"Yes, yes. Don't give me some stupid, pompous response to flatter yourself. Think."

Quickly: "Rashness."

"Yes. We have the extremes, and in the middle—"

Alexander holds out his hands, palms up, in that gesture he likes to mock me with.

"My few meagre tools with which I try to order the universe. You must look for the mean between extremes, the point of balance. The point will differ from man to man. There is not a universal standard of virtue to cover all situations at all times. Context must be taken into account, specificity, what is best at a particular place and time. You must—"

"That's interesting."

"Yes. That's where I differ from my own teacher, insisting on particulars instead of universals. A less formally beautiful system, more pragmatic, but infinitely more flexible and applicable, if you—"

"No, not that part. What you said about the balance point this time. You've said it before, but—" He holds out his hands again in that familiar gesture. He's staring at his own hands, thinking this time, not mocking.

"The truth in the body," I can't help saying.

"You can't mean to prize mediocrity."

I want to laugh at the way he's skipped across the stepping stones. "Not at all. Moderation and mediocrity are not the same. Think of the extremes as caricatures, if that helps. The mean, what we seek, is that which is not a caricature. Mediocrity doesn't enter into it, you see?"

"You." Very slowly, holding out his left hand. Holding out his right: "My father."

"Caricatures?" I say, very gently, not to discourage him. He seems very young just at the moment, a small boy trying so hard to understand.

"Extremes," he says, just as carefully, still staring at his hands. "As though my father, to counter an extreme tendency in himself, prescribed the opposite extreme in you to create a balance in me."

"That is—"

"I'm thinking, too, of my brother."

"Who?"

He looks at me.

"I mean, you told me you didn't have a brother. I've never heard you mention him since that day, how many, five years ago?"

"Am I an extreme, next to him? And what would be the mean of the two of us?"

"Do you swim?"

"Of course."

"*Do* you?"

"A little."

"I could teach you."

He says nothing, waiting for what's to come.

"I've been meaning to give your brother a day at the beach, a day out. We could all go together."

"A swimming lesson."

"A lesson in moderation. We spoke of pride before, and the excess of pride. Vanity, might we call that?"

"Yes." I know he's thinking of his father and the honours he grudged him at Maedi.

"And a lack of pride, a want of pride: shame."

The flush begins to creep up his pretty cheeks.

"You're ashamed of your brother. You are, aren't you?"

Very softly: "We share blood."

"He speaks. He's clean. He doesn't smell. He can ride, on a lead. He's like a very, very small child in a grown man's body. Once you get past the incongruity, it gets easier."

"You would come?"

At first I'm not sure what he's getting at.

"You wouldn't leave me alone with him?"

I promise.

"Only my father might summon me first. If his embassies to Athens and Thebes fail, I might have to leave right away. Tomorrow, maybe, even."

"I can't tomorrow anyway," I say. "I have some business tomorrow."

"The day after tomorrow, then, if my father doesn't send for me."

I agree.

"What business, anyway? You don't seem like a man of business to me. What's tomorrow?"

"No," Pythias says.

"Love." We're in her room, early evening. She sits in her bed, propped with many pillows. I've come to present my case, not plead it. "She's defiant. It's intolerable."

"She's smart and competent. How has she defied you? Tell me and I'll speak with her."

I won't tell her, not this truth. "She threatened to poison us."

Pythias gives me a look. "She threatens to poison everyone

six times a day. It's how we know she's happy. Since when are you such a tyrant with the slaves? Tycho refuses to bathe with the others and you haven't sold him."

"I've had Tycho for twenty years. Are you going to make a horse bathe if it doesn't want to?"

"Tycho's not a horse."

I stand. This conversation is done. I do not say: Her function is devotion to you and she cannot perform her function. Her fear is uninteresting. A hawk's fear, a dog's fear, a horse's fear is of no account. They perform the functions they are trained for or they do not. Her rebellion is more than just an inconvenience; it's an affront to the natural order of things. It offends against everything I've pinned my sanity on, sweet stability and order, everything in its right place. I won't be threatened.

"No!" Pythias says as I turn to the door. "She's mine!"

"You have others. That dark one you like, Herpyllis—"

"You said they were family. You said we don't sell family."

"They were never family. Look. Listen. It's the natural order of things, the natural ends things are fitted to. Means and ends. Some people are born to be slaves, some masters. But sometimes life interferes with the natural order, and things get—confused. We've made a mistake with Athea."

"I don't know what you're talking about."

"I've made a mistake. She wasn't meant to be a slave. She isn't fitted for it. She wasn't born to it, and she's too independent and stubborn to accept that her circumstances have changed. If she were a man, she'd make a physician. I can't in good conscience keep her."

Pythias looks at me the way my father looked at me long ago, like something is happening to me, to my face, to the words coming out of my mouth.

"It would be unethical."

"Free her, then." Pythias shakes her head once, sharply, like she's trying to rid herself of something. "Free her and pay her for her services. She'd stay with us as a freed-woman, I know she would. Where else would she go?"

"We're arguing in circles. I don't want to keep her. She's disobedient. You think that will improve if we try to keep her as a servant instead of a slave? It'll only get worse, and set a bad example to the others. They'll think we're afraid of her, don't dare tell her what to do, don't dare get rid of her. We have only one option." An idea occurs to me, a cruel idea. Little Pythias is newly walking now. She clings to Athea's skirts, following her everywhere, singsonging the slave's name in her deep little voice. "The baby will miss her, it's true."

Pythias goes still.

"And she will miss the baby. They're very close, those two, aren't they?"

"She's a witch." Pythias raises her eyes to me, slowly. "I'm sick."

"She hasn't made you so, and she can't cure you. Sticks and stones and bones?"

"You will cure me."

I bow, as though to agree. I'm out of this conversation, anyway, out of this room.

AT THE MARKET THE slaving stalls are crowded, a bad sign for me. War brings uncertainty, tightens purse strings. There's a glut in the market at the moment and the goods don't move.

The first man I approach sees me coming, gives her a single glance, and shakes his head. The second asks what she does without looking at me or her. He can't take his eyes off a cockfight a few stalls away.

"Wonderful cook. Good general house slave. Loyal. Good with children." All true enough, mostly.

"Why do you want to sell her, then?"

"My wife doesn't like her." The slaver gives her a tired once-over. "You know how women are. Likes and dislikes coming out of nowhere. You can't reason with them."

"Not much to be jealous of there." The slaver's eyes drift back to the cocks.

"Hey fuck you," Athea says.

We try another stall out of sight and hearing of the one we've just left. "No talking," I tell her. I should have brought Callisthenes, I suppose, who's better at anything requiring charm, but I'm embarrassed that he was right in the first place.

"Or what you do?"

"How much?" the next slaver says.

I quote something low.

"What's wrong with her?"

"Hey fuck you," I say, pre-empting Athea and hopefully shutting her up. "She's healthy. I just don't need her any more. Household economy and so on. Trimming the fat."

"You gamble?" He looks interested. He thinks he's got my number. It'll do.

"Mind your own business," I say, in a way I mean him to take for yes. And I probably look like a loser, too, a mild, daintily dressed man with soft hands dragging a grinning slave from stall to stall and finding no takers.

He offers a price, less than half what I paid for her.

"She cooks," I say.

"Take it," Athea says. "He look okay."

The man's eyebrows go up and a grin starts. He looks back and forth between us, waiting for something to happen. I'm supposed to hit her, I suppose.

"I'll take it," I say.

The grin blooms. Even in this market, even for back-talk, he's got a deal. He pays me and opens the cage door. Athea ducks inside. I hope she had a good breakfast.

"She's a witch, by the way," I tell the slaver, to wipe the grin off and, I hope, make him think twice about how he treats her. I don't let myself look back.

ARRHIDAEUS IS TALLER THAN ALEXANDER. For the rest of my life I will be able to close my eyes and see them walking down the dusty beach road between the long dry grasses, the ocean roaring just out of sight, just over the next rise. Somewhere they are alone in the universe on this sunny road, still walking, Alexander asking questions slowly and waiting for the answers, Arrhidaeus inclining his head to his brother's level. We of their retinue follow behind in an ever-thickening tail: royals first, myself, Philes, then maids and guards and porters and horses and carts to carry the stuff of a royal day at the beach. They'll set up pavilions on the sand, with furniture and carpets, tables of bread and fruit, couches so no one need know the feel of a sleep in hot sand, rising after to leave the form of himself behind. Only Alexander's companions are missing, though whether he left them behind out of embarrassment or consideration I can't guess. While the beach is transformed into a village behind him, Alexander walks his brother up to the top of a nearby dune to continue their conversation. He is putting himself on show. I flatter myself, believe he's doing it for me, to show he can keep his word and keep it nobly, even in circumstances I know he finds revolting, horrifying even: proximity to his shit-headed brother. I wonder what they're talking about. The failure of Philip's embassies, perhaps, and Alexander's imminent departure, finally, to join his father's army?

"Princes, come." I drop my bag in the sand. Philes hangs back, as I've asked him to. Relax for an hour, read a book, I told him; I've got this one. I strip and walk toward the waves. Little nothings today, little lickings at the blond shore. All along the beach heads turn to watch the three of us. The princes strip as I've done, Alexander easily, Arrhidaeus excitedly, tangling his head in his tunic and needing rescue from his brother. They drop their clothes in the sand as I've done. Later we'll find everything we've discarded neatly arranged in one of the pavilions, as though by reproving mothers.

Now they're in front of me, looking fine in the sunlight, waiting for what I have to offer next.

"It's like a big bath," I say, mainly for Arrhidaeus.

"I was telling him how we used to have our lessons together," Alexander says.

"No," Arrhidaeus says.

I take his hand and walk him into the water to his ankles, where he stops and squats.

"No." The water licks at him, wets his bum.

Alexander walks out ahead of us until he's in to his waist. He holds his arms out of the water like a girl afraid to wet her hands. I stride past him to piss him off, dive in, and swim a few strokes. When I look back they're in the same positions, watching me.

"Come on," I say.

Alexander holds his hand out to his brother to lead him in.

After our swim, Arrhidaeus heads doggedly for the tents and his nurse. His skin has gone grey in the way that I know, his eyes dull. He wants his nap. Alexander is happy to let him go, and throws himself down on the hot sand. I sit beside him. "Nice to get an outing."

He laughs, eyes closed to the sun.

"I used to come down here all the time, when I was your age," I say. "I should do it more often. Some days I hardly leave my library. I can't remember the last time I came swimming. I'll feel it tomorrow," I add, rubbing my legs. Truthfully, I feel it a little already.

"You sound like you're a thousand years old," Alexander says. "You want an outing? A real outing?"

I don't answer. I'm thinking about a masseur, hoping my aching muscles won't distract me, tomorrow, from my work. Annoying prospect.

"Aeschylus fought at Marathon," Alexander says. "Even Socrates was a foot soldier. What's your excuse?"

"Respect." I rummage in my bag for a towel. My legs could cramp if I leave them wet. I think perhaps they're cramping already.

"You should come," Alexander says. "March with the army, see the battle. Do you want to die never having seen a battle? Like a woman?"

"You want to teach me. You want me to become the student."

"I've been thinking." He lies back down and closes his eyes against the sun in a show of casualness. Too casual; something is coming. "I've been thinking about the forms that you explained to us that very first day. Do you remember? The chameleon? And how you said that there's something all chameleons must share, a chameleon form, but that it can't be in some other world? That it has to be in this world for us to be able to perceive it, and to account for change?"

"I remember."

"And what we spoke of the day before yesterday, about finding the mean between two extremes. The point of balance. I've been thinking the same applies to people. We're all versions of each other. Repetitions, cycles. You see it best in families, the repetition of physical traits and characteristics. My hair comes from my mother, my height from my father. I'm the point of balance between them. But even more than that. You and my father. Me and my brother." He opens his eyes, briefly, can't bear not to see my reaction. "Just versions of the same form, do you see? Opposing extremes, but also versions of the same form."

I can't help mentally adding my own pairings: my master and myself, our nephews, Speusippus and Callisthenes, Lysimachus and Leonidas, Olympias and Pythias, Pythias and Herpyllis, Illaeus—now there's an interesting fulcrum. Illaeus and my master, Illaeus and my father, Illaeus and myself. Carolus and my father. Alexander and—?

"You see the consequences, don't you?" He's sitting up again now, eyes wide. He sees what he wants to say quicker than he sees the words to say it. "Macedonians and Greeks, Greeks and Persians. The same form. All just versions of each other."

"An entertaining lay application of some extremely complex ideas. You might make a philosopher after all, with a few decades' more study and no distractions."

"That'll happen," he says.

"I wish it would. You can't develop such ideas beyond the merely entertaining if you're constantly riding off to war."

"Merely entertaining? It's a philosophy of war itself. Every battle is against a version of your own self. Every enemy—" I'm holding a hand up to cut him off. "Every Persian—"

"We've had this discussion."

"Every Athenian, then. Would you deny you have an Athenian self as much as a Macedonian self?"

I open my mouth to speak, think, stop.

"You go into every battle knowing you're fighting your own self."

"That would be a thing to see," I admit.

"So you'll come?"

Ah. "Your father wouldn't allow it."

"My father wouldn't notice. No one would ask you to fight. You could travel with the medics."

That old nightmare. But then I think of him holding his hand out to Arrhidaeus at the water's edge. He's trying to help me toward something.

"It's important to him," I tell Pythias later. "Love, you're unreasonable. He will take me under his own protection."

"Little good that will do you if he is defeated," she says from her bed.

"If we are defeated, it will not matter for long where I am. Pella will be no safer. I thought," I add, changing tactics, "I thought you had some affection for him."

"I have some affection for you," she says, but when I move closer, moved, she closes her eyes and turns to stone.

I go to the baby's room. At eighteen months she's already tall and speaks well for her age, with many grown-up words and turns of phrase all cute in her mouth. Her moods—stubbornness, rages—remind me of Arimneste and get on my nerves a little, though Pythias thinks she'll outgrow them. I'm not so sure. She took Athea's departure hard but is quiet today, fortunately, playing in-and-out with some wooden blocks and bowls from the kitchen. I get down on the floor beside her, knees popping smartly, and show her how to make a tower by building smaller onto bigger. She watches, learns. I hide her blocks inside bowls, in my fist, under my sandal, and watch her find them. I tell her I'm going away for a few days (because what are weeks, months, to her?) but she doesn't react. She pretends not to hear when I ask for a hug and a kiss. I get up to leave and she flings herself at me, *no, no.* Her little cream dress is a copy of her mother's, right down to the embroidered pink roses at the hem. I have to unpeel her fingers, push her away to get her off me, call for Tycho to hold her in the house so I can open the gate and go.

PHILIP IS ALREADY IN PHOCIS, marching toward Boetia and Athens itself. I ride with Alexander and Antipater and some reinforcements to catch up to the main force.

We are led in our march south, symbolically and for luck, by that perennial Macedonian mascot, a goat; one of a dozen transported in their very own cart so they can spell one another. If only my own circumstances were so comfortable. I walk, ride, walk, allowing the blisters and the chafing to spell each other, wondering how long it takes the average cavalier to develop a groin of hide. We are mostly foot soldiers, with only a few cavalry, friends of Alexander who ride with him. They carry knives and long lances akin to the foot soldiers' sarissae and wear only light armour. The foot soldiers are arranged into squadrons of about two hundred men, grouped geographically; I walk for a while with the Chalcidician squadron, hoping to meet someone from home. They are scouts, archers, slingers, sword- and pikemen. They too are only lightly armed. If the cavalry are aristocracy, the foot soldiers are a great hot stew of Macedonians, conquered colonials, and mercenaries, and speak more languages than I can recognize around the fires at night. They travel fast, as fast as a pampered goat, thanks to that light armour and the fact that the heavy equipment of the siege train is already with Philip. The units—the smallest being groups of ten who camp and eat and piss and screw and fight together—are fiercely loyal to one another and to Philip, and even the mercenaries are better behaved than most, because Philip takes care to pay them well and promptly.

My fantasy, perhaps, was of a comfortable ride by the prince's side, discussing Homer and the virtues. In fact I see little of Alexander, who rides now forward, now back, joking with the men, making a show of himself in his fine armour on his fine horse. He is only faintly ridiculous, and maybe only to me. He is leading as he was taught and doing it well. At night he moves from fire to fire, extemporizing speeches of encouragement to make Carolus proud. Men's faces light up when they see him coming. Mostly when I ride it's with Antipater, who's softened a little toward me now that I've joined the campaign. We talk politics: borders, taxation, military strategy. (That *is* politics, to a general.) On the fourth day of our journey, scouts report that the main force of the army is encamped in the Cephissus Valley, held there by the Greek forces. The site of the battle, then, will be a place called Chaeronea, a broad plain, almost flat, with a river to the north and hills to the south. Tomorrow, now that we've arrived.

"You've never done this before, have you?" another medic says to me.

It's early evening. I've helped pitch the tents where we'll patch the wounded, and seeing the others clean their kits, do the same. Memories of my father are strong now, in the blue quiet of nervous soldiers sitting around their cook fires, not cooking. Drinking. Stars are prickling into view but there's light enough still. I unroll and reroll some bandages. The other medic's kit is grubbier, lighter than mine. I bought all new for this and it shows. He's younger than me and more experienced. He has told me what I'll need and what to leave packed, the surgical equipment there won't be time to use.

"No," I say. "Never seen battle."

"You're fucked, yeah?" He picks through my things. "This is nice."

A new set of knives; I left my father's at home. I offer him the set.

"No shit?"

I tell him he'll get it before we leave. That's a promise.

"Sure."

He doesn't seem to care either way. I wonder if he's been drinking, too. I wonder where to get some. He points to a tent.

Here's some boisterousness, finally, some night-before bluster. Soldiers line up with their cups and flasks. The wine is bad, thin and sour; you can smell it from the back of the line. I know it won't be strong enough. My hand shakes when I hold out my father's flask, and the dispensing soldier has to hold my hand to steady it, a maternal gesture I understand he's made a thousand times. He's missing a leg below the knee, and mumbles something when the pouring's done. Some blessing: I see his lips move over each soldier.

On my way back to the medics' tents I give the flask away to a boy who watches the horses.

Antipater's tent is by Philip and Alexander's, now, under a stand of oaks ringed at all times by the royal bodyguard. I sleep with the medics, in the tent where we'll treat the wounded tomorrow. I do sleep. The journey down was hard and I've never gone so long without privacy. There's privacy in sleep. I dream of Pythias, Pythias sweet and eager as I have never known her, and wake with an erection. The medics are already moving around me, setting up their stations, and from outside I hear barked commands, the clank of metal arms, the unison stomping of feet, horses' clop.

"No, no." The head medic stops me at the tent flap. "You don't go out there, not now. Too late for that. What are you looking for anyway, breakfast? You think the prince is having breakfast? You think maybe you're invited?"

He knows who I am; knows me and doesn't want the responsibility. Fucking dilettantes, eh? "Just to piss," I say, quiet as Pythias, eyes down.

"Use the pot."

I'm not the first, at least; my flow lands in a good couple inches of yellow. So that's a rule, then: no one leaves the tent. Makes sense; everything in its place. Tidy. I don't mind that.

I watch the others and try to copy them, turning my bedroll into my own station. I lay out some of my gear and catch the eye of the young medic from the night before. "What am I missing?" Water, pliers. I should have gone down to the river before dawn like the others and drawn my own. I don't have a bucket, either, and will have to use my own drinking skin. Under the head's angry eye I fill it from a barrel by the door. Pliers I'll have to do without.

"Move over next to me," the young medic says. "You can borrow mine when I'm not using them."

A trumpet sounds from outside. Everyone in the tent looks up, then down again.

"Hurry," he says.

What was that fantasy, again? Philosophers' talk on the ride down, and then—oh, yes—a view from a high hill, Alexander too much to hope for, but Antipater, surely Antipater beside me, explaining the battle, pointing out its features, walking me through the logic of it, and then a vigorous shaking of hands when the day is won. Alexander will find his way to me then, a bit of dirt smeared across one cheek, surely no worse, and laugh and tell me how pleased he is that I came and saw his great day. And Philip behind him, Philip out of breath, a little bloodied maybe, sweatier, grubbier, more grudging, Philip saying, We didn't fuck him up too badly, then, you and I, did we? In the tents, earlier, I'll have saved a few lives, exhibited a few unexpected skills (knife skills?), earned respect and joking offers to join the medics' unit should the king no longer require my services elsewhere. Good joke! Might as well go straight on to Athens, Philip will tell me, as the setting sun dallies in the treetops, gilding our hair, as together we look back over the battle plain, go straight on and begin your work there, just as we agreed.

The trumpet sounds again and the medics stop moving, like children playing a game of statues. From far, far away, a shouted command, a long silence, another shout. A sound like the surf, and the head says, "Stations." He doesn't need to shout. I look at the ground, have the leisure to observe the kinky walk of a beetle in the dust.

After a few minutes of listening to what sounds like a distant ocean, the young medic next to me pulls out a set of dice. "Play?"

"Now?"

Around the tent, men are slowly relaxing, speaking in low voices, some even lying down.

"There won't be any work yet. Wounded who could bring themselves in will keep fighting if they can. There's a detail to bring in the fallen but they won't go onto the field until the archers are done. Head likes everyone to stay at their stations just in case, but we've probably got some time, unless it's a rout. Arrow wounds first. That's what the pliers are for, yeah? Our goal is to get men back out, get them back fighting. We treat the easy ones first. Eyes, chest, or spear arm, leave those for later. Head usually sorts them for us but he can't catch everything. If something unexpected comes up, don't waste time. Remember: eyes, chest, or spear arm, send them back to Head. If they live, we deal with them later."

"Eyes, chest, spear arm."

"Want to know what's happening outside?"

"Yes. Yes."

The young medic digs in his satchel, puts away the dice, and pulls out some tiny wooden figurines, smaller than my fingers. "Here's Philip, here on the right, the sword arm, facing the Atheni-ans. Alexander on the left, the shield arm, facing the Thebans and Boetians. Infantry between. We're a little outnumbered, but not badly." He starts to manoeuvre the figurines like a child playing toys; he actually bumps them up and down on the ground to show movement. Like toys; like theatre. "Two arms, pincers. Theban tac-tics, yeah? You know Philip was a hostage in Thebes when his brother was king?" I know. "Learned from the best. They'll regret that now. Philip's going to try to extend the Athenian line, draw it out, retreat a little even, so they think they're winning. Overextend the line and then turn on them and break through the gaps with the cavalry. Alexander on the other side, well. Might as well fight flame, yeah? That's what they say. And then the two sides come together and there you go."

"How do you know all this?"

He scoops the figurines up in a quick handful. "Up early, before Head sealed the tent. On my way to the river I got a look at the field. I could see the standards, how the enemy laid itself out. And I've seen enough of Philip's battles to know how he usually works. Overextend the enemy line, then work the cavalry in as a wedge. Use Alexander to scare the holy hell out of everybody."

"He's never used Alexander before, though."

"He's been looking forward to this one."

I reach for his handful of figurines, raise my eyebrows to say, May I? He lets me take a couple.

"Bragging about it for weeks," he continues. " 'The day my son comes. The day they see what my son can do.' "

"Did you carve these?"

"Myself." Whittled wood, cute. Little soldiers in assorted costume. He points, naming them. "Illyrian, Thessalian. Olynthian, this one, yeah? Triballian, here. I like that one."

"Stations!" Head calls.

He lifts the tent flap for our first casualty, a Macedonian with an arrow to the thigh. The soldier has already snapped off the shaft. Head points him to a station. When the medic yanks the point out with his pliers, the soldier screams.

"You, and you, and you," Head is saying.

Suddenly I've got a man in front of me, a mercenary. He's bleeding over his eye but that could be shallow. He looks at me and vomits down his front. I see the arrow then, buried in his left shoulder.

"Send him back," the young medic says, barely looking at me. He's busy with his own man now.

I tell the mercenary to lie down. "Use your pliers?"

"Send him back."

"Shield arm." I take the pliers and yank. The man screams. The arrowhead comes out, it actually comes out. I've done one. I fumble to strip his leather tunic to get a bandage on. The man opens his eyes and looks at me and dies.

"No, wait," I say.

The young medic points to his groin, to the blossom of blood there. "Eyes, chest, spear arm, groin. Head!" He points to my station.

Head sends a couple of attendants to carry the body away. Immediately there's another, and another. Soon my clothes are soaked with blood. Most of them die. As the young medic predicted, arrow wounds give way to spearings, stabbings, splintered bones. I start sending them back faster.

"Wait," this one says, as I'm raising my hand for Head's attention. "Just bandage it."

A thigh wound, pouring blood. Thighs I'm supposed to treat, but surely he'll just bleed to death. I look at the face, look again.

"Quality!" Lysimachus laughs and then grimaces. "I am the lucky man."

I tie a tourniquet, tight as I can, and press a bandage to the wound with both hands, leaning all my weight onto it.

"Curse your mother," he says.

Head looks over my shoulder, walks on.

"What's happening?" I ask.

"Retreat."

I try loosening my grip and the blood wells up again. I bear down.

"Just to the river," he says. "I need to get back. We need every man."

"The prince?"

He grins, grimaces. I ease up and the bleeding's less. I help him stand.

"I'll give him a kiss for you," he says.

The work continues. My mind categorizes automatically, ahead of my desire to categorize; I think faster than the willingness to think. Matter and form: the soul gives form to the matter of the flesh; I don't think that's merely a metaphor. It's like wax, and the impression in it. Then, some bodies are natural, some are not; some natural bodies have life, some have not. There is, too, the matter of purpose; can one say the soul is the purpose of the body? I feel a woolliness there, a gap in the teeth of my logic. Pythias has such a comb, of tortoiseshell, which she tries to use despite a gap the width of two fingers where the teeth have broken off. She brought it with her from Hermias's court, and won't allow me to replace it for her. Set aside purpose for now. The attributes of life: mind, sensation, movement in space, and the movement implied by nutrition and decay. Sensation comes first; animals, for instance, can sense before they can move. I wipe my hands on a rag, which is already wet and black with wiping. Not all creatures have all these faculties; plants, for instance, have the nutritive faculty but no sensation; animals lack what in humans is called mind, and are incapable of rational thought.

"Hey." The medic is shaking my arm. "You need to sit, yeah?"

"No."

"Yeah, go on. It's over. Don't you hear?" Roaring from outside, the ocean pulling up close. "Head!"

I wonder who's dead. Then hands are on me; I'm being sat. Head pinches my nose with two fingers, jerks my head back, pours wine down me. Something strong, not last night's. I gag.

"You're all right, old man."

He lets go of my nose and I jerk away, spluttering. "What happened?"

The young medic puts his face up to mine, his own eyes wide as he looks at my pupils. He taps his temple. "You went away."

"We won," Head says.

I retch purple. Head tousles my head, grinning, and walks on, pouring a shot for every man in his tent.

"Home now, eh?" The medic taps his temple again.

I nod.

"Lie down, if you like."

"Can we go out?"

"Soon. We've got a long day ahead still. Head will take us out to look for survivors. Each medics' tent gets assigned a different section of the field; we have to wait and see which is ours."

"All survivors, or just ours?"

The medic nods. "You're learning. Bread?"

I take the chunk he offers. It's smeared with blood off his hands, blood with substance in it, like Pythias's menstrual gore. The taste is salt; I manage a bite or two. I watch Head bend his head to listen to an officer at the tent flap, then turn back toward us.

"Macedonians and Athenians. Everyone got that? Macedonians and Athenians. If you're not sure, ask."

"What about the others?" I ask the medic.

"They have a detail for that. Bring your kit in case you get one that can't be moved."

"East field," Head repeats to every man as we file through the tent flap. "Horses down. Watch for the horses. East field."

Outside, at first I can't see. The sun hurts everything it touches. We walk into a world of men and horses, milling it seems like, the men stunned by the rent in the fabric they've just come through, the walk back from the killing field to the false world of tents and bedrolls and meals and living. They need to drink so they can celebrate. I look for faces I recognize and realize: most of them. Is that possible?

"This way."

Head leads us toward the river, toward the horses. There's a detail for that, too: a cavalry officer works grimly through the downed animals, cutting throats. Some scream; some scrabble their legs, running nowhere. Other medic teams are spread across the field, heads down, like berry pickers. I find Head close to me, keeping an eye.

"No," he says, as I stoop for a closer look at something; someone. Theban. "Walk on."

I stop.

"Walk on."

The Theban is looking at me.

"Walk on, cunt."

I kneel down and unshoulder my kit. Overhead, vultures orbit the field, singing, waiting for us to leave.

"You cunt." Head kneels down beside me. The Theban's eyes move back and forth between us. Head feels for a pulse at the side of the throat, thumbs up the brows for a better look at the eyes, tweaks the man's feet. He moves up the legs, pinching. He's at the chest before the Theban grunts. "Help me." Together we roll him on his side. Blood all down the back. "Paralyzed," Head says. "Slashed spine. Were you running away, fucker?"

"No," the Theban says.

We roll him back so he can look at the sky. "Walk on," Head says to me. "Come on. You don't want to see this."

I don't move.

"Close your eyes," Head tells the Theban. He doesn't. "I'm doing you like one of our own," he says, and sinks his knife where he recently felt for the pulse. We both jump back from the blood that leaps out. The Theban's hand slaps the ground a few times and then stops. His eyes never close.

"That's not my job," Head says. "Don't make me do that again."

"Head!"

The young medic has something; he's waving us over. I kneel down again.

"I don't have time for this." Head turns away. "You're on your own."

In my kit I have a tablet and stylus. I roll the Theban back onto his side and unlace the leather corset. It falls away in pieces where the weapon severed it. The lips of skin are plum-coloured. I pull them apart to discover a flap of yellow fat. It's bone I want; I need my knives, then something to clean my hands on so I can write and draw.

I don't know how much time passes.

"Here you are."

"Minute." I'm teasing out a long thread of something from deep in the cavity.

"What *is* that?" Head kneels beside me, squinting.

"I don't know. I'm seeing where it goes."

"Look at that." Another voice, another shadow kneeling beside me. The young medic. "All those bits came out of just this one here?"

I've laid a lot of viscera out on the ground.

"Are you all right?" the medic says.

"I need more tablets."

Head nods at the medic, who jogs off. "He'll find you what you need. What—fuck *off*." A stench rises; I've hit bowel. "You *do* this?" he says.

"*You* do this."

"Not after they're dead." Head looks around the field. I try to stand up. "Steady." He catches my arm. My feet are pins and needles from squatting so long. "They're building the pyres. You almost done?"

"No."

"He's got to go with his people."

"I haven't started the head."

Shouting at the edge of the field, behind us; some argument.

"Ah, no." Head starts kicking dirt over the viscera. "No, no, no. Roll him back, quick. Help me. Put your shit away."

"I'm not done."

"Look," Head says. "I know who you are and why you're here. I understand what you do, sort of. But soldiers are not going to get this. You left the sex alone, at least. But you have to stop now."

"I was getting there."

"Women's work." He looks over his shoulder. "Oh, fuck me." He heaves the Theban onto his back so we can't see the hole I've made there. "Kneel," he hisses.

"Majesty," I say.

"Dismiss." Alexander's looking at the Theban. Head runs; runs. I stay. "Is he dead?"

"Yes."

"Because," Alexander says, "sometimes you think they're dead but they're not. You have to finish them."

"Yes."

Hephaestion has stopped a dozen paces away. His face is white.

"I fought here," Alexander says. "East field. Is he dead?"

What's been smoking up my thoughts is clearing now. Behind Hephaestion I see Antipater and Philip himself. They, too, stop a cautious distance away.

"Child," I say. "Has something happened?"

"What are you doing?"

I hold out my tablet for him to see.

"Can I help?"

"I'm just done. Another time. I think we need to go wash."

"I fought here."

"Alexander." Hephaestion steps forward. Alexander draws his knife. Hephaestion steps back.

"Child," I say again. "Will you show me where to wash?"

He's looking at the Theban. He kneels down beside him, as I did hours ago.

I walk a wide circle around him, over to Philip and Antipater. They're arguing in whispers.

"It happens," Antipater is hissing. "You know it as well as I do."

"What happens?"

Philip shakes his head. "He stabbed Ox-Head's groom," Antipater says. "Thought he was the enemy. The battle was over."

"Like after Maedi."

Antipater looks haggard.

"What?" Philip says.

We look over. Alexander is working at the Theban with his knife, up by the hairline.

"This is your fault," Philip says to me. "You teach him this shit. What kind of animal are you, anyway? Who does this to a body? What happened after Maedi?"

Antipater shakes his head.

"That's my son."

"He still is," I say.

"He's supposed to be king someday."

"Look," Alexander calls. He's leaning over the body. "It comes off. Come look."

Hephaestion is backing away.

"Deal with this," Philip says. "The two of you, since you know so much about it. Get him into a tent, for fuck's sake, before anyone sees." He draws his own knife far enough to slam it back into its leather. "Do I have an heir or not?"

Hephaestion is green on the side of his face, the phenomenon Arimneste tried to describe to me so long ago.

"This isn't happening," Philip says. "I'm going back to camp."

I go see what Alexander's doing. He's got the face peeled down from the forehead. He's working it down with his knife, ripping and jiggling. He's got it peeled to the eyes.

"I tried, at Maedi," Alexander says. "I tried to bring one back. But I couldn't get it off."

"For me?"

"For Carolus. I was thinking it could be dried. He said they couldn't afford masks."

"May I help?" I reach for his knife. He lets me have it. I take the flap of forehead and hold it delicately taut, as he did. "May I finish this for you? I think you are required back at camp."

"I want to stay here, with you."

"Your father is very proud of you," I say slowly. "Of the work you did today. He wants to celebrate with you. He wants the world to see you together." I feel Antipater behind me, closer. "Your father needs you now."

"Majesty, come," Antipater says.

Alexander looks at Hephaestion. "Hey." His face lights with pleasure. "When did you get here?"

Hephaestion looks at me. "Just now."

I nod at him over Alexander's head, *That's right. Go on.*

"Hey," Hephaestion says. "So, hey. I'm starving. You want to find something to eat?"

Alexander slings an arm around his shoulders and they walk

back toward the tents that way. I try to smooth the Theban's forehead back down but the fit is ragged now, and the lips of skin won't meet at the scalp.

"He won't remember any of this," Antipater says. "Alexander. He didn't last time, either."

The young medic comes running up, panting, three tablets under his arm. "Is this enough? It's all I could find. Theban, yeah? They're asking at the pyres. I'll help you carry him over when you're done."

"He's done," Antipater says.

We carry him the hundred paces to the Theban pile, already spitting and crackling in the golden late-afternoon light. Gutted, he's not very heavy. We heave him onto the other bodies while the presiding officer makes a note on his tablet, keeping count. The medic runs off. Antipater and I stare at the fire and the heated air wobbling around it.

"I get nightmares," Antipater says.

A long silence.

"I work," I say. "It's like the ocean. I go in, way down deep, and then I come out."

He nods, shakes his head. The setting sun gilds our hair. The Theban—smoke—rises to the spheres.

ANTIPATER AND THE PRINCE leave for Athens, escorting the bones of the Athenian dead. A courtesy: defeat has made the Athenians respected allies again. I secured a bag of poppy seed from Head before we broke camp and showed Antipater how to administer the proper dosage. Philip will spend the fall in the Peloponnese tying up loose ends and arranging a great conference in Corinth, where he can get down to the business of ready-ing all his new subjects for a Persian war. Philip has never been to Athens, and to forgo this opportunity is extraordinary. My guess is he can't stand, right now, to be near his son.

I travel home to Pella with a convoy of walking wounded. No goats, this time; no luck; no hurry. I change bandages, clean wounds, lance infections, sedate the delusional.

At home I give Little Pythias her present, a tiny Athenian sol-dier carved for me by the medic in exchange for my knives. I visit her mother in bed, where she spends most of her time now. I can't persuade her to take exercise, and when she does get up she creeps along the walls, or supports herself on a slave's arm. I can't bring myself to accuse her of malingering, but nor can I dispel that suspicion.

"Athens," Pythias says. "Athens, Athens. Perhaps Philip is right. What would you have done there, really, other than more of the work you do now, for a more attentive audience?"

"Is that nothing?"

"To him it is."

I shake my head. "Look at this city. Look what he's done with it. He's brought in actors, artists, musicians. He knows what it means to be cultured, to feed the mind. He understands the—the diplomacy of it."

"You think it's personal?"

I don't answer.

"Practically, then. What would he do with you? He can hardly force you back into the Academy if they won't have you of their own free choice. He knows that much, at least. So what could you do for him?"

"Run my own school," I say, to be contentious, but I see the pain is returning and she's lost interest in the argument.

"ANH," THE OLD ACTOR SAYS when he sees me, a consonant of pleasure that becomes a guttural, wet coughing. "Long time," he adds when the coughing subsides, gasping for the breath to make the words.

A housemaid has led me to the bedside, where Carolus lies in odd relief: what's under the sheet seems shrunken almost to flatness, but his hands and head seem enormous. Hands hairy, knuckly, worked with surpassing fineness and detail by some master carver. Head leonine, the white hair longer than I remember and styled back in a greasy plume that still shows the ploughmarks of the comb, chin stubbled, eyes two gems sunk in soft pouches.

"She's a good girl," he says of the housemaid, when I ask if there's anything I can do for him, anyone I can send; we can easily spare someone to sit with him at night if he wants it. "No. Nights aren't so bad; sometimes I almost sleep. I remember a lot at night. Performances I've been in, actors I've worked with, audiences I've played for, travels, lovers. My childhood, too, and stories my father and grandfather told me about their performances, their days. I have a lot of company at night."

"I'm sorry it's taken me so long. I've been travelling with the army, if you can believe it, as a medic."

"I hadn't thought we were so short of men."

"We're not. Alexander wanted me to come. Get me out seeing the world."

"Through his eyes," Carolus says.

"Through his eyes."

He nods, closes his own, opens them with an effort. "He likes you. That's good."

I wait while he closes his eyes again, and am thinking I should slip away when he opens them. "I'm here," I say.

"You were going to leave."

I can't tell if he's frightened. "Should I?"

"No."

I look around the room while he does the work of breathing, preparing his next sentence. A shelf of books, plays I assume, that I covet a closer look at. Masks on the walls, and props placed here and there. He's surrounded himself with the things that make him happiest.

"Under the bed," he says.

I bend down from the chair I've drawn up next to him and lift aside the trailing linens and furs. There's a box.

"Yes," he says, and I pull it out.

His fingers twitch a little so I lift it onto his lap where he can reach. He fumbles with the lid. Inside is a mask.

" 'How dreadful knowledge of the truth can be when there's no help in truth!' " I quote. " 'I knew this well, but made myself forget. I should not have come.' "

" 'Let me go home,' " Carolus replies. Of course he knows his *Oedipus* as well as I do. " 'Bear your own fate, and I'll bear mine. It is better so: trust what I say.' "

His grandfather's Tiresias mask is fine and light and old; the ribbon that would secure it around the actor's head has yellowed and frayed away to scant fibres. At first it looks almost feature-less: the eyes are shallow, unpainted pods, the nose and mouth minimally marked. The cheekbones are high and wide; the brow is delicately wrinkled, in the moulding rather than the paint. It's large, larger than a human face so as to be seen from the back of a theatre, but light; my hands almost seem to rise as I hold it, tricked by the illusion, the contradiction between size and weight.

"Have you ever worn it?"

He lifts his hands and slowly takes it from me to lower it onto his face. After a moment's rest he struggles to raise his hands again to lift it off. I help him, and lay it gently back in the box. "First time," he says. "Last time."

I lid the box and replace it under the bed.

"I miss my father."

After a long moment I realize he's crying.

"May I look at your books?" I ask.

They're well used, torn and marked, some lines underscored and others struck through. He has some I don't. When I turn back to the bed, he's watching me.

"Yours," he says.

"I'm greedy. Even now, and I let you see it. Forgive me."

"I don't forgive you. To be alive is to be greedy. I want you to be greedy. I want everyone to be greedy. You know he came to see me?"

I've lost the thread. "Your father?"

"My father's dead. Alexander. Speaking of greedy. One day that monkey's going to open his mouth and swallow the whole world."

This costs him; he coughs until his whole being is concentrated in a long, gagging exhale that purples his face and closes his eyes to slits, like blind Tiresias himself. The housemaid, hearing, returns to the room with a cup of water and lifts him upright with a practised grip until his breathing eases. He sips, sags, sips again. She settles him back, smooths the covers, puts a palm briefly on his forehead, and gives me a nice look to say hurry up.

"You need to sleep," I say.

I rise and arrange myself to go. I'm not sure what gesture to leave on. Perhaps I'm too aware of my own movements because of his stillness, or because he's an actor after all and would know just what is needed, how to hold your hands when you leave someone for the last time. I bend to kiss his forehead. He opens his eyes again, obviously in pain now, and I hesitate.

"You need to love him better," he says. "Alexander. He knows the difference."

I go the last distance, let my lips touch his wrinkled forehead, which is not cool, not feverish, but warm, humanly warm.

FOUR

Poor Proxenus. My sister's husband tried so hard to be a father to me in those obscene first weeks after my parents' deaths. He spoke gently, patted my back, frowned in concentration on the rare occasions that I spoke. But I was already such a cool boy, and my physiology was such that grief made me cold. So I overheard him telling my sister, Arimneste, on the ship from Pella to Athens, when they thought I was asleep in my bunk. He presented his bafflement to her as a medical diagnosis. I had rare blood and humours, and ran cool in the tubes where others ran hot; was it his fault he found my company distasteful? He was a naturally warm man, as she was a naturally warm woman. They wept, they spoke their love for the dead, they found succour in the rites of mourning, and then they moved on. They were like friendly dogs, but I was a lizard.

"Ssh." Arimneste was feeding the baby again; I could hear the rhythmic sucking. Arimnestus snored quietly in the bunk above mine. "He's not a lizard. His skin is warm when you touch him."

"That could come from the outside, absorption from the sun," Proxenus said. "I really do think he's afflicted. The body needs to weep to release the excess fluid caused by grieving. How is he releasing the fluid if he isn't weeping?"

Arimneste said something I couldn't hear and they both laughed quietly. I rolled over in my bunk and they stopped.

After a minute Arimneste said, barely above a whisper, "Mother used to say he had the ocean inside him, but that it was his great secret and I must never tell anyone. She said if he wanted to talk about it he would, but we must never push him. We have to let him go about things in his own way." She was weeping herself now. "Oh, Mummy," she said, and to Proxenus, "I'm sorry."

"No."

The creak of a bunk. I risked a look: Proxenus getting down to sit with her and the baby on the floor, to kiss her cheek and stroke her hair. I closed my eyes again.

"Is he finished?" Proxenus asked, meaning the baby.

"Almost."

After she settled the baby in his basket, she and Proxenus had sex in their bunk: delicate sex, almost silent, mindful of the baby and of Arimnestus and me. I listened with interest. Their love culminated in Proxenus sighing heavily, once.

"I can't see that school being good for him," Proxenus said after a while. "More brooding and living in his head. Maybe we should take him back to Atarneus with us after all and find him a wife. He can work with me, as my apprentice."

Arimneste said something I couldn't hear.

"We'll find him his own house, then."

Arimneste murmured again.

"You're a bit cold, yourself," Proxenus said. "All right. You know him better. Maybe this Plato will work wonders. Can't say I'll miss your big brother, though, in the meantime."

. . .

"WHAT DO YOU MEAN, he's not here?" Proxenus said.

The one named Eudoxus explained that Plato had recently departed for Sicily, to attend to the education of the young king there.

"And when do you expect him back?"

Four, five years? But I was welcome to begin my studies with this Eudoxus and his companion, Callippus, in the meantime. As acting director of the school, he would oversee my education as scrupulously as the great man himself.

"Years?" Proxenus said. Surprised; not distraught.

That night we ate with Eudoxus and Callippus, and sometime during the meal it was decided we would stay the night. The twins and the baby were staying in the city with relatives of our mother.

Proxenus went to his room early to write letters. Restless, I visited our cart in the courtyard and helped myself, quietly I thought, to a fist-burying handful of raisins.

"Still hungry?" a voice said.

"Always." Carefully lidding the amphora.

Eudoxus gestured for me to accompany him, and led me through his gate and into the road. "We'll walk, yes? This way our voices won't disturb your guardian, or Callippus."

"What's he working on?"

Eudoxus laughed. "He's sleeping. He keeps bird's hours. He'll be up at sunrise tomorrow, piping his little song."

I told him I didn't know what that meant.

"Working, writing," Eudoxus said. "We work a lot around here. What do you think of that?"

It was a lovely road we were walking, lined with olive trees, fragrant with flowers from the public gardens we were passing. The school was on the city's outskirts. Quiet, almost like country, but no country I knew: sweet and warm and comfortable, even at night. The South, then. Eudoxus (*trim* was the word I wanted for him: trim of beard and belly, trimly clothed, so trim and tidy and modest in his appetites, I noticed at supper, waving away meat and wine for a little fruit and water, that he probably could have trimmed a few years off his age without anyone guessing) put a brief hand on my shoulder, squeezed, and let go.

"I was so sorry to hear about your father. Your guardian does him great honour, bringing you to us, and so promptly."

"I don't think he knows what to do with me." My voice was rusty; I'd barely spoken to anyone these past weeks. "He's trying to find me a place to live."

"You might stay with Callippus and me," Eudoxus said. "If you should choose to stay. If your guardian should make that choice. Several foreign students lodge with us."

I thanked him.

"Whose decision is it, anyway? As a matter of interest?"

"I'm not sure," I said.

"I'll show you around, tomorrow."

I liked him for that, for not leaving a beat. "Will there be a lecture?"

"In the morning." Eudoxus himself would speak on a mathematical problem set by Plato before his departure for Sicily. "It should be well attended; you and your guardian will get a good sense of our students and of the atmosphere here."

I asked him if he remembered Illaeus.

He laughed. "Very well. Excellent poet, horrible mathematician. I shall have his mess to undo, I suppose, in you." When I told him that was an empty room rather than a messy one, he laughed again. "Come on." He cut into some trees. "Want to see where you'd live?"

We had circled back without my noticing. Set away from the main building, deep in the garden, was a smaller house with lights in the windows although it was late. We could hear low, young voices and laughter. Eudoxus tapped a knuckle lightly on the door, then pushed it open. Half a dozen young men sat around a low table, drinking and arguing about something on a piece of paper they passed from hand to hand.

"New student," Eudoxus said.

I saw I would be the youngest. They greeted me, smiling, friendly. The one who'd answered the door led me deeper into the house to show me the dormitory with its rows of sleeping mats, all clean and comfortable enough, while Eudoxus stayed in the front room, grinning, to look over the piece of paper.

"Do you want to stay here tonight?"

"Yes."

The young man had a flop of hair like my brother and a lazy eye. I was prepared to like him. I was prepared to like all of them, why not, and their math problem too.

The next morning, Proxenus and I hung back under the colonnade while the big courtyard filled with members of the Academy who had come to hear Eudoxus. I struggled to follow the talk, while Proxenus looked around, performing a more pragmatic calculation. Afterwards, at the meal, he told me he liked what he saw. Well dressed, serious men from good families. He had recognized some faces. Later he took Eudoxus aside for a little stroll. I knew they were talking about money. The school didn't charge tuition, but my board would have to be covered. I knew I had plenty of money and land: an estate in

Stageira from my father and another at Chalcis from my mother. Money would not be a problem.

My housemate with the lazy eye drew me over to some other young men. "We're going into town. Want to come?"

I nodded. "I have to say goodbye to my family."

Proxenus had sent a messenger ahead to the house of our city relatives, so that the twins were already waiting in the street with the carts when we arrived. I kissed the baby, Nicanor, that Arimneste held out for me, and embraced Arimnestus.

"Those yours?" my brother said of my housemates, who hung back a little, respecting our farewells.

Eudoxus had told them of our parents' sudden deaths, and told them too, I guessed, of my own numbness. At least, they hadn't yet asked me why I didn't talk. They probably looked freakish to my brother: indoor skin, no weapons, skinny arms hanging down. Freakish brains, like mine.

"Friends," I said.

Arimnestus knew I didn't know how to make friends. I could see he wanted to say something, some advice he was afraid to offer. Finally he brought our foreheads together in an affection-ate butt and whispered, so Proxenus wouldn't hear, "Relax. Drink a little more."

I nodded.

Arimneste hugged me long but said only, "Take care."

Proxenus had never dismounted. I was sorry, in that moment, that he so disliked me, read me so wrong.

"You come to us in Atarneus when you're done here," he said.

"Write," Arimneste called, holding the baby up to see me.

The carts were already moving, sending up dust. I held my hand up, kept it in the air while they moved away. I wanted to die.

"All right?" my housemate said.

They knew a place where we could eat, a two-storey house on a busy street in a commercial district. Over bread and meat skewers at a long table someone produced the piece of paper from the night before, and they were off again. I wandered away from the table, deeper into the house, looking for somewhere polite to piss.

"Through there," a woman called from the kitchen. She waved a shooing hand at me. "Through, through."

I went through the door she meant, into a bedroom, and found the pot in a corner. When I turned around there was a girl sitting on the pallet on the floor.

Outside, I took my place again on the bench. "All right?" my housemate said again.

It was an hour's walk from the door of the little garden house to the door to the girl's room, a walk I made many times over the next few months. It never cost much; we hardly spoke. Back at the school there was a library where I spent most of the rest of my time. Occasionally there were public lectures in the mornings; occasionally a symposium in the evening. I could attend or not; my time was my own. I thought of Perdicaas and Euphraeus and their snotty dinners: the ritual measuring and watering of the wine, the blessing, the rehearsed disquisitions on set topics, the learned quips, haw, haw. One night I spoke too, some ideas I'd been putting together about the forms that everyone here talked so much about, the ineffable essences of things. I was not much keen on the ineffable, and said so, carefully. Surely things had to be rooted in the world to make any sense at all?

"The boy smells of the lamp," someone said, making them laugh. They were pleased, and curious too. So they'd been watching me after all, waiting.

I would always smell of the lamp, I knew that. I lacked spontaneity; my wit was dry as mouse droppings, and as measly. I needed to put in the hours, yes, late hours over the lamp, exhausting myself. I had lied to Eudoxus. The inside of me was not empty, but viciously disordered. On the ship to Athens we'd been sitting below at a meal, my sister passing out plates of food, when a sudden swell sent everything sideways, she and the baby tumbling over, food swept to the floor, plates and cups shattering, everyone crying out. My mind was like that now, prone to such sudden upendings. Some days all I could do was wake and roll over and sleep some more. My housemates, by some instinct, left me alone. Some days I knew I would never have to sleep again, and produced monuments of work that were pure luminous hammered gold genius. Less so, the next day. I learned never to show or speak of my ideas to anyone until I'd sat on them for weeks like a broody hen, checking and rechecking, making sure everything was strapped down tight and shipshape. Oh, good, steady, studious, boring me, who worked that girl over and over, used her hard, and came shouting when there was no one to hear.

In my nineteenth winter, word came that Plato was returning early from Sicily.

"What's he like?" I asked Eudoxus at supper. I'd almost forgotten he was the reason I was here at all. I could more or less manage my life as it was, my Illaeus-life of sex and books and a fair amount of privacy, and I feared change.

I had pitched my voice quietly but it made no difference: because I spoke little, people stopped to listen when I did, and because I was bright, people loved what ignorance I let show. It turned out I was the only student who hadn't met him. He liked to approve admissions himself, and I was the last he'd considered before leaving for Sicily. Voices around the room competed to enlighten me. He was nobility, descended from the great Athenian statesman Solon on his mother's side and the god Poseidon on his father's. His family had been active in politics and he had been expected to go that route, but he was too fastidious, too moral, and occupied himself instead with political and pedagogical theories, theories he had tried to implement in Sicily. But the young king there was already well schooled in tyranny and debauchery, and wasn't interested in the kind of beatific restraint Plato preached; so interpreted Eudoxus from the letter he read to us over our meal. Plato would be home in two weeks.

"It'll be all right," he added, so only I could hear.

WE WENT DOWN TO the port to meet his ship, the whole merry gang of us, led by Eudoxus, and Plato's nephew, Speusippus. Everyone spoke too loudly and they might as well have worn flowers in their hair. I wandered some little distance away to watch the unloading. The sun struck coins in the water where I stared, dazzling my sight, and when I looked up the great man himself was on the quay being mobbed by my teachers and classmates. My name was called but I was already on my way over. I would not reveal sullenness.

Speusippus introduced me, a hand on my shoulder, as though he knew me well and my accomplishments were his. Plato was slightly younger than my father would have been, and looked tired. He had close-cropped greying hair and lines around the mouth and eyes. Thin, not as tall as me, simple light clothes, hard chips of light in the eyes. I liked the look of him despite myself. I had expected someone soft and jolly, with seriousness represented by the cryptic.

"I'm sorry I wasn't here when you arrived," he said, as though three years ago was last week. "I wanted to be. I was so sorry about your parents. I thought I could do good work in Sicily, influence many fates, and that it was the better choice. So it seemed at the time."

"The moral calculus, the choice to serve the greatest good for the greatest number," Speusippus announced, as though interpreting an oracle.

Around us the crowd murmured and nodded. Plato looked annoyed.

"I would have waited longer," I said. More murmuring and nodding; a good answer; only I meant it. *Your parents,* he had said, not *your father.* He and I shared a bubble: we were both stuck together back in that moment three years ago. I was only now arriving at his school, in his mind; my parents had only just died, in mine. Every morning as I woke they died all over again. Today my true studies would begin.

"I want to spend time with you," he said.

We were moving away from the ship, swept along by the crowd eager to get him moving, to reinstate him at the school, like a city craving her king back in the palace, or a child his parents in the house.

"Later. I'm too tired right now. I want to tell you a lot of things, and hear a lot from you also. I don't like not knowing you. Eudoxus has written me——"

I allowed Speusippus to slip between us then and the crowd to peel me away. Was that flirting? At a stall I bought apricots and hung back to eat them while the crowd I had come with disappeared in the distance, sheep guiding the dog. Musicians had already been hired, I knew, and a great supper was being prepared; no one would be working this afternoon. Had they heard him say he was tired?

"You," the girl said, surprised, when she saw me sitting alone at one of the long tables. Unusually, I had been told to wait. Her hair was loose and her face puffy. I followed her to the back room, where she rubbed hard at one eye with the side of her finger while I undressed. The bed was made.

"Where do you sleep?" I asked.

She pointed at the ceiling. Business quarters downstairs, living up.

"Mornings. You sleep mornings."

She shrugged, nodded.

"I'm sorry."

"No, no." She dropped her dress and yawned, then laughed. "*I'm* sorry. I'm not very sexy today. I worked last night. Need a bath."

Could have been a slut's patter—*I'm so dirty*—but she looked at me a moment too long. I wondered if this too was something I should offer to pay for, or if she was trying to tell me something else entirely: *I don't belong to you. Just to you.*

"How about we don't talk," I said.

I got back late to the Academy. The sun was setting and the grounds were almost deserted. I could hear the music from the big house, glimpse the light and the movement of dancers through the windows. Laughter, clapping, smell of roast. At the guest house I washed quickly and changed my clothes. Teeth-marks in the soft places. A big meal would be perfect.

In a niche by the front door I passed Speusippus in linen, reviewing some notes. We looked each other up and down and looked away. A roar went up when I walked through the inner door. They were drunk already, my classmates, and roared at every appearance: me, Callippus with a scroll under one arm, a slave with a tray of new delicacies. Plato sat with Eudoxus, but broke off his conversation to look up and smile every now and then at this or that student and mouth some pleasantry. *So long,* I read many times on his lips, and *thank you.* Something something something *so long.* He had not changed clothes, or his travelling clothes were his only clothes. I saw him notice me. He raised his hand for silence.

"Nephew," he called.

Speusippus had entered immediately behind me, and made a show of putting his clammy hand on my head to move me aside. "Uncle. All here now."

Speusippus released me. I stepped back into the crowd, back and back, as he made his speech of welcome, until I found a slave against the wall with a tray I could pick clean. I finished in time to applaud with the others.

"Water," I told the slave with two pitchers on his tray. My hands still smelled of the girl, or I imagined they did. I plucked a large flower from an arrangement and shoved finger after fin-

ger down its white throat, reaming for scent. Plato was responding to Speusippus. He had taken the scroll from Callippus and
unrolled it and held it up. It was a map of the world, fly-specked
with black dots. Plato was explaining that each dot represented
the birthplace of a member of the Academy. We all edged closer,
looking for our dots. There was no Stageira-dot. The Pella-dot
was probably supposed to be me.

"I'm so proud of you all," Plato was saying. "I've been away
for so long. Too long, I know. I'm very tired, and can't imagine
travelling again anytime soon. You're all stuck with me, is what
I'm trying to say." Laughter. "We have a lot of work to do, a lot
of problems to solve. Difficult problems. But there is no problem without a solution. We are the world in miniature here,
and together we will solve the problems of the world. Problems
of geometry, problems of physics, problems of government,
problems of justice and law. What we achieve here will be
incorruptible down the ages." Applause. "And I apologize for
the rubbish they're feeding you. I see standards in the kitchen
have slipped unconscionably since I've been away. We'll remedy
that problem tomorrow." Laughter and applause. A rebuke: the
food was fine and fancy, the master a known ascetic. "Tomorrow," he repeated.

I made my way over to him as the party resumed.

"Did the new boy like my speech?" he asked.

"All problems have solutions and the food will be worse
tomorrow?"

He laughed, and leaned forward to look into my cup. "He
doesn't drink?"

He spoke like Illaeus. Illaeus spoke like him. "Not much."

"Why not?"

Callippus was rolling the scroll, listening to something Eudoxus was saying in his ear. We were alone for a moment in the middle of the crowded room. "My master in Pella drank. It stopped him from getting his work done."

"Illaeus."

I nodded.

"I remember his time here. A lovely boy. Lovely mind. A gift for languages, and for language. Loved poetry. He drank then, too, and liked to go into the city, alone, at night. It seemed harmless at the time."

I held his look.

"His letter moved me," Plato said. "Unexpected, first of all, because he left angry. I hadn't heard from him in years. Then he says, I have a boy here. You must take this boy."

I smelled my fingers.

"I had a master myself, years ago. Will you come with me, please? I'm having trouble hearing in this room."

He led me through a curtain. I felt my classmates watch us go. We sat in a room I had never entered, a cell with a bed, table, two chairs, and a shelf of books.

"My master was a father to me," he said. "I will be a father to you, if you'll let me. You are already so many people to me. Illaeus, again, and my own younger self, and your own self too. Eudoxus tells me the others are frightened of you. He says you spend a lot of time alone."

"Yes."

"That's not a bad thing. It doesn't have to be."

"Why did Illaeus leave angry?"

"He wanted me to love him the most. I failed him."

We sat listening to the party sounds from the big room.

"Not all problems have solutions," I said.

We spoke for a while about that. I too wanted him to love me the most, already, and suspected the way to achieve that was to fight him. He had enough fawns in the other room. He said he believed in perfection; I said I believed in compromise. Perfection was an extreme, and I had a need to avoid extremes, perhaps because I was so subject to them.

"I will help you," he said.

A tap on the door frame, and Eudoxus looked in. "Food." He set a plate on the table.

"Sleep, rather." Plato rose, handing me the plate. "Eat for me. Boys are always hungry. Our conversation will last years; we needn't finish it tonight."

Eudoxus led me back to the party. "You may not want that." He nodded at the plate. "It was prepared specially for him. No honey, no salt. He likes you. What did you talk about?"

Bread, figs, yogourt, a duck egg.

"Lucky!" My friends gathered around, staring at the plate, at me.

The girl had licked and bitten, licked and bitten, until I didn't know myself. I knew I had seen her for the last time. Giddy, I gave the plate away.

FIVE

YTHIAS IS DYING. Her pain is a bright ribbon drawing her
on through dun days and sleepless nights; it's all that's real
to her. She lies in her room, in her bed, in sheets sweet-
scented by fruits left to ripen in the cupboards, fanned by the hour
by her maid. I can't help thinking of her pain, also, as a rational
being, one with whom she must argue to rescue herself, but as a
poor reasoner she cannot. I see the perplexity in her face, the lines
in the brow, as pain's logic bests her again and again. Sometimes, in
a low voice, she speaks of her girlhood in Hermias's court, of her
mother and of a younger sister, whom she's never mentioned
before; sometimes she cries out, and I can't tell pain from grief. In
her sleep she thrashes, gripped by nightmares, and wakes white-
faced, eyes and mouth black with fear. It takes a long time to persuade her to tell me what she sees.

"A road," she'll say, or, "I am walking," and then the terror
will grip her again and she'll refuse to say more. I know she
believes these dreams to be prophetic.

"If you tell me the dreams, I might find a way to stop them."
But this, too, troubles her: if the gods want her to watch her
death, it would be impious to refuse the vision.

"So you die in the dream, then?" I ask, relentlessly. I've never
had a recurring dream, never had dreams of any coherence, in
fact, and am fascinated.

Pythias closes her eyes, and with a great effort opens them again. She looks directly into my eyes while she speaks, and my attention to her words is overlaid with the revelation that throughout our marriage we've rarely made eye contact. She's always gazing just over my shoulder, or at my chest, or my feet.

"I am walking," she says. "I am alone. There is a wind and the sky is black. Then the sky begins to melt. It falls away in strips, and behind the sky is a white fire, and a huge noise. Soon the heavens are on fire, and the sky is a few black tatters, peeling away in the wind. The wind and the noise and the heat are unbearable, but worst of all is that I am alone."

She clings to my hands, her knuckles gone white.

"I barely have to close my eyes and it comes," she whispers. "Have I done wrong to tell you?"

I comfort her as best I know how, in the language of reason, explaining that the body's sense-organ, the heart, needs natural intermissions, called sleep; that the goal is to give rest to the senses. I explain the relationship between digestion and sleep (privately taking note to question the maid about her eating habits), and tell her that dreams are the persistence of sensory impressions, playing upon the imagination. Many factors can affect the nature of one's dreams, such as slight sensory input during sleep—a room too hot or too cold, say—which will then become exaggerated in the dream, producing an impression of freezing or burning. Perhaps her dream of great heat was suggested by her fever, or too many blankets. (Her eyes follow mine throughout this lesson, like Little Pythias's when I tell her she will one day be a great beautiful lady like her mother; doubtful, yet wanting to believe.) I explain further that certain people are particularly susceptible to violent dreams, these including people who are excitable, or under the grip of some strong emotion, or those with vacant minds, vacuums that need to be filled. (I don't suggest to which category she might belong. My own dreams are negligible; my mind is too busy in waking to suck for fuel during sleep.) As for impiety, I explain gently, dogs have been known to dream—they run their legs in sleep—and why would the gods send visions to a dog? No, dreams might be coincidental, or prescient, but then some people respond to almost any stimulus, the way water trembles throughout when the smallest pebble is tossed into it, and see visions in straw and cooking pots and fingernail clippings as much as in dreams. It means nothing.

"I had thought, perhaps, it was a memory." Pythias is calmer now. "When you told me of the heavens, of all the—the spheres, and the outermost sphere that was black but all full of pin-holes, so that the great fire behind shone through as stars. It frightened me at the time, when you explained it to me, and I thought perhaps I was remembering this in my dreams."

"Now, you see." I feel a simultaneous rush of gratitude and affection and amazement and pain at the inevitable, impending loss of her. "You have already thought it through, without me. I am proud of you."

She lies back, then, and closes her eyes in a show of bravery.

"She is comfortable," the maid says later, when I ask. "She slept this afternoon, a little, while you were out." This maid, Herpyllis, is a warm creature, not especially young, with a tidy bent and a sympathetic face. The dark one with the green eyes, the one Pythias likes. Now that Pythias is utterly bedridden, Herpyllis has taken over the running of the household. I've seen her coddle Little Pythias with hugs and cooing, affection the little girl accepts with total, unsmiling attention. I suspect her of trying to comfort me. I don't resent the effort, but am curious about the audacity it implies. She's a servant, not a slave; still.

"You take it very calmly," I say to her as she closes the door to the sickroom. Her arms are full of the bed linens she has just changed, her face flushed with the effort of stripping them without disturbing Pythias. I'd been meaning to spell her by the sickbed, as I do every evening now, but Pythias waved me away, saying I would only try to make her think.

"You can talk to Herpyllis instead," my wife said. "She will listen."

"I've seen it before," the maid says now, in the hall. "When I was a girl. Sometimes in the stomach, sometimes the breasts. My mother used to sit with the sick. She would take me with her."

I stand aside to let her precede me, and follow her to the kitchen, where she drops the laundry in a corner. "And can you guess," I say, but courage crumples inside me and I stand unhappily without finishing the sentence.

"How long?"

I nod. She, in turn, shakes her head, which I take at first to mean she doesn't want to venture a guess, but then she says, "She won't suffer much more."

I watch her move around the kitchen, tidying, and beginning to prepare my meal. She plucks a hair from her head, a coarse white strand from the dark, and with it sets to slicing a hard-boiled egg for Little Pythias's supper. Not so young, but not so old. Her hands, the nails especially, are clean for a servant's. The pans are burnished, the floor scrubbed. My own bed linen, I'm only now realizing, is always changed before I have a chance to smell myself on it. My meals are prompt and hot; my favourites appear without me asking for them. Even the court-yard garden appears more kempt, weeded and watered and clipped and staked. I'm noticing everything, now.

When I clear my throat, she turns away from her chopping board, wipes her hands, and pulls up her skirts—from some wet-ness on the floor, I think at first. When she smiles, laughter in her eyes, I start back, as though from a cinder. The rest of the evening I spend in my study with the door closed, which the ser-vants know means I am absolutely not to be disturbed.

THERE ARE HISTORICAL PRECEDENTS for certain territor-ial borders—Sparta, Argos, Arcadia, Messene—that Philip, busily redrawing the maps down there, should know about. So I tell myself, planning to send him a letter of advice. Perhaps I'll compare him to Heracles while I'm at it. Voices at the gate; Tycho will send them away; I'm sick; I don't leave my study; I see no one. But footsteps.

"Ears full of shit and skull full of shit," I say to Tycho without turning away from the maps on the table in front of me. "I told you, I'm not home."

"Can't hear you."

I look up.

"Ears full of shit," Alexander explains.

What is it? Taller, deeper voice, what? Oh, what?

"I came to see Pythias."

"Did you?"

"She said I could come whenever I wanted."

The corner of my mouth twitches. A smile, if I could smile.

He kneels in front of me, looks at my face. "She's not—"

"Not yet."

He takes my hands.

"No." I pull back. No warmth, no touch. "She's sleeping. Will you stay until she wakes?"

He nods.

"How are you? When did you get back?"

"Yesterday." He tells me briefly of his past few weeks, closely monitored in Athens and then promptly sent home. "They don't know what to do with me. My father and Antipater. They think I'm going to hurt someone, or myself. Antipater told me as much. I haven't seen my father since the battle. At least they gave me my knife back."

So there it is, out on the table between us at last. "Do you remember much of what happened that day?"

"Some. I know what Hephaestion's told me." He hesitates. "He told me what my father said about not having an heir. Is it true?"

"Philip was frightened."

"No, I don't think so. My father doesn't get frightened."

"Pissed off, then. You—we were doing something he didn't understand."

"We?"

"You, then."

"A gift. Carolus liked the head."

So he does remember. "How did you get that thing, anyway?"

He looks blank, and I shiver. It chutes me back six years, that same look of incomprehension when Carolus asked him where he'd find one.

"You remember. The head was my job. I was going to sculpt one out of clay and paint it. I went to the actor's house to get a look at him, to make it accurate, and the minute I saw him I knew he wouldn't be performing. It was obvious to anybody. There was an old woman there who said he'd been sleeping for days and wouldn't wake up again. He was feverish. She lifted the sheet and showed me his belly. He was swollen from not having had a shit in so long. She said that's what was killing him: there was a blockage and his body was filling with shit. Can that happen?"

I nod.

"So I sketched his face, for my sculpture, and went home and worked on it, but I couldn't get it right. It looked silly, like a child had done it."

"You *were* a child. Sculpture is difficult enough for a master artist."

He waves this away. "I should have been able to do it and I couldn't. But I realized why. It was because I had already had a better idea. It was a waste of time to work on the lesser idea. So I went back to his house."

I want to know and not to know. "And did you—" I flutter my hands. Soon I will be half a hundred years old. "Help?"

He hesitates; changes what he was going to say. In six years, this is the first time I've seen him do this. "The old woman did, with a pillow. She said he had suffered enough."

"And she let you take the head?"

"I took the whole thing. She knew who I was. What was she going to do? I had him buried properly, afterwards. I'm not an animal."

The greatest insult one man could level against another, I remember telling him once, and it's the achievement of my time here that he believes it. "Would you do such a thing again? Today?"

"You have to admit it was effective."

"I admit it was effective. Would you do it again?"

"You want me to say no. No, I wouldn't do it again."

"Why not?"

"Because Carolus is dead."

"There's no one left to impress?"

Alexander looks at his lap.

"Forgive me. I inflict pain with words, the tragedian's art. Tell me, if you were to write a tragedy, what would it be about?"

He looks up.

"What makes you feel fear, pity?"

"That's easy. You. Stuck here, with me, when you could be great in the world. Put in a little box by my father and the lid nailed down tight. An animal dying in a cage."

"You're not dying."

"I was talking about you."

"No, you weren't."

"And when you're done and all the juice is sucked out, someone will come along and cut open your head and say, here, look at this enormous brain. Look at the waste."

"No waste," I say softly.

"Waste of mind, waste of body, waste of time. What would you write a tragedy about?"

"Master." Tycho stands in the doorway. "My lady is awake."

We stand.

"I want to see her alone," Alexander says.

I wait in the courtyard, picking over my herbs. Late fall again, everything dying again. Even the perennials have gone woody and brown. They aren't long together.

"She asked if you'd fed me," Alexander says when he returns after a few minutes. "I told her you hadn't, and I was starving."

"Now I'll have hell to pay." We walk to the gate together. "How is your mother?"

"Happier. I'm seeing a lot of her, these days. Who's going to stop me?"

In the street wait Hephaestion and a handful of others I recognize, boys I've taught. Men, now, who take no notice of me, except for Hephaestion, who nods and looks away.

"My escort," Alexander says.

"Will I see you again?"

"My father forbids it. So, of course."

I return to Pythias. The bedroom is hot and dark and smells of the spices that burn in a little brazier to scent the air.

"He can't sleep," she says. "Loud sounds startle him. He can't concentrate on books. He can't always remember how he spent his day. He gets angry and then he comes out of it and wants to die."

"It's a kind of battle sickness. Soldier's heart, they call it."

"Soldier's heart." I watch her turn it over in her mind. "Sounds like praise."

"I've thought that, too. I'm told they often recover."

"He says it's getting worse."

I remember him limping for his mother. "He's worried about you. He wants you to fuss over him so you'll forget yourself. He'll be fine."

The answer, of course, is that I wouldn't write a tragedy. I don't have that kind of mind.

PHILIP RETURNS TO PELLA early in the winter a changed man. He chews parsley to sweeten his breath, and dresses fashionably, and drinks noticeably less. It's said he's infatuated with the daughter of the general Attalus, a girl named Cleopatra. She's a living blank, fresh and pretty and unremarkable. Her mouth sits in a natural pout, like the petals of a flower, probably the source of the attraction. She has the guileless serenity of a favourite not old enough to appreciate the danger of her position, and a shrieking laugh.

Herpyllis is from Stageira, and that is the point of the dagger that nicks my heart. Pythias tells me this during one of our long afternoons when our conversation ranges loose and wide and it's not difficult for me to mention the woman's particular good care of me during her illness. The next time we happen to be alone together, as Herpyllis is serving my supper, I ask her if it's true.

"You don't remember me?"

"I wish I did," I say, truthfully. "I think you're younger than me, though."

"Maybe a little. I remember your father's house. Beautiful flowers. My father helped yours remove a wasps' nest from under the eaves. I would have been seven or eight. I remember sitting in the garden, watching with a bunch of other children from the houses around, and you kept herding us farther and farther back so we wouldn't get stung. Just like a sheepdog."

"I remember." And with a thump I do—the high heat of summer, the drone of the wasps, the extraordinary noise from all the visitors in the garden, and my own excitement and exhaustion to be around so many children when I was used to spending my time alone. The day was like a festival. "What else?"

"You were always swimming. We would see this head out in

the water, my sisters and I, and know who it was. But our mother told us we must never laugh at you because you were a favourite of the sea-god."

"You laughed at me?"

She waves this away, laughing now, refilling my cup. "My father was a fisherman. You wouldn't have known me, but I remember you. I went to work for your mother's people in Chalcis, and they sent me to you when you married."

"Yes." Though this is a watery memory; I could see only Pythias then. Perhaps I remember a woman a few years older than my new wife, taller and heavier, readier to smile. I never had much to do with my wife's women.

Over the next days and weeks we trade these little reminiscences—the big snowfall, the bumper crop, the terrible storm, the festivals of our shared but separate childhoods. The kitchen offer has not yet been repeated, though I have an idea it will be. She's not the green sprig Pythias was; her breasts are heavy doughs to Pythias's apples. For a while I decide I actively dislike her: too easy and pleasant and smiling, too close to my own age, too familiar, and most of all too disconcerting: a black smudge on my memory, a little empty place, a face I should recall and can't. She becomes annoying, a constant chafing, and I listen for her step, her voice, just for the irritation it produces in me. Her smell, too, a perfume of my wife's (Pythias told me of the gift; "I have too much; I'll never get through it all now"), transformed by the alchemy of her different skin from lighter to darker flowers: so I imagine. Her mannerisms—the way she smooths her hair behind her ear with curving fingers, her habit of grunting softly when she sits after long standing or stands after long sitting, the constant light smile, the occasional unconscious cupping of her own breasts—become intolerable to me. Of course I am falling in love, and know it. Sex is not a cure, but a treatment I'm saving for the height of the fever.

One day she tackles the books in my library, takes them out into the sun to blow the dust off and dry them out to inhibit mould, a process I find distracting: the coming and going, the books out of place, fear of my daughter's grubby hands, fear of rain. I move from my work table to the doorway every minute or two to make sure Little Pythias isn't sucking on my *Republic*, or a cloud hasn't blown over to ruin everything.

"Still blue sky," Herpyllis says, pointing up. The next time I glance out she doesn't notice: she's looking at one of the books.

I go up behind her and look over her shoulder. "You read?"

She starts and rolls it up. "No."

I take the book from her hand. It's sticky. I unroll it, read a few lines, and laugh. Drawings, too, what she must have been looking at. "Perfect. I needed a gift for the wedding."

THE DAY AFTER THE WEDDING, Alexander and Olympias and their entourage leave Pella for Dodona, the capital of neighbouring Epirus, where Olympias's brother is king.

"I don't see the fuss," Callisthenes says to me in my study. "Philip's had other wives since Olympias. Why does she run away now?"

I hear in the turn of phrase the condescension of the court.

"And Alexander. A lion in battle, but at home he's as hysterical as a woman."

"Who says so?" I ask.

"If you'd gone to court, you'd have seen it. He's been as twitchy as hell, picking fights with people over nothing. Like last night. Attacking Attalus? Threatening his own father?"

Callisthenes attended the wedding as Philip's guest; I wasn't invited.

"What happened, exactly?" I've heard only a garbled report from Tycho. Slaves get their information fast, but it's rarely accurate.

"Attalus gave a toast saying what handsome children they'd produce, or something like that. Alexander took offence and threw a cup at his head. Nailed him." Callisthenes mimes Attalus taking a blow to the temple. "*Doof.* Then Philip jumps up and falls flat on his face, and Alexander asks how's he going to make it to Persia if he can't make it off his own couch—"

"Cute."

"—and then something about everyone insulting his mother for the last time. He kind of lost me there, but I'd had a lot to drink."

"Olympias isn't Macedonian, she's Epirote, so that makes Alexander half-and-half. A pure Macedonian son would move ahead of Alexander in line to the throne."

"Alexander won't allow himself to be supplanted by a baby," my nephew says smoothly.

It never ceases to amaze me how the man can glide right over his own ignorance and carry on a conversation as though I'm the one in need of instruction.

"I don't see how he will prevent it. A regent can rule through a baby until it's of age. It wouldn't be the first time."

Though I'm mostly housebound now, I pick up the gossip;

inflamed from my nephew when he visits, calmer from Herpyllis. Alexander installed his mother at her brother's court, in Dodona, and himself visited the celebrated oracle there, a massive oak tree full of nesting doves and hung with bronze vessels that sound in the wind. Thereafter he rode north, alone, and is rumoured to be reflecting deeply. (Herpyllis smiles; I smile; then we put our smiles away, carefully, without further comment.) Meanwhile a mediator, Demaratus of Corinth, a family friend, is now in Pella, now in Epirus, relaying messages of respect and contrition between father and son. All this the Macedonians watch with their usual voracious affection, as though the two men are a tussling lion and cub. Eventually Alexander returns alone to Pella, head held high, and resumes with dignity and magnanimity his former role of heir apparent. It helps that the child Cleopatra has made herself scarce; it's said she's pregnant and ill with it, and rarely leaves her bed.

I begin a little work on respiration, a booklet to keep myself busy at Pythias's bedside. She slips in and out of consciousness, and I spend hours watching the sunlight move across the walls, listening to the rhythm of her breath. I myself slip too easily, these afternoons, into a kind of drugged stupor, with memories and erotic daydreams twining themselves together as I remember Pythias in the bloom of youth, Pythias on our wedding night in her veils and garlands as I led her to my door, where the women waited with burning torches, and later at the wedding feast, eating sesame cake and quince; Pythias who after that first night I had to coax with infinite patience out of her clothes and into my bed; Pythias who lies bed-bound now, who won't rise again. I even masturbate once as she lies struggling for breath. I write down everything I know about breathing, in men and animals and fish and birds, and try to dispel the memory I have not been able to resist, the memory that hurts my heart now, of our wedding night, when I laid my head on her breast and felt the rise and fall of her breath, and thought that I would never again have to sleep alone.

PYTHIAS DIES IN THE NIGHT. When she starts to rasp I go to the kitchen for a cup of water, and by the time I get back she's gone. I close her eyes and put the coin on her tongue and lie down beside her, pressing my face into her shoulder, her neck, her breast, into the last warmth there. Mine at the last.

A FEW DAYS LATER, a courier appears. Together we ride up to the palace. Summer is coming; the light is flattening out and heat stays longer in the ground. I think briefly of taking Herpyllis to the coast, of teaching her to swim, but know I won't. She'll be too ready, too smiling.

My audience turns out to be a private one. After I've waited a few minutes alone in a small anteroom, Philip strides in and embraces me roughly.

"I heard. I'm sorry."

The king sits with me for a long time, speaking with his familiar rough gentleness, with a catch in his voice that sounds genuine, and moves me. He is more patient with me than I am with Little Pythias, who has cried herself into a fever and vomits up everything she eats. She keeps asking for a coin for the ferryman so she can go see Mummy. I can't bear to be near her.

Eventually I force myself to say to him, "I'm keeping you from your duties."

"You're not. I keep thinking of my little one, if she were to have died. I don't know what I would have done."

I remember, then, to congratulate him on the birth of his daughter.

"Eurydice, we're calling her, after my mother." Philip shakes his head. "I'll tell you what else. I've had the satrap of Caria offering his daughter to Arrhidaeus."

"In marriage?"

Philip laughs and wipes his eyes.

"Caria." I try to think clearly.

"Not too big, not too small. Strategic. It might just do. We're having a dinner for him, you must come."

"For Arrhidaeus?"

"For Pixodarus. The satrap. That's a thought, though. I suppose he should be there?"

"Arrhidaeus?" I say again.

"You're right, of course. I hope he doesn't fuck it up. Feeds himself, does he?"

"When was the last time you saw him?"

Philip squints fiercely. "Can't remember," he says finally. "How long have you been with us?"

"Six years."

"That sounds about right."

I get up to go.

"Wait, wait, wait. You're in a fuck of a rush today. I haven't told you the main thing yet."

Apparently not the death of my wife, nor the birth of his daughter, nor the marriage of his son is the main thing. I sit back down.

"You look like I'm going to hit you."

He feints a punch at my head and I duck automatically. Sometime in the last twenty-five years I've acquired the reflex.

Philip laughs. "I never thanked you for my wedding gift, did I, in all the commotion? You always were funny."

So that is the main thing: a sticky little book, a bit of nostalgia still smelling slightly of raisins. "I was?"

"You had a face like a clown. You were always trying to make everybody laugh. I remember you could mimic people. You used to do your father, and my father. That was a little spooky, actually."

"Not me."

"Oh, yes. And you did me once, too, and I beat the shit out of you. Funny as hell, but I had to. I think you were pretending to screw an apple."

"You did love apples," I say, slowly, trying to remember.

"Still do." He swats his own leg conclusively, as though I've settled the matter. "And that's a funny thing. Alexander loves them, too. I used to share mine with him when he was a toddler, feed him off my own knife. He couldn't get enough of me, once. Where did that little boy go, do you suppose?"

"Got his own knife."

He bumps my jaw with his fist, gently, a blow I see coming and this time let happen. "We should have been better friends."

It's the closest to an apology I'm going to get. I nod.

"Cleopatra says Olympias might be telling the truth about the boy having been fathered by one of the gods. Never mind that face, you've heard the rumours. Olympias herself spreads them. Has done for years, but I never paid any attention before now. Little Cleopatra, eh? Already a politician. We both know what she's really getting at, of course, only she knows better than to come out and say it. Though I don't think it can be true. Another lover? Not back then, anyway. We were white hot for a while, his mother and I. Do you think he looks like me?"

"What a thing to ask."

Philip laughs. "See? Funny. After all, what are you going to say? All right. Though he has always favoured her, the hair and skin and so on. Is it ridiculous to start wondering only now?"

I decide my grief will buy me some indulgence. "He's not very tall."

"That's nice of you to remind me." Philip looks annoyed, which was the danger. But then he says again, "That's nice of you to remind me," his eyes no longer focused on me, and I know I've given him what he wanted, a little polished stone to hold on to in the night and rub with his thumb, a worry-bead, a talisman: two short men in a kingdom of tall.

I wonder how long this will hold him, and how clever his new little wife really is. A daughter this time, but a son next time, maybe, and then what? Not so blank and guileless, if she's already looking that far ahead. She's learned quickly, or someone is teaching her. And how long before Alexander hears that his father is wondering if he's a bastard?

"All right," Philip says. I wonder how much of this he's already figured out for himself. Most of it, would be my guess. "You see, it's always good for me to talk to you. Now I'm going to give you something. This probably isn't the right time, and you may not care right now in your time of mourning, but I want you to take it away with you, if you know what I mean, and let it sink in. I'm rebuilding Stageira."

"Stageira?"

"A repayment, for all you've done with the boy. A gift. Call it whatever you want. I know things haven't turned out the way either of us expected, but you can't look at him and think you've wasted your time."

"No. I don't."

"You can't. Anyway. I've ordered the work started, and I want you to go there later this summer and oversee it. You can tell me what needs doing and I'll have it taken care of. Fields, crops, buildings, boats, whatever it needs. We could bring the people back, too, try to. You'd know where to find some of them, maybe?"

"Maybe."

"I remember you had a brother."

"Yes." I don't tell him that Arimnestus died in his eighteenth year after a fall from a horse, nor that the following year Arimneste died giving birth to her second child, a daughter who died with her, and that Proxenus and Nicanor left Atarneus before I ever got there and are settled now in Eresus, on Lesvos. Pythias and I visited them there once or twice during our years in Mytilene. Stageira doesn't mean anything to them. And it surely isn't Athens, but I understand that promise is in the spheres now, with the Theban.

We rise together and embrace one last time.

"He's like a god, isn't he," Philip says. "Who understands the gods? You can't blame me for making backup plans. Some days I just look at him and wonder what he'll do next."

"WATCH THIS," ALEXANDER SAYS.

At his sign, the actor begins to declaim.

"You can't do that," I say, within a couple of words, when I've caught the gist of the speech.

The actor stops. Alexander turns to me with his old look of amused incredulity.

"Majesty," I add quickly.

We're in the palace library, where Alexander summoned me ostensibly for a lesson.

"But I can, and I will," Alexander says. "Who do you think he'll prefer for his daughter, Arrhidaeus or me? Would he dare refuse me?"

The actor is tall and slender and handsome, and stands with an unnatural stillness while others speak. I recognize him as Thessalus from Corinth, the famous tragedian, a new favourite of the Macedonian court.

"Again," Alexander says, and the actor starts over. He speaks lengthily of Alexander's qualities while the prince beats time on the arm of his chair.

"You've met this girl?" I ask when he's done.

Alexander tosses a few coins that the actor catches neatly and pockets. He bows low and slow, with tragic dignity, and leaves the room.

Alexander brushes away the remark, and by implication all casual conversation, with a toss of his hand, as though at a fly. "He arranges a marriage for my brother. My feeble, idiot, older brother. Why not me, then? Am I not marriageable? Does he think Arrhidaeus has something I lack? Caria is our most important ally against the Persians."

I wonder if I dare point out this isn't true.

"He's trying to replace me. He doesn't trust me. He had a daughter, you see, so now he must find another way. He'll take Arrhidaeus's whelp before me, even."

I notice a pile of papers on the table at his elbow. "Do you hear from your mother?" Olympias has remained in Epirus with the king her brother, sulking, the Macedonians say.

"She writes me." Alexander indicates the papers.

I counsel him to reconsider.

"I suppose you think I am not fit for marriage either."

"Not for this marriage, no. It's beneath you."

I watch the boy consider my words, holding himself nobly still, as the actor did.

WHEN PHILIP FOUND OUT about Alexander's scheme, he banished four of Alexander's companions, including Ptolemy, but not Hephaestion. Never a fool, Philip, even in anger; he wanted to punish his son, not break him. When Philip learned Thessalus was already on his way back to Corinth, he sent soldiers out after him and had him brought back to Pella in chains. This indignity the actor bore with great nobility and quiet suffering.

"I can imagine," I say.

Herpyllis, who's telling the story, pokes my arm reprovingly. We're in bed. We're screwing now, a nice salty business I don't have to explain to anyone. She went to see the actor dragged through the streets, as did most of Pella, while I stayed home to work on my book.

"That poor girl, though," Herpyllis says. "Not knowing which brother she's getting."

I turn onto my back to help her. "She's getting Arrhidaeus. I think Philip took care of that pretty quickly."

"Poor girl."

I close my eyes. "Poor boy."

My mind goes to work on the categories of pleasure and how to teach them. The first time or two, Herpyllis let me go at it in my own way. When she began to guide me a little, I assumed she was offering me liberties she thought I was hesitant to take: tongue at the tit, fingers in the hole. Then, one night after I had spent myself, she continued to grunt and shift until I asked her what was wrong. I ran my fingers down her arm to her own fingers to see what she was doing.

"Do you need a cloth?" I asked. Not wiping, though, but rubbing. She tried to use my fingers but I pulled away and told her to be more modest.

"What?" she said.

"I am finished." I was aware of sounding like my father. "That is not necessary."

"You're finished. I'm not."

Not knowing what to say, I let her continue. She arched her back a little and then collapsed in a series of spasms, moaning weakly with each exhale. An annoying sound.

"And what was that?"

I assumed her answer was a lie. My father had taught me what she claimed to experience was not physically possible.

"Next time, you can help," she said.

I asked her to describe her pleasure.

"Like honey," she said, and, "Like a drum." And other similes: cresting a hill, waves breaking, the colour of gold.

She said when I came I sounded like a man lifting something heavy and then, with a great effort, setting it down.

THE FIRST GREEK KING in Macedon was told by an oracle to build a city at the place where he first saw the *aigas,* the goats. Twenty-four years ago, Philip's first military outing as king was the defence of Aegeae—former capital, site of the royal tombs—against Athens. Late this summer, the court relocates to Aegeae.

The palace, protected from behind by a mountain, faces north, with a view across the shrine and the city to the plain below. It's smaller than the palace at Pella but older and holier; all important ceremonies are held here. At the heart of the complex is a square courtyard forested with columns; then reception rooms, shrines, living rooms. The circular throne-room has an inscription to Heracles in mosaic; elsewhere the floor is worked with stone vines and flowers so that it's like walking across meadows in bloom. Near the west wall is the outdoor theatre. A tall stone wall shelters courtiers on their way from the palace to the theatre, cutting them off from the public space of the city. The theatre is stone and beaten earth, with platforms for the audience and an altar to Dionysus at the centre of the pit.

In addition to the court from Pella comes the king of Epirus, Olympias's brother Alexandros. Philip, politicking to the last, has arranged for his and Olympias's daughter to wed her own uncle. The marriage is widely understood as a tool to confirm Alexandros's loyalty to Philip, rather than to Olympias. It's an important wedding, too, not so much because of who the bride and groom are—Philip, presumably, still has a thumb free for each of them—but as an opportunity for Philip to display his grand greatness before all the world. Macedon itself will be on display. There will be a festival of the arts, games, and massive banquets over many days. Foreign guests come from everywhere; this is not the season when foreigners are refusing Philip.

On the morning of the first day of celebrations is to be a performance of Euripides, the *Bacchae*, again. Is Philip indulging in a little irony, reminding his brother-in-law of the last performance they attended together, all those years ago? We all love the *Bacchae*.

I sit in the audience with my nephew, toward the back, waiting for the play to begin. Below us sit a few hundred of Philip's choicest guests, men all bright and lovely in their festival clothes, flowers in their hair, their many languages glorifying the air. The rest of the guests—a thousand all told, I've heard—will be feasting already, waiting for this afternoon's games. The heat is oppressive and I'm missing Herpyllis, who's remained behind in Pella to care for Little Pythias and our newborn son: Nicomachus, after my father. I miss my son's small self in the bed, where Herpyllis matter-of-factly put him between us that first night, where he sleeps with his arms stretched wide, a hand on his mother and a hand on me. He gives me a deep animal pleasure—his fat little heat and snoring, a cub in the den, tangling limbs—that I never had with my daughter. Pythias insisted she sleep in her own room with her nurse, who for nighttime feeds roused us formally with a ritual knock at the door, as though fearing to interrupt us in some act of uxoriousness. Little Pythias was a fretful baby and took forever to get back to sleep once woken. Little Nicomachus, so far, eats like a wolf—Herpyllis feeds him on her lap, cross-legged next to me in the bed, like a peasant girl—and sleeps like a sot, a white trickle of his bliss still in the corner of his mouth. He will be an uncomplicated sort, I think. I miss him. I take pleasure, too, in Herpyllis, who is naturally kind and competent, who shares my childhood memories and has a reassuring earthiness to my dead wife's absentee etherealism. But my work frankly bores her, and when I speak of it she always has another task in hand, mending, or trimming vegetables, or feeding the baby, or braiding Little Pythias's fine hair.

It's time to start choosing a future: somewhere with people I can talk to, or at least ghosts I can live with. "I see a journey," Callisthenes said to me yesterday, waggling his fingers in front of his eyes like a priest having a vision. So do I; but journeys need hope and courage and planning and a desire to get up in the morning. It's going to take me a while to muster those troops.

The procession starts, the drums and trumpets, the statues of the gods, and then Philip himself a few steps ahead of his bodyguard. The crowd roars. One of the bodyguard ducks suddenly and draws a knife. Philip seems to say something, seems to raise a hand to the soldier's shoulder, and then the knife is sticking in Philip's chest. What? Philip looks over his shoulder, kneels carefully, touches the knife's handle, and lies down.

I don't see what happens onstage after that. All around me men are shouting profanities, naming the gods, denying what they've seen. What? No! Then the crowd is pushing and stumbling and running and we are borne along in it, Callisthenes and I, particles in a current. We link elbows to stay together. Outside the theatre, soldiers are yelling at people to go back to wherever they're lodging and stay there. For us, that's the palace library. We're searched for weapons several times as we make our way there. Callisthenes is bleeding from a kicked ankle.

"Is the prince all right?" I ask a soldier at the palace gate. He recognizes us.

"The king, you mean."

"Is he all right?"

"He's the king," the soldier says.

The library is silent. Our bedrolls are where we left them this morning. So many foreigners are here, every spare room is taken. I don't like eating and drinking and washing and pissing in here, bringing moisture in with the books, but we weren't given a choice.

"You saw who it was?" Callisthenes tears a strip from his bed linen to bind his ankle. "Pausanias."

"Why?"

Callisthenes knows. There's a story told about the officer—a bookend to the story Carolus told me about his promotion, long ago—that he quarrelled with Attalus, the new queen's father, and that Attalus, pretending reconciliation, invited him to dinner, got him drunk, and threw him into the yard with the stableboys. When Pausanias went to Philip for justice, the king refused to punish his own father-in-law. Instead, he sent Attalus off in command of an advance force to Persia to prepare for the coming invasion, and promoted Pausanias once again, this time to his personal bodyguard, in an attempt to pacify him.

"They held him down and took turns," Callisthenes says. "He shit blood for days."

"He attacks the king because of some rough trade? That doesn't sound right." Though, as Carolus once reminded me, *they celebrate with it, they make people suffer with it, they do their business with it, they run the kingdom with it.* "You don't suppose Philip's dead?"

The room has one tall slit of a window overlooking vine-yards. Callisthenes cranes his neck, trying to see something, any-thing. "Do you think anyone remembers we're in here?"

The answer comes at midnight. We've lit lamps and drunk this morning's stale water but we haven't dared go look for food. Now we're lying in our bedrolls, wide awake, when a sol-dier opens the door. A soldier: Antipater.

"Not you," he says to Callisthenes.

I follow him through the unfamiliar halls. Aegeae is older and rougher than modern, expensive Pella; the halls are narrower, darker, with lower ceilings and uneven floors. We pass sentries and patrols, antsy soldiers with white faces who startle and bris-tle until they recognize Antipater. I'm glad we didn't try to leave the library ourselves.

"Face me," Antipater says outside a door. "Spread your arms." He pats me down for weapons. "Go in."

"What is this?"

"Go in."

A bedroom. Alexander sits on the bed, head in his hands. He looks up when I come in. I sit down beside him and put an arm around his shoulders.

"Maybe I wanted it," he says.

"All young men want their fathers dead. I did. And then when it happens—"

"I sacrificed for it."

"What did you sacrifice?"

"A black cock. I wanted a bull but you can't hide a bull. But the gods knew what I meant."

"When was this?"

"After Maedi, after he said he'd cripple me if I went out again on my own."

"Three years ago?"

"The gods knew."

"Three years," I say. "Child, the gods don't wait that long. You didn't do this."

"I knew about Pausanias."

"His argument with Attalus?"

"And if it wasn't Pausanias, it would have been someone else. The gods heard me."

Accept the guilt. Accuse yourselves.

"He looked at me," Alexander says. "I was behind him, under the archway, waiting for my turn to enter the theatre. After Pausanias—my father couldn't speak, but he turned to look at me. He knew it was really me. The gods opened the door."

Opposing extremes, but also versions of the same form.

"I've been waiting and waiting for you," Alexander says. "No one knew where to find you. Where were you?"

"In the library."

He starts to cry.

"My father died of plague." I take my arm from his shoulders. "Your father was killed by an assassin. The body needs a balance of fluids. Grief creates an excess, which we release through tears. Too many tears and the body becomes parched; the brain shrivels. You need to grieve, and drink water, and sleep. In the morning you'll ask the gods to turn the guilt you feel into a tiny fish. You'll hide that fish somewhere inside yourself." I touch my temple, my heart. "Here, or here. You can live like that. No one will know."

"Antipater thinks Pausanias was paid."

"Who by?"

He looks at me.

"He doesn't think that."

"My mother, then."

"That's ridiculous. Wipe your nose." He wipes his nose on his sleeve. "Any number of ambitious men would perceive a benefit in your father's death. Antipater will see that."

"You think so?"

"It makes sense. Some disgruntled chieftain who fancies himself in line for the throne, maybe, who found a sharpened tool in Pausanias. I'll have a word with him." I stand. "You need to sleep. Shall I bring the lamp?" He nods. I light a table lamp from a torch on the wall and bring it to his bed, where he's lain down. "All right?"

He nods.

"You didn't do this."

He closes his eyes.

Children hold hands. Men walk by themselves, you see?

AFTER PURIFICATION RITUALS AND a period of lying-in-state, Philip is buried with his weapons under a great tumulus of earth. Pausanias's mutilated body is burned on top of the pile. The sons of Aëropus, a disgruntled chieftain, are tried, convicted, and put to death. Ritual sacrifices, funerary games, full pomp and honours in the high, golden, late-afternoon summer sunlight, pollen twinkling in the air all around.

I grieve. There's a tiny place deep in my chest where a little man sits, a manikin, weeping. I tell him to settle down. In the evenings, when I drink, he clambers up onto my shoulder for a shy look round. He thinks the same thoughts I do, in his small way, highly spiced thoughts, meat skewers, tiny and intense memories. He's a bit of an Arrhidaeus, my manikin, with his crust-nosed gibbering, probably diapered, probably can't feed himself, but he remembers exorbitantly, lavishly, complexly, in flashes of super-saturated colour. Here's one: Philip opening his eyes under water for the first time and laughing, bubbles streaming silently from his mouth, reaching to touch the bubbles that streamed from mine, looking over his shoulder, at his feet, over his head to the surface, and back to my face. Philip with both eyes open, laughing under the sea.

"Be safe," Herpyllis says.

It's bronze-dayed, crisp-nighted harvest time. Callisthenes and I are taking a trip while we can, before the weather turns. We'll ride Tar and Lady; Tweak is for the bags. He huffs and snuffs, annoyed at the unaccustomed weight. Callisthenes scratches his nose and tells him he's gone soft.

I pick Little Pythias up in a hug and tell her I'm going to find us a new house to live in.

"Me too?" she says.

"You too."

She bumps her forehead to mine. I put her down and she goes to stand beside Herpyllis, who holds the baby.

We mount and ride away. "It hasn't been all bad," Callisthenes says as we turn back to wave, meaning Pella, meaning the three of them.

"You think we should stay?"

"In Pella? No."

"In Macedon?"

"That's what this trip is about, isn't it?"

We ride east, in sight of the ocean for a while and then

inland. We toast bread on green sticks over our nightly smudge of fire and sleep rough. We're quiet together, each looking inward. I have a feeling about my nephew, an idea there's something he wants to tell me. No matter. I won't mind what he decides either way, though I'll miss him.

Philip's army—Alexander's now—has been busy in Chalcidice. Even just a few weeks' reconstruction have brought some of the prettiness back, some of the prosperity, the fruit and the birds and the colour. Go still at sundown and you can hear the earth itself humming. The ground stays warm long into the night; strange-familiar faces smile up at us from the fields; the stars are a splash of silver liquid across the sky, a spill pattern as familiar as the stains on my mother's kitchen table. I'm almost home; all this time, it's been only two days' ride away. Callisthenes smiles at me once or twice without saying anything, at something he sees in my face. It'll take a good month to pack up the house in Pella and conclude my affairs there, and by then it'll be too late in the season for the women and children to travel, too wet and cold for the baby especially. We'll make this journey again, for real, in the spring. This is just reconnaissance.

As Antipater warned me, the east coast is still bleak; Stageira is the exception. The fields lie fallow and the vineyards are overgrown but the village has been patched back together, old stones and new wood. I show Antipater's letter to the officer in charge, who gives us stew in his own tent and says he's grown fond of the place these past couple of months. Nice manners. I tell him his men have worked fast.

He pours more wine. "We know where our orders come from. Who you are."

We throw dice together for a while, and then I walk down to

the shore in the moonlight. Callisthenes follows after a couple of minutes.

"You're happy," he says.

"Am I?"

"Comfortable. You belong here."

"I guess I do. I don't know. It's a good place for a childhood. I like to think of Nicomachus running around here the way I did when I was a child."

"Playing with your ghost."

I point at the sea. "That little boy is about fifty feet out and twenty feet down, diving for shells. Anyone who wants to go look for him can try."

Callisthenes hugs himself and rubs his biceps up and down. "I'd rather see the house."

My father's estate is set back from the sea. The big house is dark but from a distance we can see light in one of the outbuildings. Closer, the window of the garden cottage. When our footsteps sound on the pebbles, an old woman appears in the doorway.

"Hello, Beauty." Callisthenes ducks down to greet her.

She's a hunchback and twists herself so she can look at our faces with sharp eyes. I don't recognize her.

"Do you live here?" he asks.

"I know you."

Callisthenes smiles. "I don't—"

"Not you." She looks at me. "You."

I tell her my name and my father's name. "If you know me, you know where you're living."

"No one's been here for years. They rebuilt it first and it stood empty. I keep it nice."

"May we see?"

We follow her inside the cottage.

"Ah!" I say. It's small; they rebuilt it small, or my memory did. Six years ago it was half-burnt, roof gone. It's clear the old woman lives in this one room with the neat hearth and the dried lavender hanging from the ceiling. How is it possible the place smells the same after all that's happened, all this time? "Do you keep the big house, too?"

"As I can. I sweep it out most days. I'm trying to bring back the garden, too. Can't manage the orchard, though, except for the windfall."

"You're alone?"

"I'm too old to leave. My boys aren't far. I lived with them for a while after the war, after the exile order, but I belong here. I came back last month when I saw the big house was finished. Army knows I'm here; army don't care. Nobody cares. My boys check on me every few days, bring me what I need."

I'm scouring my brain, trying to place her. "Sons. No daughter?"

"You should know my little girl."

"Should I?"

"My baby, Herpyllis. She serves your lady." She sees my face. "No. Not my baby before me."

"No, no. It was my wife who died."

"Ah." She relaxes, shakes her head, pats my arm. "I'm sorry. How long?"

"A year and a half ago. Herpyllis—" I look at and then away from Callisthenes, who's considering the ceiling. "Herpyllis was a great comfort to her lady through her sickness. To me, too."

"You didn't get rid of her, then, after."

"Ah."

Callisthenes is humming faintly, eyes closed now.

"No. As a matter of fact—" I've never had a mother-in-law. "Shut up," I tell Callisthenes.

"Sorry."

The old woman laughs. "That kind of comfort, is it?"

"A son is a great comfort."

"A son!" She claps her hands; pulls her dress wide with her fingertips and describes a slow circle in the middle of the room: dancing. "A grandson!"

"Herpyllis is very happy," Callisthenes says.

The old woman has gone pink in the cheeks. "Will I show you the big house? It's ready for you. You'll bring them here, bring them back. Won't you? Get the lantern for me, love. Up on that shelf."

"Tomorrow."

Callisthenes begins to talk about my household, Herpyllis and the baby, the good food they eat, the nice clothes they wear, all easy and expansive, distracting her from the answer he knows I haven't given. She asks us to stay, but the officer expects us back for a tour of the reconstruction first thing in the morning.

"In the afternoon, then."

"The afternoon."

Callisthenes and I walk back to the soldiers' camp.

"You'll break her old heart," he says eventually.

"I can't help that."

"I know." It's late; cold. Our breath smokes. "This is why we came. For you to decide."

I can't speak.

"You've seemed better, lately." Callisthenes doesn't look at me. "Your illness. It was so bad for a while, but just lately—"

"Illness?"

We're on a small rise overlooking the soldiers' encampment. I raise my hand to acknowledge the sentry, who's spotted us. He sits back down at his fire.

"Please," Callisthenes says. "Won't you talk about it, even to me? Haven't I known you long enough?"

I shake my head.

"You're better when you have someone new to love. Alexander, at first. Herpyllis, now. Me, once. You pull out of yourself. It helps you. I remember when I first came to you, in Atarneus. Everyone warned me what a miserable man you were, but I was never happier in my life. You always had time for me, always wanted to talk to me. You gave me gifts, encouraged me, made me welcome, made me feel brilliant. I wondered for a while if it was sex you wanted. But it wasn't; you just loved me. Then you got married and it was Pythias. Then we came to Pella and it was Alexander."

"You're jealous?"

"No. Yes, of course. But that's not— I'm trying to say I've been watching you for a long, long time. You have a sickness. Everyone who loves you sees it in you. When you were in Mieza, Pythias and I used to talk about how to help you. She said you needed Alexander. She said if ever they took him away, you'd die."

"Black bile," I say.

"She wasn't resentful. She was more astute than I think you ever—"

"Not in her, in me. My father taught me long ago that black bile can be hot or cold. Cold: it makes you sluggish and stupid. Hot: it makes you brilliant, insatiable, frenzied. Like the different stages of drunkenness, you see? Only my father didn't realize that none of this had to be bad. The people who find the balance between the extremes—"

Callisthenes puts his hand on my arm.

"—the very best teachers, artists, warriors—"

"Plato, Carolus, Alexander—"

"I swung back and forth for a long time. I'd find a girl and fuck myself empty, and then afterwards I wanted to die. Lately, though, as you say, it's better. Not so high, not so low. Maybe it's Herpyllis; maybe. Does it matter, if it holds?"

"You think it won't hold here?"

"You saw the orchard by the big house?"

"Plums."

"Plums. One of my oldest memories, the taste of those plums. I looked at them as we walked by just now and thought, too small, after all these years. Those damn trees are still too small to hold a noose. That's the furniture in my mind, here, still."

"Athens, then."

"For me. For you?"

He looks shy, surprised.

I nod. "Your work is solid. You don't need me any more. I'll give you this place, if you want it."

We start the walk down to the camp. "Remember how I hated Macedon when we first got here?" my nephew says.

"I do."

"Stageira," he says. "Comfort and leisure and time to write. I could do worse."

"Or you could come with me, stay with me. Colleague, rather than apprentice."

"Or I could do something else altogether. Fall in love, maybe. Travel."

"Both."

He laughs. "Both, then."

"Fucking cold one tonight," the sentry says. "Extra blankets in the storage tent. Help yourself to what you need."

"MAJESTY."

"Master," Alexander says.

We embrace, briefly. I feel the dry, slightly feverish heat in his skin that corresponds precisely to the ruddiness of his complexion, feel the strength of him, and smell the faint, pleasant spiciness that so endeared him as a boy to my dead wife. We're in the palace library, back in Pella, for the last time. He's been king for eight months.

"I can't believe you're going," he says.

I give my student two gifts: a volume of Homer, and one of Euripides.

"But these are your own." He looks through them. "Your notes are here."

I nod.

"I will always sleep with them beneath my pillow," he says gravely, and I bite back a smile. I rise. "No, no. For all I'm giving you, I want one more gift."

"Anything." What else can I say?

Alexander laughs and says, to an invisible audience, "Look at him. You'd think I was asking for his first-born."

I feel a last pang of jealousy. Here is a mannerism I've not seen before; already Alexander has fallen under new influences. That I'll no longer be close enough to watch him adopt and adapt, to watch his mind fill in as his body has—this is love, then, finally, I think, what I feel as I watch him. Maybe Callisthenes was right. As good as love.

"A lesson. I want a last lesson."

We take our seats.

"I suppose it would be a waste of time to speak to you of moderation." I hook a smile. "Therefore I will speak to you of excellence. What is human excellence? When is a man a good man? What does it mean to live a good life?"

"To triumph. To act to the furthest extent of one's capacities. To flourish."

"To flourish." I nod. I talk about the exercise of a man's faculties, and all the ways in which he might excel: in character, in friendship, in intellect. I linger over the intellect, explain that it is the divine seed in man that no other animal shares. In the hierarchy of excellences, intellect is at the top; therefore the best human life is that spent in pursuit of intellectual excellence.

"In philosophy," Alexander says.

I turn away from the glibness in my student's voice, the smooth amusement. I want at this moment to bury my face in my books the way Little Pythias once buried her face in her mother's breast, obliterating the world thereby.

"Lysimachus used to say the same thing," Alexander says. "That it was in my nature to excel in all things, and anyone who stood in my way was thwarting the will of the gods."

"I don't think that's quite what I'm saying, is it?"

"Not quite." Alexander smiles. "Lysimachus flourishes, these days."

"Does he?"

"I've promoted him to my personal bodyguard. Oh, the face! You don't approve?"

"Not for me to approve or disapprove. Only—"

"Only?" He leans forward.

"Only I would have thought he had all the preconditions to pursue the kind of excellence I'm describing to you. A well-rounded man, an athlete, an artist, a lively mind, just the mind to appreciate the innate superiority of the contemplative life. Not to mention the means, the leisure. I'm pragmatic enough to know that's a necessary part of the equation."

"I have the same qualities, don't I?"

"If your father left you an impression of a Macedonian king having time for leisure, you weren't paying very close attention."

"Don't avoid the question."

"You have the same qualities. No. You have these qualities superlatively. You know it. You know I don't flatter you. Have I ever?"

"Wouldn't love you if you did." Before an awkwardness can grow up he says, "I should retire to one of my father's estates and spend my time in a comfortable chair, drinking water and considering the wonder of creation?"

"Not too comfortable a chair. My father's estate is in Stageira, by the way." I make sure he looks at me. "I never lived there as an adult."

"A self-made man."

"That can be hard to pull off. Harder than you know."

He laughs. "You think your life is perfect. You think every-one should want to be you. All our years together, you've made your theories out of the accidents of your own life. You've built a whole philosophy around the virtue of being you. Seashells are worthy of study because you love to swim. Violence should be offstage because you never got to leave the tent at Chaeronea. The best government is rule by the middle class because you come from the middle class. Life should be spent in quiet contemplation because life never offered you more."

"Tell me what more is."

"There's a whole world more." His eyes go big. "You could travel with me, you know. I'm not staying here. I'm going east, and east, and east again. I'm going as far as anyone's ever gone and then farther. Animals no one's ever seen. Oceans no one's ever swum in. New plants, new people, new stars. Mine for the taking. Yours, too. I'll make sure you're comfortable. We'll carry you in a palanquin, cushions, scribes, wagons groaning with all the specimens you'll collect. You'll never even notice the army. We'll just be clearing the way forward for you. To make the unknown known, isn't that the greatest virtue, the greatest hap-piness? Isn't that exactly what we're talking about?"

"You conflate pleasure and happiness, real enduring happi-ness. A few thrills, a few sensations. Your first woman, your first elephant, your first spicy meal, your first hangover, your first ascent of a mountain no man's ever climbed, and your first view from the top to the other side. You want to string together a life of thrills."

"Teach me better, then. Come with my army. Come with me. You've been a father to me. Don't orphan me twice."

"You worked on that line."

"I never please you. Not when I'm polished and not when I'm dull. Yes, I worked on that line. Is that so terrible? We're not so different after all, you and me. We both work for what we want. Nothing comes easy. Does your work come easily to you?"

"No."

"Look at me." He stands up. "I'm short. I fumble when I talk. I blush. I'm afraid of the dark. I black out in the middle of battle and can't remember anything afterwards. They look at me, they say, Great warrior, well-spoken, charming, worthy student of the greatest mind in the world. I'm holding on by my fingertips and so are you."

I nod.

"Maybe you've made me into yourself after all. A fine, fierce surface on the mess underneath. Like you polished up my brother, teaching him to speak, teaching him to ride. That's you, isn't it? That's you, and me, and him?"

I say nothing.

"I'll tell you what I accept, in your theory of happiness," he says. "I accept that the greatest happiness comes to those capable of the highest things. That's where we leave my brother behind. That's where you and I walk away from the rest of the world. You and I can appreciate the glory of things. We walk to the very edge as everyone else knows and understands and experiences it, and then we walk the next step. We go places no one has ever been. That's who we are. That's who you've taught me to be."

"Did I teach you that?"

"I've made you sad."

"Yes." I touch my forehead. "Yes, you have."

"We're so alike. I'm your child."

The boy who knew where to find the head, the heart, the breath, the brain. The boy who smelled so nice. The boy running in from the rain. "Majesty."

He says, "Stay with me. Don't make me go the next step alone."

WE LEAVE ON A SUNNY DAY, when the sunlight sparkles on the marsh and makes the ocean blinding.

Alexander has loaded me down with goods and gear and servants and money until I begged him to stop. Herpyllis rides with the children on a cart lined with furs; she is cheerful and placid, nursing the baby, chatting with Little Pythias, almost four, who's excited and fretful and already looking strained around the eyes, a sign of the headaches that afflict her. I gesture to Herpyllis to remind her about her hat. I know I am seeing in Little Pythias the anxiety her mother would be feeling about such a trip. Herpyllis, in contrast, could be going to the seaside, or back to Mytilene; it's all the same to her. The slaves, Tycho and Simon and the rest, have a cart to themselves. Philes is mounted beside me, my plan for him realized at last. He can't speak. He's terrified.

"Uncle." Callisthenes holds out his hand.

He'll serve Alexander on his expeditions as official historian. Travel, then; with luck, love is still to come. We embrace and bid each other farewell.

I'm about to mount when he says, "There's someone else here who wants to say goodbye."

A tall young man with a familiar loping gait steps out from behind a cart, where he's been hiding with the little groom who is now his companion. Both their grins are enormous.

"Now who is this?" I say, knowing.

"I don't want you to go," Arrhidaeus says.

The young man clings to me, even weeps briefly, while I pat his shoulders and his hair. "I'm very proud of you, Arrhidaeus."

This, then, is what I see as I ride out: my nephew, his heart a Macedonian heart now; and the fool beside him no longer quite a fool, one hand raised in farewell, until they've dwindled, in my sight, almost to specks.

As soon as there's no one to see, I dismount and get onto a cart so I can write. No more doctoring, politicking, teaching children; no more dabbling. Soon I'll be alone in a quiet room where, for the rest of my life, I can float farther and farther out into the world; while my student, charging off the end of every map, falls deeper and deeper into the well of himself. *Never be afraid to enter an argument you can't immediately see your way out of.* Can anyone tell me what a tragedy is?

C LEOPATRA AND HER BABY DAUGHTER were murdered shortly after Philip's death, supposedly by Olympias. Leonidas once rebuked the boy Alexander for wasting incense on the altar, saying he should not be extravagant until he had conquered the countries that produced such spices. Years later, from Gaza, according to Plutarch, Alexander sent Leonidas "five hundred talents' weight of frankincense and an hundred of myrrh." Alexander conquered Persia and Egypt, and led his army as far as India and Afghanistan. At the oracle of Ammon at Siwa, he is supposed to have asked whether any of Philip's murderers had gone unpunished, and whether Philip was really his father. He strove to synthesize Eastern and Western cultures, adopting Persian dress and manners. His behaviour during his long campaigns became increasingly erratic: he drank heavily, suffered fits of violent rage followed by crippling depression and guilt, and refused to go home. He took two wives, and died in Babylon of a stomach ailment at the age of thirty-two. Ptolemy became one of Alexander's greatest generals and later ruled Egypt, where he established the Ptolemaic line of rulers that ended, in Roman times, with the death of his great-great-great-great-great-great-great-granddaughter from the bite of an asp. Hephaestion remained Alexander's constant companion and died in battle scant weeks before Alexander himself. Callisthenes accompanied Alexander on his campaigns as a historian, but lost favour after criticizing Alexander for accepting obeisance from his soldiers in the Eastern fashion. The ancient biographer Diogenes Laërtius says Callisthenes was "confined in an iron cage and carried about until he became infested with vermin through lack of proper attention; and finally he was thrown to a lion and so met his end." Arrhidaeus became regent of Macedonia during Alexander's long absence in Asia, and king after his death. He was assisted by the aging general Antipater. Olympias quarrelled frequently with Antipater and eventually had Arrhidaeus murdered so she herself could serve as regent.

Aristotle returned to Athens to direct his own school, the Lyceum, until a rise in anti-Macedonian sentiment following Alexander's death forced him to leave that city a second time. He spent his final year at the Macedonian garrison at Chalcis in Euboea, where he died at the age of sixty-one.

Aristotle's will survives:

All will be well; but, in case anything should happen, Aristotle has made these dispositions. Antipater is to be executor in all matters and in general; but, until Nicanor shall arrive, Aristomenes, Timarchus, Hipparchus, Dioteles and (if he consent and if circumstances permit him) Theophrastus shall take charge as well of Herpyllis and the children as of the property. And when the girl [his daughter Pythias] shall be grown up she shall be given in marriage to Nicanor; but if anything happen to the girl (which heaven forbid and no such thing will happen) before her marriage, or when she is married but before there are children, Nicanor shall have full powers, both with regard to the child and with regard to everything else, to administer in a manner worthy both of himself and of us. Nicanor shall take charge of the girl and of the boy Nicomachus as he shall think fit in all that concerns them as if he were father and brother. And if anything should happen to Nicanor (which heaven forbid!) either before he marries the girl, or when he has married her but before there are children, any arrangements that he may make shall be valid. And if Theophrastus is willing to live with her, he shall have the same rights as Nicanor. Otherwise the executors in consultation with Antipater shall administer as regards the daughter and the boy as seems to them to be best. The executors and Nicanor, in memory of me and of the steady affection which Herpyllis has borne towards me, shall take care of her in every other respect and, if she desires to be married, shall see that she be given to one not unworthy; and besides what she has already received they shall give her a talent of silver out of the estate and three handmaids whomsoever she shall choose besides the maid she has at present and the man-servant Pyrrhaeus; and if she chooses to remain at Chalcis, the lodge by the garden, if in Stageira, my father's house. Whichever of these two houses she chooses, the executors shall furnish with such furniture as they think proper and as Herpyllis herself may approve. Nicanor shall take charge of the boy Myrmex, that he be taken to his own friends in a manner worthy of me with the property of his which we received. Ambracis shall be given her freedom, and on my daughter's marriage shall receive 500 drachmas and the

maid whom she now has. And to Thale shall be given, in
addition to the maid whom she has and who was bought, a
thousand drachmas and a maid. And Simon, in addition to
the money before paid to him towards another servant, shall
either have a servant purchased for him or receive a further
sum of money. And Tycho, Philo, Olympias, and his child
shall have their freedom when my daughter is married.
None of the servants who waited upon me shall be sold but
they shall continue to be employed; and when they arrive at
the proper age they shall have their freedom if they deserve
it. My executors shall see to it when the images which
Gryllion has been commissioned to execute are finished, that
they be set up, namely that of Nicanor, that of Proxenus,
which it was my intention to have executed, and that of
Nicanor's mother; also they shall set up the bust which has
been executed of Arimnestus, to be a memorial of him
seeing that he died childless, and shall dedicate my mother's
statue to Demeter at Nemea or wherever they think best.
And wherever they bury me, there the bones of Pythias shall
be laid, in accordance with her own instructions. And to
commemorate Nicanor's safe return, as I vowed on his
behalf, they shall set up in Stageira stone statues of life size
to Zeus and Athena the Saviours.

Acknowledgements

MANY THANKS TO Denise Bukowski and Anne Collins. I gratefully acknowledge the financial assistance of the Canada Council for the Arts.

The following books were particularly helpful: for Macedonian history, Plutarch's *Life of Alexander*, N.G.L. Hammond and G. T. Griffith's *A History of Macedonia Volume II: 550–336 BC* and *The Cambridge Ancient History, Volume IV: The Fourth Century BC*; for ancient medicine, *Hippocratic Writings*, G.E.R. Lloyd, editor, translated by J. Chadwick and W. N. Mann; for Aristotle's life and thought, Werner Jaeger's *Aristotle: Fundamentals of the History of His Development*, translated by Richard Robinson; Jonathan Barnes's *Aristotle: A Brief Introduction*; W. T. Jones's *A History of Western Philosophy: The Classical Mind*; and Martha Nussbaum's *The Fragility of Goodness: Luck and Ethics in Greek Tragedy and Philosophy*. For translations of Aristotle's work, I have relied primarily on the Loeb Classical Library series and Penguin Classics. The translation of Aristotle's will, above, is R. D. Hick's (Loeb Classical Library).

For a fictional account of Aristotle's time in Macedon from Alexander's perspective, see Mary Renault's excellent 1969 novel *Fire from Heaven*.

The translations I have quoted directly are *Meno* by Plato,

A NOTE ABOUT THE AUTHOR

ANNABEL LYON's short-story collection, *Oxygen*, and book of novellas, *The Best Thing for You*, were published in Canada to wide acclaim. Her juvenile novel, *All-Season Edie*, has been translated into three languages. Her first novel, *The Golden Mean*, is a Canadian best seller and is being published in six languages. It won the Rogers Writers' Trust Fiction Prize, and was nominated for the Scotiabank Giller Prize, the Governor General's Award for Fiction, and the Commonwealth Writers' Prize. Lyon's short fiction has appeared in *Toronto Life*, the Journey Prize anthology, and the *Harvard Review*. She lives in British Columbia with her husband and two children.

A NOTE ON THE TYPE

THE TEXT of this book was set in Centaur, the only typeface designed by Bruce Rogers (1870–1957), the well-known American book designer. A celebrated penman, Rogers based his design on the roman face cut by Nicolas Jenson in 1470 for his Eusebius. Jenson's roman surpassed all of its forerunners and even today, in modern recuttings, remains one of the most popular and attractive of all typefaces.

The italic used to accompany Centaur is Arrighi, designed by another American, Frederic Warde, and based on the chancery face used by Lodovico degli Arrighi in 1524.

Composed by Creative Graphics,
Allentown, Pennsylvania

Printed and bound by RR Donnelley,
Harrisonburg, Virginia